OMEGA

OMEGA
THE PENTON LEGACY

SUSANNAH SANDLIN

Montlake
Romance

The characters and events portrayed in this book are fictitious. Any similarity to real persons, living or dead, is coincidental and not intended by the author.

Text copyright © 2013 Susannah Sandlin

Published by Montlake Romance
P.O. Box 400818
Las Vegas, NV 89140

ISBN-13: 9781612183596
ISBN-10: 161218359X

Dedication

*To Dianne, who saved Penton from the CIA,
and so much more.*

❋

❧PROLOGUE❧

D avid Jackson's back slammed into the wall with enough
force to crack the plaster, sending a cloud of dust, splintered lathing, and blood-covered plaster chips pluming outward.

"A whole town can't just disappear. Tell me where they
went." Matthias Ludlam hefted one of the ugly primitive paint-
ings he'd pulled off the wall of his new headquarters in the Penton Clinic office and cracked it over the back of an upholstered
chair with a crash of splintered wood frame and torn canvas.

He wielded a jagged spear of framing and punched it into
Jackson's chest, just hard enough to use *its* point to make *his*
point.

"You will talk to me, Mr. Jackson. You obviously left the
Penton scathe and your memories were scrubbed, but guess
what? Memories can be retrieved." He lowered the makeshift
stake and poised it over the man's groin. "Here's my next tar-
get."

"Please. I don't remember anything, I swear." Jackson, a
short and slender black-haired vampire, looked like a teenager

and couldn't have been turned more than a decade. Matthias recognized the vacant expression and the man's dilated pupils and knew his memory had been scrubbed thoroughly. But even altered memories could be retrieved sometimes if the pressure were great enough.

Matthias knew how to exert pressure.

After months of targeting them in different ways, he finally had trapped the Penton rebels exactly as he'd planned—Aidan Murphy, the Slayer Mirren Kincaid, and their whole band of humans and vampires, including his ingrate of a son, William. Three days ago, he'd received backing from the Vampire Tribunal to shut down the entire town. Better still, permission to kill Murphy for illegally turning a human doctor into a vampire—a crime in these days when vampires were on the brink of starvation and civil war. And permission to kill Mirren Kincaid for murdering that pain-in-the-ass Tribunal member Lorenzo Caias.

Then that goddamned squaw Kincaid had taken as a mate used her telekinetic powers to throw the whole town into chaos and they'd escaped. All those people—he'd estimated a hundred vampires and humans combined—had just vanished from a little town in the middle of nowhere. It was impossible.

He shifted the stake a few inches to the left and jammed it into Jackson's thigh, proving the stupid fool could still cry like a human. Murphy had bonded a bunch of weaklings who'd rather cower in the protective cover of a herd, hiding behind Murphy and Kincaid, than stand on their own. "Where did they go?"

Jackson's legs collapsed, forcing Matthias to back out of the way or get blood on his tailored suit.

"Omega." Tears, mucus, and blood mixed on Jackson's face. "They're in Omega."

Another half hour of persuasion yielded nothing more, and Matthias finally turned the man over to Shelton Porterfield. Former manager of Matthias's Virginia estate, Shelton was now his second-in-command in what he'd come to think of as Project Penton.

The Vampire Tribunal wanted Penton shut down, but Matthias needed Aidan Murphy, Mirren Kincaid, and their mates dead. They knew enough to ruin him if they could ever get enough ears on the Tribunal to listen. Luckily for him, the Tribunal was threatened by Murphy's power and not prone to giving him a sympathetic audience. They also didn't like getting their hands dirty, which meant they'd leave Matthias alone to handle things however he wanted.

He looked down at Jackson. "Might as well kill him. He can't remember more, or he'd have coughed it up by now. And he's too pathetic to be of any use to us as a fighter, even if I enthrall him."

Shelton flicked a glance over the prostrate man and ran the tip of his spongy tongue across his lips. His thinning white-blond hair made his blue eyes look almost electric. "Pretty, though. Care if I have a little fun with him first?"

Jackson whimpered, already healing enough to understand Shelton's intentions, and Matthias looked at Shelton in disgust, brushing the remaining dots of plaster dust off his jacket and smoothing down his hair. "Do whatever you want—just get him out of here."

He watched Shelton hustle the man out the door. His lieutenant liked to play with his prey, especially the ones who barely looked old enough to be legal, and Matthias almost felt sorry for the hapless David Jackson. Almost.

Omega. What the hell did that mean? Obviously, it had to be some kind of last-ditch escape plan for everyone to have disappeared so quickly. And only a master vampire could alter the memories of another vampire—even a weak one like Jackson—which meant Murphy or Kincaid had wiped the memories of everyone not going with them into Omega. If they went *into* Omega, it sounded more like a physical place than a plan.

Before Murphy had done his Houdini act with most of the bonded humans and his key lieutenants, including William, Matthias had laid waste to the town with a few dozen mercenaries lured by money and the hope of unlimited feeding. The more time that passed after the vaccine to prevent a human pandemic had turned the blood of vaccinated humans poisonous to vampires, the more desperate his kind became. There was no shortage of bodies willing to help break up Murphy's town of vampires and bonded, unvaccinated humans.

As soon as Murphy and Kincaid were dead, the whole structure of Penton would crumble. Matthias would be a hero for doing the Vampire Tribunal's dirty work. And his foolish son William would be back under his control.

Omega.

One little word, but it might be enough to fire up Matthias's secret weapon. He'd been keeping this treasure to himself until he figured out what to do with it.

He stuck his head outside the clinic office, making sure Shelton and his evening's entertainment had left the building. Then he crossed the office to the back corner and shoved aside an area rug. At first glance, it looked like the same oak parquet pattern as the rest of the floor. Not on second glance, however.

His people had set off one of their explosives on the west side of the clinic. The east wing, where the office lay, was still usable but had been jolted enough to show off the cracks in the floor where an intricate wooden lock lay hidden. Matthias recognized William's work, and an uncomfortable mixture of pride and anger filled his chest. His son was smart in his own way—and stupid in others. The boy had learned to make these kinds of puzzles at one of a million summer school sessions he'd taken to make up for failing his studies during the school year.

William was soft. It was unthinkable that he'd spurned the life of immortality and power and wealth Matthias had offered him, despite his mental limitations, and had thrown in his lot for an easy, uncomplicated life with that Irish peasant Aidan Murphy. Yet it had happened. And if he didn't retrieve him soon, Matthias knew he'd never get his son back. If William hadn't already been too brainwashed by Murphy and his peace-loving scathe members to be salvageable.

He still hoped to get the boy out of this situation alive, without the Tribunal accusing William of treason and himself of favoritism. His son would have to be punished, and severely, for supporting the rebels. And punished again for leaving Matthias's household.

At the end of it, Matthias would take William home.

At the end of it, once William had been broken enough to accept his role, they'd be able to take over the Tribunal.

At the end of it, Matthias would be untouchable.

Using the makeshift stake covered in the blood of the unfortunate David Jackson, Matthias wedged the pointed end under the crack at the edge of the floor panel and hefted it up. It opened into a narrow vertical tunnel with a ladder attached to the wall, leading downward into a basement. Matthias descended slowly, testing his weight on every rung as he'd done on each prior trip into the bowels of underground Penton. In his suit coat pocket, he'd stuffed a folded sheaf of papers.

Murphy had come up with a clever living system, Matthias had to admit. Below the clinic was the building's original basement, an empty shell that Matthias was surprised hadn't been put to use. At the far end, under another elaborate locked hatch, was yet another stairwell into a deep subbasement. However the people of Penton had gotten out, it had likely been in some kind of underground passage, since they'd already proven adept at building them. He just had to find out where they had escaped *to*.

In the subbasement, the concrete and rebar gave way to a carpeted hallway lined with lavishly furnished suites. The far end had collapsed in the explosion, so Matthias had no idea how many suites lay beyond the six on this side. It had been a brilliant setup, with lighttight guest suites. Although a couple of them locked from the outside to keep "visitors" in, he'd found the keys in the clinic desk drawer, and these plush, lockable rooms made the perfect place to stash his secret weapon.

He slid the key into the lock and swung the heavy wooden door inward. The room was dimly lit with a couple of fluorescent lanterns, but he could see the woman well enough. Her riot of strawberry blonde curls partially covered a drawn, pale face. And if looks really could kill, her silvery-green eyes would have shoved a stake right up his ass.

Matthias smiled. In his previous visits, she'd been too racked by the pain of her transition and physical healing to talk, but he'd brought one of his two humans down to feed her for a few minutes at a time, and now she was hungry but lucid.

Exactly the way he intended to keep her.

He'd expected the woman to scream or beg as soon as she recognized him—and she did recognize him, whether or not she knew his name. It would be hard to forget the man who'd been responsible for ending her human life.

"I'm Matthias Ludlam." He closed the door behind him and walked into the suite, taking a seat on the edge of the bed. Silver-laced rope bound her ankles and secured her arms to the bedposts at an angle that would make it impossible for her to get comfortable. Not that a newly hatched vampire ever got truly comfortable—or posed much of a threat. "I'm head of the Vampire Tribunal Justice Council."

"I know who you are, you bastard. What do you want with me?" Her transition hadn't wiped out that horrendous Southern drawl, unfortunately, and she still had that wholesome country-girl look.

"Let's start by telling me your name."

She paused. "Lucy Sinclair."

Matthias laughed. "I met Lucy Sinclair a number of years ago, and she's dead. We found what was left of her in the ruins of the Penton municipal building. Besides, she was vampire, and until three days ago, you were quite human. Let's try again, girl—it will go more easily if you cooperate. Your name?"

She clenched her jaw, but spat out two words: "Melissa Calvert."

"Let's see if we can confirm that." Matthias extracted his sheaf of papers and unfolded them. He scanned the list of names printed in two columns on one of the last sheets and began laughing again. He'd been assembling this partial list of Penton residents for over a year from various sources, trying to find a way inside Murphy's organization. It had finally paid off.

"You're Aidan Murphy's familiar?" A flush of pleasure sped up his heart rate. This was perfect. "No wonder he had such a reaction when we twisted that pretty little neck of yours. My instincts to quickly have you drained and turned were exactly the right move." Murphy had looked ready to explode when he'd seen the woman killed a few feet from where he stood, and only the intervention of one of his lieutenants had held him back from getting his own neck snapped.

The irony that he'd committed the same crime for which he planned to kill Aidan Murphy wasn't lost on him. But the Tribunal had told him to take Murphy down by any means necessary. And turning Melissa Calvert vampire was just another means.

"If you think I'll give you information on Aidan, forget it." She struggled against the ropes. "All you accomplished was creating another pair of fangs to feed."

"Perhaps. But you'll have to give me some useful information before you're allowed to feed again. You'll be amazed at how long you can last without feeding, and how painful it is." A lot of his kind were learning that hard lesson, and it would only grow worse as more time passed. All the more reason to break up a place like Penton, where the vampire citizens were bonding humans so they couldn't be shared outside the scathe.

"Now that I know who you are, I imagine you could say a lot I'd be interested in hearing. When you get hungry enough, your devotion to your precious Aidan Murphy will pale beside your desire to survive." Matthias stood and walked the length of the suite, hands in his pockets. Aidan Murphy's human familiar. This was better than he could have hoped for. Matthias didn't keep single fams—it was more intimacy than he was willing to grant a human. This one was important to Murphy. He'd seen agony in the man's face when he thought he'd seen her die.

Familiars, or fams, were loyal, however, and she hadn't been turned long enough to lose that loyalty. There was no point in trying to get her to tell him anything directly about Murphy, even under enthrallment, not until she was truly desperate.

Matthias looked at her thoughtfully. Would Murphy be able to tell she was alive because of her bonds to him? If so, all the better—it would bring him out of hiding faster. He'd want to play the hero.

Matthias had spotted another person named Calvert on the Penton list. It wasn't that common a name, so chances were good that Mark Calvert was related to this one somehow, which might give him leverage without resorting to torture. Torturing a newly made vampire was rarely effective. They had an annoying tendency to die.

He perched on the edge of the bed again and laid a hand on her ankle. She flinched. "Don't you want to help Mark? Don't you wonder what happened to him?"

Melissa stilled and clamped her lips shut, but Matthias saw the streak of fear cross her face. Good.

"Is Mark your brother?" His name was next to that of Krystal Harris, the woman who Murphy had turned vampire against Tribunal law and who was also his mate, so this Mark Calvert was strictly a feeder and not a lover. Mated vampires didn't stray. "Ah, husband, perhaps." Even better. How cozy for Murphy and his mate to have a human couple as their feeders. Almost like a foursome.

Melissa said nothing, but she dropped her gaze, which told him what he needed. They hadn't captured Mark Calvert, but his wife couldn't know that for sure.

Matthias sat on the edge of the bed again. "Mark wasn't as stubborn as you're being. He's cooperating, and that's how I know about Omega. Mark's already told me they went into Omega."

Her eyes widened. "Mark would never tell you where..." She pressed her lips together again.

But she'd given herself away. She knew plenty, and Aidan Murphy's sentimental willingness to share information with his human familiar made her more valuable than Matthias ever could have hoped.

Yes, Melissa Calvert had much to tell him.

Beginning with how a whole town of humans and vampires had suddenly disappeared, and where they'd gone.

❦CHAPTER 1❦

"You must be planning something big. Hope it's gonna be fun."

The building supply checkout clerk was dark haired, pretty, and pink cheeked. Not to mention a flirt.

Will Ludlam studied the woman's name tag. "I always find a way to make work fun, Cindy."

He lifted his gaze to her face, gave her a smile that showed off his dimples, and felt her heart rate jump a few notches in response. Oh yeah, he still had the touch. Too bad the scent from that same heartbeat told him she'd been vaccinated for the pandemic virus that had turned human blood poisonous to vampires three years ago.

Then, he'd have waited around until her shift ended and taken her somewhere private for a good feed. She'd have finished the night with a love bruise on her neck and a regrettably vague memory of the best orgasm of her life.

Those were the good old days. Now, in the bad new days, he paid for his supplies and pushed his oversized cart into the dark edge of the megastore parking lot. Not that there would be members of his father's Tribunal hit squad hanging around the Home Depot in Opelika, Alabama, but one couldn't be too cautious, especially if one lived thirty miles away in Penton.

Correction: if one lived in the underground bunker outside Penton known as Omega, where what was left of Aidan Murphy's vampire scathe and their bonded humans had been forced to flee after his father blew up half the town.

He did a quick inventory as he unloaded the flat cart and piled supplies in the back of the beat-up black pickup that belonged to one of the Penton humans. His own wheels, a sweet cream-colored vintage Corvette, was too conspicuous to drive around in these days, and most of the town's vehicles had been blown to smithereens by one of Dear Old Dad's minions three days ago when they'd torn through Penton like Sherman burning Atlanta.

Of course, to be fair, Will had done a fair share of the burning himself. He'd torched his own home and all those belonging to the Penton lieutenants. No point in leaving anything Matthias might find instructive or incriminating.

Their escape hadn't exactly been well-timed and leisurely—thus, his shopping trip.

Plywood. Nails. Screws. Lots and lots of batteries. Two more generators. More filters for the air-cleaning system. Every fluorescent lantern in stock, in case the generators failed. Soundproofing panels for the generator room. Those noisy, noxious things were even causing the vampires to have headaches, so acoustical tiles on walls and ceilings would help.

Ninety-eight people had gone into Omega. Some of them were in for the long haul, but most of the newer scathe members and familiars were having second thoughts now that they'd had a couple of days to realize what living underground really entailed.

Aidan had met with Will, Mirren, and the other lieutenants last night to plan an exit strategy for all but their core group.

Moods had been bleak, and everyone agreed they had to start wiping memories and getting people out of there a few at a time. They couldn't go en masse. Most of the people in Penton had lost their vehicles, and retrieving the ones left in town was too risky. Besides, Matthias would have the roads out of Penton watched, as well as the streets of Atlanta, looking for an influx of new vampires and bonded humans. But they could take out a few at a time, put them in transitional safe houses owned by the Penton scathe, and make sure they didn't remember anything that would play into Matthias's hands.

The Penton scathe would be easy to identify, being pretty much the only well-fed vampires around these days. Aidan's peaceful community of vampires and their willingly bonded human familiars had been perfect until their numbers grew large enough to threaten the Tribunal and their old ways of doing things.

Now, thanks to Will's father and a bunch of trumped-up charges, they were all in a clusterfuck nobody knew how to escape. Some of the newer scathe members would leave, and he couldn't blame them. They'd joined the Penton community to live peacefully, not end up in a war with the vampire ruling body. But the lieutenants like Will would stay with Aidan, no matter what. Penton was worth saving and rebuilding. They just had to figure out a way to survive.

Will had designed the Omega facility with three access points. The entrance from the community center basement had been destroyed by the first of Matthias's bombs, killing a lot of people who'd been gathered for a town hall meeting. The second, located in the sanctuary of the Baptist church downtown, was known to the townspeople but had been well camouflaged, unless one knew where to look. But how many people Matthias had looking was the big question. Will had sensed patrols around Penton as he went in and out for supplies. The old bastard himself might be in town.

The third Omega access point, with a location known only to the lieutenants, was the safest. It was an earth-covered, locked hatch just beyond the tree line behind an automobile plant about ten miles east of Penton, just across the Georgia state line near West Point. A variety of cars could be parked in the lot without attracting attention since the plant operated multiple shifts. He'd brought out a trio of the Penton humans tonight. The vampires to whom they'd been bonded had been killed in Matthias's attack, and they'd elected not to stay.

The four of them had traversed the tunnel in a battery-operated cart, gotten into the scathe-owned pickup truck parked in the factory lot among the vehicles belonging to the automotive workers, and then Will had driven them to Opelika. The scathe had a safe house in this city of about a hundred thousand. The former Penton citizens could live there until they decided what to do. At least it was safe so far, and Matthias was less likely to be watching here. He'd expect them to run to Atlanta, where there was a more organized network for vampires.

Aidan had wiped the humans' memories of Penton, but the scathe's leader was so torn up and guilt racked over losing his fam that he hadn't done a thorough job of it. Melissa had been Aidan's familiar for at least five years, and she'd died right in front of him. In front of them all, on the orders of his father. Mark, her husband and Aidan's business manager, had been injured in the attack and taken unconscious into Omega, but now he was asking for his wife and demanding answers.

And if all that wasn't enough to make Will feel like one guilty asshole, he didn't know what it would take.

Aidan was going to have to pull his shit together, though. One of the humans tonight, Ethan, had begun asking questions about when it might be safe to move back to Penton and if they could come back and visit their friends when the fighting was done. At first, Will had thought he'd have to haul Ethan and his wife back to Omega and have their memories re-wiped.

But the damnedest thing had happened. He'd done it. He'd been able to scrub Ethan's memories himself, operating on instinct. He'd enthralled the guy and concentrated hard, replacing Ethan's real memories with a set of false memories Will had devised on the fly. He'd tested and retested him to make sure it worked. Now Ethan didn't even remember Will, much less Penton.

Will didn't know what that meant. Only master vampires did shit like that, and he was no master vampire. How did one become a master vampire, anyway? Something to ask Aidan before taking the next people out of Omega. If he could do the memory scrubs, it would make things easier on Aidan and Mirren, the real master vampires.

Will pulled out of the parking lot and saw a neon ice-cream cone on a sign at the mall across the street from the interstate entrance. He pulled in the lot and went inside a shop so bright and self-consciously cheerful it hurt his eyes. Mirren's mate, Glory, liked to eat stuff the big guy could taste when he fed from her—turns out the six-foot-eight killing machine formerly known and feared in vampire circles as the Slayer had a serious sweet tooth. Of course, he'd probably beat the shit out of Will if he knew Glory had told him.

He didn't bother to study the signs on the glass counter front, but ordered a pint of each flavor, enough to give all of Omega's humans a sugar buzz. The unexpected purchases sent the shop's small night staff—unfailingly polite college kids from a nearby university—into a frenzy of dipping and packaging.

He loaded the last boxful of pint cartons into the truck cab and, on his final trip out of the store, noticed a small display of American flags attached to cards.

"It's a fund-raiser for my fraternity—they're musical cards." One of the store employees, a tall, thin boy wearing a navy-and-orange T-shirt with a tiger on the front, plucked a card from the stack and opened it to a rousing military tune. "The money goes to support the families of the servicemen and women at Fort Benning."

Fort Benning, Georgia, about thirty miles from here—where Will's partner on security detail, Randa Thomas, had gone through basic training before getting shipped off to Afghanistan. Her mortal life ended, not at the hands of a soldier, but a vampire. Aidan had told him Randa's whole family was tied into the US Army, and Will owed the woman an apology for ditching her a couple of times in the last few weeks.

Well, OK, he might even have knocked her out once. She was such fun to torment he couldn't help himself, but he didn't want her to hate him. Maybe the card would mend some fences and help them work together better.

He picked up one of the cards. "How much?"

"Whatever you want to donate." The kid smiled. "Most people give a dollar or two."

Will handed him a twenty and took a card, then, on impulse, caught the boy's gaze and rolled his mind, replacing his memories with the idea that Will hadn't made any other purchases.

When he broke eye contact, the boy shook his head and blinked a few times. "Uh, could I help you with something else?" He looked at the twenty-dollar bill in his hand and frowned.

"No, thanks." Will smiled on his way out of the store. This new trick could come in handy. He didn't like the idea of enthralling anyone or altering minds, but it could prove useful in an emergency.

He thought about it on the thirty-minute drive to the auto plant, pulling into the edge of the lot nearest the encroaching woods. A few seconds after he turned off the truck's engine, five dark-clad figures slipped away from the tree line. He recognized Mirren Kincaid because, well, it was hard to disguise six foot eight inches of vampire massiveness, even dressed in black on a dark night. The others had to get closer: Aidan, with the grim smile that hadn't reached his eyes since Melissa died; Cage Reynolds, the new lieutenant who'd come from England not long before all the shit hit the fan; and a couple of lower-ranking scathe members.

"If you guys can get all this, I want to look around town a little before I go back to Omega. I'll bring what you can't carry—ice cream needs to go first." They began loading boxes on the back of the John Deere Gator cart they kept parked in the back of the parking lot under a tarp, near the equipment shed. So far, no one had managed to steal it.

"Why the hell'd you buy ice cream?" Mirren hefted one of the big cardboard boxes the kids from the creamery had given him from their storeroom, then took a second. The former Tribunal executioner was not only big, but strong.

"The treats are a good idea." Cage's voice was quiet with its clipped British accent, but it carried authority. "It'll cheer up the humans, and we need to do what we can to keep them from going stir-crazy."

Will didn't know much about Cage—as with all the lieutenants, Aidan chose who got into the inner circle, and he'd never erred. He and Cage were sharing a room in Omega, but they'd hardly been in it except for daysleep. If they had to stay underground long, though, he had a feeling he'd get to know Cage Reynolds quickly enough.

He agreed with the guy about keeping the humans happy. Without them, the vamps would have to leave Omega as well and hit the streets in search of food. They were all out of practice at hunting, even if they had the desire. One of the reasons for founding Penton in the first place had been to avoid that predatory shit and shield their bonded humans from hungry vampires growing increasingly desperate.

Plus, he noticed Mirren might be grumbling about ice cream, but he also was the one carrying the boxes rather than sticking them on the Gator. Will couldn't help himself. "I have it on good authority that a certain oversized vampire has a sweet tooth and it's virtually turned his mate into a diabetic. Ice cream's for you and Glory, big guy."

Mirren speared him with a glare from eyes the color of storm clouds, but Will grinned at him. After a second, Mirren turned and headed toward the tree line with his load of ice cream, but not before Will caught the edge of a smile. Glory, a Muscogee Creek woman with telekinetic powers, had come to Penton under bad circumstances—rescued, along with Mirren, from

Matthias's compound in Virginia. She had a straight-talking, spirited nature that had tamed the Slayer, much to everyone's surprise—especially Mirren's.

Will scoured the parking lot and surrounding areas while the others loaded up materials and blended into the shadows. Someone, probably Mirren, would return the Gator to the parking lot once it was unloaded.

Aidan was last, hefting the remaining generator to carry in by hand. "Be careful out there. And don't be surprised if you see Randa—she's patrolling." He frowned and paused, looking like something else was on his mind.

Will might be getting the ability to roll humans' minds, but he couldn't read the mind of a master vampire, and it wasn't like Aidan to be indecisive. "What's up? Anything in particular you want me to look for?"

Will planned to visit the densely wooded area behind his former house and dig his spare laptop out of its hiding place. If Aidan needed him to handle something else, though, the laptop could wait.

"This is going to sound weird, but it's about Melissa." About the same height as Will's six feet, but with long dark hair and blue eyes that grew downright icy when he was hungry or angry, Aidan had retained a hint of his native Irish accent. "I know she died. I heard her neck snap, for God's sake. But I swear a trace of my bond to her is still there, and it shouldn't be. It blinked out when she died, but it came back. It feels different and it's faint, but I swear I feel it."

Aidan rubbed his eyes. "I know this is nuts, but...keep an eye out for her, you know?"

Will pondered the nature of blood bonds, at least what little he knew of them. He'd performed them with a lot of Penton's humans—well, OK, with a lot of Penton's women, since all the humans had to be bonded to a scathe member. He'd never been close enough to any of them to have that kind of emotional connection, however, even with his fams. He couldn't feel any ties to his current feeder, Olivia. The fact that he still thought of Liv as a feeder and not a familiar probably spoke volumes.

In other words, this bonding issue was way outside his wheelhouse. "What do you think it means?"

Aidan shrugged. "Don't know. Probably just wishful thinking. But...oh, holy hell, forget it. Just be careful out there. My guess is that Matthias has stayed close. He has to be trying to figure out how we all escaped and will be waiting for one of us to resurface. Don't play into his hand."

No problem. A run-in with the dad from hell was not on Will's to-do list.

After Aidan disappeared into the hatch entrance to Omega and the lock clicked, Will jammed on a black hat to camouflage his blond hair and loped toward Penton. It was after midnight, and Matthias's patrols would be sniffing around.

He stopped frequently, scenting the air for vampires or humans, and picked up his first whiff of eau de vampire about a mile from downtown, or what was left of downtown after Matthias had tried to blast it to hell.

He stopped and scented the air again. Normally, all he could distinguish was whether something warm-blooded nearby was vampire, human, or animal. But he knew there were two vampires nearby; one belonged to the Penton scathe, and one didn't.

What the hell was going on? He was suddenly able to alter memories, and now he was able to tell not only that vamps were nearby, but what scathe they belonged to? This was not normal. Maybe he was on the verge of a nervous breakdown and his senses had become heightened in advance of a total shutdown. If so, he wished he'd go ahead and get it over with so he could quit freaking himself out.

He ignored both vampires and skirted to the back of the street, where the burned shell of his house still smelled of smoke and ash after three days. Aligning his position with the oak tree twenty feet behind what was left of his chimney, he paced forty steps into the woods.

A thorny bramble draped over a small scrubby bush pricked his fingers when he pulled it back. Grasping the trunk of the bush, he eased it from its loose grasp in the soil, exposing the top of a metal box.

The loud click of a cocked pistol preceded the cold press of steel against the back of his head by less than a second.

He inhaled, annoyed. A rookie mistake. He'd gotten so engrossed in his task he'd let someone slip up on him.

Vampire.

Penton scathe.

Female.

Freaking Randa.

❧ CHAPTER 2 ❧

"If I were your father, I'd already have the silver spoon back in your mouth, Willy. He'd have you trussed up like a rodeo calf by now, hauling you back to wherever it is he lives when he's not terrorizing innocent people."

Will Ludlam was the kind of guy Randa Thomas had hated as a human, and she didn't like him a bit more as a vampire. Less, in fact. Not only was he a spoiled rich boy, he was now a virtually immortal spoiled rich boy. He had probably been a blue-chip jock in school with a 4.0 GPA and a string of girls trailing his every step.

Plus, he annoyed the hell out of her. The consummate smart-ass.

"No, if you were my father, you'd have slit my throat—not enough to kill me, but enough to make sure I couldn't fight back." His voice was soft, calm. "Then you'd hand me over to your sadistic freak show of a second-in-command, Shelton, who would play with me until I couldn't take it anymore. Only when I was good and broken would you return the silver spoon to my mouth."

Good God, would any father really do that? Will didn't really sound as if he were joking. Randa relaxed her stance for only a split second before the world tilted and she hit the ground, landing on her back, with Will stretched out on top of her in a full-body press. And he had her gun.

"Damn it." She pushed against him, but it was like pressing on bedrock.

He propped on his elbows and grinned down at her. His hat had fallen off in the scuffle, and the moonlight glinted off his hair, making it look silver instead of a naturally streaked blond. And he had dimples, as if God hadn't already rewarded him with enough in the looks department.

"And if I were my father, you would be dead. Or worse. Believe me, with Matthias, there's always much worse. Give up?"

She squirmed some more, but froze when she realized he was getting turned on by her movements. There was definitely more of him pressing on her than there had been a few seconds earlier.

He laughed, a white glint of teeth in the moonlight. "Oh, don't stop moving, sweetheart. This is getting more and more interesting."

Yeah, she could feel exactly how interested he was getting. She felt a very un-vampire-like flush of heat as he wedged a knee between her legs. *Damn it.* She clenched her teeth at her body's betrayal—which he'd be able to sense. She hated being a vampire; there was no sense of privacy. "Get. Off. Me. Now."

Will lowered his head and, damn him, inhaled deeply, with his face pressed against the side of her neck. Her carotid artery also thumped in a very un-vampire-like cadence. She waited for the sarcastic comments to start.

Instead, he lifted his head and looked her in the eye. She could swear his heartbeat sped up, although it was hard to tell over the pounding of her own. Well, this was damned awkward. He blinked and opened his mouth to speak, then closed it again.

Well, that was one good thing. Will had been stricken dumb, at least for a moment.

Finally, he rolled off her, rose to his feet, and held out a hand. "Come on, help me dig my computer out of the dirt, and let's get out of here."

Avoiding his eye, she batted his hand away and got to her feet without anything near his gracefulness. She might as well not be embarrassed by her reaction to him. He was sex on a stick and he knew it, with his just-wavy-enough hair and dimples and brown eyes the color of antique gold. And if he ever forgot it, there were plenty of women in what was left of Penton to pump up his ego, or anything else that might need pumping.

Including her Omega roommate, Olivia, a human who'd been Will's familiar for a few months and obviously wanted to be a lot more. If Randa had a pint of unvaccinated blood for every time Liv had mentioned Will's name in the past three days, she'd have enough to feed for eternity.

They knelt on opposite sides of the metal box and had it unearthed after a couple minutes of digging. "Why is your computer buried, anyway?"

Will wiped off the loose dirt and tucked the box under his arm. "It's my backup. I updated it every few days and reburied it in case we ever had to leave in a hurry and I couldn't get to my primary computer. It contains all the diagrams for Omega and underground Penton. I knew I could probably get back to retrieve it even if something happened to the house."

He looked at the blackened shell of his home, a jagged outline in the moonlight. "You know, like if I had to burn it down myself, computer and all, to keep my dad from finding it."

Randa felt a stab of sympathy for him, then shook it off. A quick roll around on the ground didn't mean she should forget what a brat Will Ludlam was. As the only girl growing up with four brothers at a string of army bases across the country, she knew brats. "We need to take a look in town first—before I spotted you, I thought I saw movement around the clinic."

"Yes, sir, Veranda, sir." Will stashed the metal computer case beneath a pile of brush and covered it up.

Asshole. Randa stalked along the tree line, not looking to see if he was behind her. He could fend for himself.

Silently, they took side streets into what was left of the small downtown area. "Wait a second." Will put a hand on her shoulder and jerked his head toward the remains of the Penton clinic. "Damn, he *is* here."

A middle-aged man in an expensive-looking suit, thin, with salt-and-pepper hair cut stylishly short, left the clinic and got into a late-model silver sedan in the parking lot. "That's Matthias. We should go in and see what he left behind," Will whispered. "The clinic office is in the undamaged side of the building. I bet he's using it."

"You do what you want. I'm going to follow him—he's driving toward downtown." Randa began moving away, then looked back at Will. "If I get a good shot at his head, I'm going to take him out. You OK with that? Even though he's your father?"

Anybody would balk at murdering a parent, even a bad parent, and a large-caliber head shot directly into the brain—the only way a bullet could kill a vampire other than multiple close-range shots to the heart—made a gory mess even if you didn't know the person. It would be better if Will went back to Omega and left Matthias to her.

He moved closer and softened his voice. "My father deserves whatever he gets, but Aidan and Mirren have made their position clear. If we kill Matthias, it's the same as declaring open war against the Tribunal. They'll come down here with an army, and we won't stand a chance. We need to leave him in place while we come up with a strategy to swing the Tribunal to our side."

Randa wasn't buying it. All her training—and, hell, her whole life had been training—told her that if you wanted to kill the snake, you took off its head. She closed the distance remaining between her and Will.

She expected him to back off, but he stood his ground, his brown eyes lightening to a tawny gold as she found herself inches from his face for the second time tonight. She kept her voice low. "You sure that's all there is to it? He is your father. It's understandable if you don't want to kill him. Go back to Omega and let me do what I was trained to do."

Will's whisper was fierce. "You weren't trained to handle the likes of Matthias. Don't ever, *ever* underestimate him. And if you think I'm going to get all sentimental over the possibility of some father-son reunion, you're full of shit." Will's gaze held hers for a moment, then dropped from her eyes to her mouth.

Randa felt his heart speed up, kicking up hers to beat in sync. This was so not going anywhere. It had to be the stress.

"Stop that—I'm not one of your women." Randa spun away, not wanting him to see her eyes, which she suspected had lightened as much as his. Life was screwed up enough right now without getting the hots for the Penton playboy.

"That's the God's truth." Will pushed his way past her, and she followed, happy to leave the conversation behind. She'd met a million guys like Will Ludlam. Cocky. Arrogant. Ready to fight the whole Afghan rebel army single-handedly. One look at the results of a roadside bomb always took the wind right out of them. Admittedly, Will was better looking than most, but he knew it, and arrogance never stayed pretty for long.

They moved silently into downtown Penton, until Will stopped so suddenly in the alley beside the superette that Randa crashed into his back. She looked around the empty street, listened, sniffed the air. She got nothing; Will was just trying to annoy her.

He grabbed her elbow when she stepped around him, and jerked her back. "Wait. He's coming this way."

"Who's—" A crunch of gravel sounded from down the street, and Randa looked toward the destroyed municipal building a block to their west. Matthias and a man with white-blond hair and a cruel mouth walked down the middle of Main Street toward them. They took a turn into the Baptist church. How had Will known they were coming so early?

"Give me a diversion so I can see what Matthias is up to."

Randa's first instinct was to tell Will to create his own diversion, but she sucked it down. Whether she liked him or not, Aidan had made them a team, so it was important for them to work as a team. "OK, I'll circle behind the municipal building and make some noise. Who's the guy with him?"

"Shelton Porterfield, who seems to have been promoted to second-in-command." Will glanced back at her. "Buy me a few seconds, then get to the outlying Omega entrance—I'll meet you there as soon as I can."

She wasn't sure why Aidan put so much faith in Will. He had great fighting skills, but he joked around too much. And as he'd proven by leaving her behind a few times—including once when he'd left her unconscious on his living room sofa after a blindside—he wasn't a team player. In her experience, rogues got people killed.

Aidan did trust him, though, and they'd been together a long time, long before Aidan had established Penton. If she bitched about Will too much and forced Aidan to choose, she'd lose.

She needed Penton more than Penton needed her, and at least she had the sense to realize it. The scathe's situation might suck right now, but Randa didn't know what she'd do if Aidan made her leave. Living here was the closest to normal she'd felt since she'd been turned vampire, even with the town under siege.

Randa locked gazes with Will for a couple of heartbeats before slipping back into the alley and taking a circuitous route around and behind the municipal building, avoiding the church grounds. She crouched in the trees behind the old city hall and waited a few seconds, but sensed no movement nearby.

Her military-issue pistol slid smoothly from its shoulder holster, and she took aim at a bit of exposed metal in the wrecked rebar. Three quick shots echoed through downtown, and in seconds, Shelton Porterfield stepped out of the church door, scented the air, and raced toward her.

That was her cue to leave. Randa holstered the pistol and ran into the woods. The day had been a warm, humid one for late March. She could still feel the heat collected in the trees and rocks as she passed them, zigzagging erratically in case Matthias's companion tried to track her. Every half mile, she'd find something with a scent—a dead possum in one spot, an abandoned carton full of soured milk in another—and kick it across her path to muddy the trail.

It took an hour, but the remote tunnel entrance finally came into view. She started to move aside the brush that camouflaged the hatch, but decided to delay going underground as long as she could. Even after five years, she still got tired after a run like that, and the fresh air helped her recuperate faster. Plus, the less time she had to stay in the hole, the better. It was a well-equipped hole, but still a hole. Will had said to wait for him, so she'd wait.

Randa sat on the ground and leaned against a tree trunk, stretching her legs out, still amazed at how quickly her burning muscles repaired themselves. What a waste it had been, all those hours she'd spent in the gym and on the track before she'd been turned. She'd pushed herself hard to keep up with her brothers and convince her dad that Colonel Rick Thomas's daughter had the stuff to make it just like his boys. She didn't think she'd ever succeeded in convincing him.

Then, *wham*. One wrong turn in a Kabul alleyway, a flash of fangs, two or three days of horrific pain and growing thirst, and everything changed. Her view of the world. Her idea of what it meant to be physically strong. Reality.

Randa inhaled the scents of sap and bark, closed her eyes, and, unwillingly, turned her mind back to Will. She'd never admit it to him, not under threat of being staked and left in the sunlight, but she'd wondered more than once what it would be like to be with him. Well, maybe not him specifically, but another vampire. She'd avoided intimacy of any kind since she'd been turned. It felt too predatory to take a human lover, plus she was afraid she'd hurt a human guy. She still couldn't gauge her own strength.

And yet the male vampires intimidated the hell out of her. If they weren't alphas before they were turned, they sure as hell were afterward. Even someone like Aidan, for whom violence was a last resort, had scary strength and skills and wasn't afraid to use them.

She'd grown up surrounded by big, pushy men, and they both turned her on and put her on the defensive—a really screwed-up combination. And nobody intimidated her more, and put her more on the defensive, than Will Ludlam. She realized that she acted like a raving bitch around him, but that's how she reacted to people who were in danger of getting too close.

Maybe she was afraid she'd be attracted to him enough to act on it, and he'd reject her.

Or worse, he *wouldn't* reject her, and she'd learn she was just the latest among his million conquests.

Or, God forbid, he'd get attached, and she couldn't. Or wouldn't. Not to him. Not to any vampire.

She just flat-out didn't want to be a vampire. But the alternative was being dead, and she didn't want that, either.

Still, she wondered, if it could be just one night, with no consequences and no ties, what might it be like to take on Will Ludlam?

Until tonight, she'd been convinced he wasn't attracted to her. She went out of her way to not play up her looks—an important self-preservation tactic in the army. Minimal makeup, even now when the vampirism had made her hazel eyes greener. Shoulder-length red hair in the casual pileup she'd always worn in the military because she could fit a hat over it.

Tonight, though, Will had wanted her. She'd wanted him. They both knew it. The problem was, Randa wasn't sure what to do about it.

Maybe if she ignored it, it would go away.

❧CHAPTER 3❧

Will crouched beneath the stained glass window depicting a shepherd tending a flock of sheep on a green hillside and waited until he heard Randa's shots, followed by the footsteps of that sorry SOB Shelton racing toward the municipal building ruins to check out the noise.

Matthias was still inside the old redbrick church—something Will's suddenly enhanced sense of smell told him without looking.

If he could scent the old bastard, did that mean Matthias could scent him as well, or would he just assume Will had been in that building at some point?

He didn't plan to hang around any longer than necessary. He wanted to see what the old man was doing and then go back to Omega and charge his laptop, maybe feed before dawn. Nothing more entertaining, though. Liv was rooming with Randa, of all people, and that killed his libido as far as Liv was concerned, for reasons he didn't want to think about too deeply.

Getting a hard-on courtesy of Randa tonight had shaken him. Talk about dangerous liaisons. His ego couldn't deal with both his father and a woman with bigger balls than him. A man had to have limits.

As soon as he was sure Shelton was well gone, Will risked a peek through the window, squinting between the legs of a particularly corpulent sheep. Matthias seemed too occupied to scent him, so Will stood upright and pressed closer to the glass.

His father paced around the church sanctuary, pausing every few steps and cocking his head as if listening for something, then scanning the floor around him. A chill stole across Will's shoulder blades. Was Matthias looking for a hatch? Had he found out about Omega?

Surely not. He might have pieced enough of it together to figure out they'd escaped underground, though. Matthias was smart, as he'd certainly told Will often enough. It was usually followed by a diatribe about Will's stupidity.

Matthias would have realized all the Penton people had disappeared too fast, and he could easily have unearthed at least one of the subbasement hatches while combing through the buildings. It was a logical leap to assume there was an underground escape route, and the church was the last place Matthias had seen any of the Penton scathe.

He was likely on a fishing expedition and nothing more. Will had designed the hatch to lock beneath the edge of one of the heavy old oak pews, with a lever from below to move the pew in case they needed to climb back out from below. But so far, Matthias hadn't gone anywhere near it.

He was still too close, though. The tunnel beneath the church needed to be filled in with dirt and packed tight. With Matthias in Penton, any coming and going would have to be done through the remote hatch into the Georgia woods. Maybe they could start tunneling a new exit in case the fail-safe was compromised, at least until they could get everybody out that wanted out.

Matthias raised his head and stared toward the window. Will froze, holding his breath as his father frowned and scanned all the windows in the outside wall. "William?"

Shit. Will forced himself to remain still. If his father heard movement, he was as good as caught.

"Matthias, I couldn't find anything." Shelton pushed his way in the front door of the church, and Will took advantage of the diversion. He eased away from the church building and moved quickly from street to street, ducking in and out of shadows and avoiding other vampires, making as little noise as possible. He scented quite a few now but none from the Penton scathe.

It was only a couple of hours until dawn, so they were all coming in to find lighttight daysleep spaces. Will was tempted to hang around and try to get a head count, but he didn't want to risk getting stuck outside Omega at daybreak.

He slipped through the woods behind the remains of his house, retrieved his computer from its hiding space, and loped back to the Omega entrance. He slowed at a familiar scent and paused at the edge of the clearing, watching Randa as she sat with her back against a pine tree, her knees propped up and her head resting on them.

If she'd been human, he would swear she was crying. But this was Randa. Ms. Army-Navy-Air Force-Marines. Armor-plated Randa, who lived duty and mission, rules and regulations. Still, she'd only been turned four or five years and had come from a big family—as least that was what he'd gathered from Aidan. Maybe there was a human beneath the robot; she'd sure felt human lying beneath him tonight.

Oh, wait. Not going there again. Ever.

Randa never talked about anything personal. Will didn't know where she'd grown up or how many brothers or sisters she had. They'd been so busy pushing each other away and trying to one-up each other, as hard and fast as possible, that those introductory chitchats never took place.

She finally sensed him and raised her head. No, she hadn't been crying, but her hazel eyes were dark pools despite the brilliant lights the moon played off that amazing dark-red hair. If she'd still been human, there would have been tears.

Will stepped out of the shadows and dropped to the ground next to her, stretching out on the pine straw. It wouldn't kill him to be nice for a change, give the woman a break—unless she started being bossy or argumentative, which was guaranteed to bring out his inner smart-ass.

The cool, damp air was weighted with the approaching dawn, and no other vampires or humans stirred nearby. Just moonlight and an unhappy partner. He pulled the card he'd bought from inside his jacket pocket and handed it to her. "You OK?"

He waited for the sarcastic answer, and she opened her mouth as if to provide it. Instead, she rattled the small paper bag and pulled out the rumpled card. When she opened it, a tinny version of "Halls of Montezuma" echoed through the forest, and she slammed it shut.

"What the hell is this?" Randa's voice sounded strangled, and at first, Will thought she was angry—until she burst out laughing. "That's the most awful thing I've ever heard."

"Hey, I bought that especially for you, soldier." He laughed too, and it felt good after all the stress of the last three days. Hell, the last three months.

Randa sighed and ran her fingers through her hair, letting it spill out of its loose pile. Her voice rang in the still air like fragile crystal. "Thanks. I needed to laugh. That was awfully"— she squinted at him in the dim moonlight—"thoughtful of you. What did you do with Will the Asshole?"

Will grinned. "I can get him for you if you miss him. Seriously, though. You OK?"

"It just gets to me sometimes." Randa leaned back against the tree again. "How wrong I was about the world. How the things I thought were important really aren't. How hard I fought to prove myself. And now here I am again, still stuck in a world I don't fit in, still a rookie, still having to prove myself."

She stopped raking the tangles out of her hair. "Sorry, that sounds a lot like self-pity, and I hate that. I guess somebody like you would never understand what it feels like to not fit in, but believe me, it sucks."

It would have been easy to throw back an insult, to point out that to fit in, you had to at least try. But it wasn't that simple, and Will knew that better than anybody. He was just better at hiding what an outsider he was.

Plus, somehow, they'd made a step in their relationship tonight—well, not their *relationship*. They didn't have a relationship. They weren't even friends. But maybe they could at least be civil patrol partners.

"I've never fit in, not when I was human and not as a vampire. At least not until Aidan found me in Atlanta and showed me..." He'd almost admitted what it was Aidan had proven to him: that he was smart, not stupid. That there was a reason his mind worked the way it did. That the things his father had done to him as a vampire weren't, in the long run, as damaging as what Matthias had done while they were both still human. "Aidan showed me what it meant to have a family."

Randa winced and looked away. "But you have a family. Matthias..."

Will blinked back the rage that rose like bile whenever his father's name was mentioned. Rage at the things he'd done, not just to Will, but to his friends. He'd kidnapped Glory and let his buddies feed on her until she had ropy scars on her neck she'd carry with her forever. He'd sent Aidan's brother to kill him and forced Aidan to turn his mate, Krys, vampire in order to save her. He'd kidnapped Mirren, starved him, and had thrown Glory at him so he'd kill her and turn back into the Tribunal's pet executioner.

"Matthias is nothing to me. Worse than nothing," he said. "What you think you know about fathers and sons doesn't apply to us."

Randa pressed. "I know he turned you vampire, but I thought you agreed to it, wanted the everlasting life of a play-boy."

Will clenched his jaw and leaned against the same pine tree as Randa, their shoulders almost touching, but at least he didn't have to look her in the eye. After all, what she thought of him was the image he'd intentionally handed people—for a good time call W-i-l-l. But for some reason, he wanted her to think better of him.

"I was twenty-two, and completely under my father's influence. I was stupid." As he said the words, snippets of memory slapped him with almost physical force. Matthias pulling him out of yet another school. Taunting him about being the slow-witted son no man deserved. Matthias wondering what he'd done that God should punish him with an offspring who wasn't even smart enough to pass first grade.

Will had bought into the whole sorry shit pile. But his sharing with Randa wasn't ever going that deep.

She wouldn't let it drop. "Most boys your age would say the same thing. My dad was a total hard-ass, especially with my brothers. Didn't mean he didn't love them—or me. I wish I could tell him..." She trailed off.

She was so off base; their families had nothing in common. Absolutely nothing. "Matthias turned my mother and sister and me at the same time. Did you know that? Wanted to make us a big happy vampire family, all serving him as our master."

Randa's intake of breath was barely audible, but he heard it. "No. Are they..."

"Dead. My mom never revived after he tried to turn her— you know it only works about half the time, anyway. Catherine, my sister, lived for three days of agony, blood seeping out the corners of her eyes, her skin withering, begging me to end it. I finally did."

Matthias didn't know that. Didn't know Will had fashioned a homemade stake and pierced his eighteen-year-old sister's heart because it was the only thing he knew to do. Matthias assumed she died naturally.

He regretted a lot of things in his life, but not that. He'd been Cathy's big brother. It was his job to take care of her. And if he couldn't take care of her, at least he could see her at peace.

They sat silently for a few minutes. He couldn't believe he'd just spilled his guts like that. The stress was obviously getting to him.

Enough already. He got up and grabbed his laptop. "I'm heading down."

She climbed to her feet beside him. "What was Matthias up to?"

They pulled the brush away from the grass-and-straw-covered hatch entrance and unlocked it, then pulled it aside and climbed down. Will closed it behind them and locked it with a loud click. "He was nosing around the church—I think he's figured out we went underground."

Randa frowned. "You mean he knows about Omega? Do we need to start moving people out faster?"

"Maybe. We definitely need to get the lieutenants together, see what Mirren and Aidan have to say." They took the golf cart through the tunnel to the Omega entrance in silence, stopping it at the bend in the tunnel that led to the solid-steel entry doors.

Will knew Cage Reynolds was there before they rounded the bend. He sat in a metal folding chair tilted on its back two legs, his shitkicker-clad feet hanging in midair and a small unlit cigar dangling from his mouth. "'Bout bloody time you two dragged in."

His chair legs hit the concrete floor with a thud, and he pulled open the heavy door into Omega, gesturing for Randa to go inside, then following her before Will could take a step. Jerk.

"You didn't have to wait up for us." Will followed them inside, narrowing his eyes at Cage's hand resting on Randa's shoulder. What did they know about this guy, anyway? He was a vampire, he'd wormed his way into Aidan's good graces almost immediately, and Glory said all the women thought he was "hot" and liked his stick-up-the-arse British accent. Even Liv had commented on his green eyes.

Will stared down the length of the hallway into the big Omega common room, watching Cage and Randa walk away like some kind of *couple*.

He shook his head and began working the combination lock on the heavy door to secure them all inside for the day. It had to be near dawn, and he had to be hungry if he was concerned about who freaking Randa thought was hot.

❧CHAPTER 4❧

Cage walked Randa to the conference room, answering her questions about whether smoking was as satisfying to him as a vampire as it had been in his human life—the answer was no, but habits were no easier to break as a vampire than as a human. At least he didn't have to worry about lung cancer.

He turned to ask Will if he smoked and realized the young lieutenant was still back at the Omega door, working with the lock.

"Your chum William is an interesting guy."

"He's not my chum," Randa said quickly—too quickly, Cage thought. "We're just patrol partners—Aidan's doing."

Cage nodded. Definitely on the defensive. "He designed this place, didn't he? It's rather amazing."

They passed through the Omega common room, which was filled with sofas and chairs and gaming tables. The room was like the body of an octopus, with corridors for tentacles that branched out in five directions. The whole thing had been carved out of red Georgia clay and lined with steel panels that held sleeping quarters, a large kitchen, and restrooms for the humans. One wing was utilitarian—rooms holding systems for waste treatment, water filtration, and air treatment. A room for generators. For food and other supplies. And at the far end of the back corridor sat a silver-lined locked room in case a vampire misbehaved and needed to be contained. Next to it, another locked steel door led into the tunnel beneath the Baptist church.

"Yeah, Will designed it," Randa said. "He's brilliant. Just ask him."

Cage raised an eyebrow. "Harsh."

She shrugged. "I don't...I think...Will's OK."

Poor girl. She liked the bastard and didn't know what to do with it. Cage pegged her as a classic guardian personality type. Driven to succeed. Liked to be in charge. Straightforward and horrified by messy emotions. He'd met hundreds like her since the Second World War, when he'd been turned vampire while assigned as a psychiatrist to the British army.

Turned by one of his own fucking patients. How was that for a laugh?

He'd become a bit of a professional shrink-turned-soldier in the years since, from the Falklands to Iraq. He liked to fight and he liked to analyze people. Perfect scenario.

"Remember one thing," he told Randa. "People who seem arrogant are often hiding major insecurities. Your partner, Will? I'm guessing he's got some serious issues, given who his bastard of a father is."

Randa glared at him. "Who do you think you are—Dr. Phil?"

Who? Cage was prevented from inquiring about Dr. Phil by the arrival of Mirren and Aidan in the hallway outside the small conference room. Everyone filed inside, and Cage wasn't surprised to see young Hannah already there. He left the others and went to sit next to her.

As a doctor, he found Hannah fascinating. The daughter of a Creek shaman, she had inherited psychic powers. As a child, almost two centuries ago, she'd been turned vampire before really learning how to control her visions. Aidan had killed her maker and kept her with him ever since. If they all survived this current maelstrom, Cage hoped to work with her. He'd been reading books and scientific journal articles on psychics to learn as much as he could.

Mirren's mate, Glory, also had a special power—telekinesis—but she'd learned to control it. Hannah hadn't grown old enough to have the emotional maturity Glory did, so it was harder for her, despite her vampire age. In many ways, she was like an old soul trapped in a young body, but in others, she was still very much a child and probably always would be.

Will arrived last, taking the seat on the other side of Cage and pulling a laptop computer from a metal box. Cage had been watching Will Ludlam for a while as well—it was an occupational hazard for a psychiatrist. The man had some demons he covered up with a bounty of jokes and flirtations.

"OK, we've only got time for a quick talk before daysleep." Aidan propped his elbows on the table and leaned forward. Cage was struck, as he often was, at the man's calm demeanor. A natural leader, Aidan picked his people carefully and let them do their jobs. But he didn't tolerate disloyalty or carelessness. He was the only one here who knew what Cage was and that he'd come to Penton on behalf of the British Tribunal leader, who was secretly contemplating a similar string of vampire-human communities in the UK.

Cage wasn't convinced Penton could be replicated. Each community would need the kind of person in charge who attracted and held people's trust and loyalty the way Aidan did. Such people weren't common, especially among vampires, and especially during the current state of panic that gripped the vampire world over dwindling humans from which to feed.

"I think Matthias has figured out that we got out of town by going through some kind of underground exit," Will was saying. "And he's snooping around the church. He hasn't found the hatch, but I think we should fill in that tunnel so, even if he finds it, he can't find us.

"Fuck me. That would leave us only one way out. I don't like it—we need to find another way out before we close it up." Mirren's voice was a deep rumble from the side of the room, where he stood propped against the wall. Now, *there* was someone whose psyche Cage would like to dissect, but he suspected he might not live through the experience. The man carried a goddamned *sword*, and rumor had it he owned an honest-to-God battle-ax.

Aidan leaned back in his chair, fingers steepled in front of him. "Can we dig another tunnel that branches off the back so we aren't left with a single exit?"

Will opened his computer and clicked through screen after screen. Schematics, diagrams, and pages of drawings filtered past. Finally, he paused on a computerized map.

Cage leaned forward. "Is that the Omega site from satellite?" He thought the large rectangle at the top of the screen might be the bulk of the automotive plant.

Will nodded and shifted the screen to give Cage a better view. "I wanted to see if there were any dead spots that might give us a good place for another exit. Although, we have to think about a lot of other issues—soil moisture, where the displaced dirt would go, even oxygen. Humans doing manual labor suck up a lot more air than humans at rest."

"But the labor would be good for them—for us too," Cage said, and he felt the room go still. He was the new guy and, as such, tended to keep his mouth shut. He could feel the chill of Mirren Kincaid's suspicious gaze from across the room.

"Explain," Aidan said.

Bloody hell. He'd opened his piehole, so he might as well continue. "We've only been here three days, and already people are getting restless, especially the humans. At least the vampires can leave at night as long as we're careful, but they're stuck here twenty-four/seven. The ice cream Will bought tonight was brilliant." He nodded at Will, who returned the gesture. "It cheered them up, broke up their tendency to think too much about all the bad stuff that might happen."

Mirren snorted, but shut up at a glare from Aidan. "So we need to come up with things for people to do, to keep them occupied? Randa, what does the army do for soldiers who are in close quarters?"

Randa shifted in her seat, and Cage thought if she were human, her fair skin would have blushed a similar color to her hair. "Well, when we go on lockdown, there are jobs for everybody to do, to keep them busy. Also, games. You know, those handheld computer games, board games, cards. And quiet space where you can go to get away from people, even if it's just a corner of a tent. Someplace to get a little privacy."

"That should be easy enough to do." Aidan turned back to Cage. "You think that sounds about right from your military and other experience?"

Aidan's question drew all eyes back to him again. Terrific.

"And you're asking him, why?" Mirren shifted positions to the wall nearer Cage. If it was meant to intimidate him, it was working. Mirren Kincaid was kind of like a half-tame grizzly when he was with his mate, Glory, but she wasn't anywhere to be seen right now, and yeah, he freaked Cage out a little. The guy was a bloody giant.

Aidan simply raised his eyebrows at Cage.

"You fix people's minds," Hannah said. "You're going to help me learn how to use my visions better!" Her black eyes lit up, and then just as quickly, the light faded from them. "But not until whatever happens, happens. And I can't see what that is."

"Fix people's minds how?" Randa frowned at him, probably thinking back to his comments about arrogance and secrets.

He let out a breath. "OK, you guys know I came to the States two months ago from London. I'm a psychiatrist, first with the British army and then for private security outfits after I was turned, only taking night missions. I didn't want anyone besides Aidan to know because it makes people uncomfortable, although he wanted me to tell you from the outset." People always thought he was assessing them. With good reason.

Cage had always thought that bit about silence being deafening was stupid—until now. It was.

Will cleared his throat. "Well, I, for one, think having a shrink here is a good thing. He's right—people are already getting antsy. Our fams are starting to look like trapped animals, and God knows Mark needs all the help we can give him. We need to either come up with a plan to start getting people out of here faster—which means getting us out as well, since we'll freakin' starve if all our fams leave—or else we need to come up with a way to take Matthias down without pissing off the Tribunal."

Aidan nodded. "Agreed. We'll get back together first thing after rising to talk more. Randa, you and Hannah talk to Cage, make a list of things we can do to keep people's minds off our situation, and we'll buy what we need. Will, after daysleep, do some logistics on starting a new exit. Mirren, work with Will on how to make it happen and how to disable the hatch into the church."

"What about Mark?" Mirren's question brought a hush to the room, where everyone had been rustling, getting ready to leave.

Aidan ran his fingers through his hair, and Cage wondered how he was handling the tension. Losing his fam, losing his town, feeling responsible for endangering those who had pledged loyalty to him. Cage wouldn't want the responsibility.

"Krys says he has a concussion, and he's in and out. We finally told him about…" He paused, and everyone looked away, down, anywhere but at Aidan. "We told him about Melissa tonight. He's a wreck. Although, on some level, I think he already knew. Otherwise, she'd have been there when he regained consciousness."

Aidan pushed his chair back. "In fact, I want to see him before daysleep. Anything else we need to talk about?"

Cage cleared his throat. "Just this. I think one way to bring Matthias down without major casualties is to infiltrate his organization. We need to get someone inside who can get word back to Omega so we know what's going on and can make the best decisions, maybe gather more evidence to present to the Tribunal. As we've said before, we can't just go into Penton and kill the bastard—the Tribunal would see it as a declaration of war."

Silence. Well, that idea had been well met.

"Who the fuck would we send that wouldn't end up at the end of a stake before the night was out?" Mirren said. "He knows all of us."

Cage shook his head. "Wrong. He doesn't know me."

❧ CHAPTER 5 ❧

"Aidan, wait."

Randa paused until everyone else had left the conference room. Will shot a curious look over his shoulder but was deep in conversation with Cage. Listening as everyone warmed up to the idea of infiltrating Matthias's organization had made her itch to get more involved.

"What's up?" Aidan made her nervous. As always when he turned his attention solely to her, she felt his light-blue eyes laser through every layer of defense she'd built up around herself, exposing her as weak.

"I don't want..." She didn't want him thinking this was about Will, because it wasn't. And she didn't want to sound like a defensive woman who wanted to prove herself, because that's exactly what she was, damn it. "I need something more useful to do. Let me start taking some of the humans and scathe members out of here. Will can't take all of those runs if he's planning a new exit."

Shit. She'd brought Will into it anyway.

A small smile played at the corners of Aidan's mouth. "I thought you and Will were getting along better."

God help her, they were getting along too well if tonight was any indicator. "It's not that. I just need to be more—"

"Look," Aidan cut her off, "I know you can do a lot more than what we've given you. You handled yourself really well last month when Tanner died."

"This has nothing to do with Tanner." Randa looked at the floor, tracing the outline of a ceramic flooring tile with the toe of her boot. She and another new lieutenant, a guy named Tanner James, had gone to Virginia to try to take Matthias out before they realized how effectively he'd turned the Tribunal against Penton. Instead, they'd been caught. She'd been able to fight her way free, but not before Tanner and his heart had parted company. Cage had taken his spot among the lieutenants.

This wasn't about Tanner, but his death was one more reason Randa needed to prove herself.

Aidan rolled his head from side to side, tendons popping. God, he had so much on him Randa felt like a whiny jerk for bringing up something just to stroke her own ego. That's all this was, and she'd been raised better. "Sorry, I shouldn't have—"

"I'm glad you did. I know you're frustrated. But there's a couple of reasons I've had you paired with Will." Aidan ran his hands through his hair and nodded at his mate, Krys, who stood in the hall beyond, waiting for him. She was tall, almost lanky, with dark-auburn hair and intelligent dark-brown eyes. Her heart-shaped face gave her a sweet look, but Randa knew she was smart and strong willed, with an offbeat sense of humor. She could actually make Aidan laugh. The two of them completed each other, much like Glory and Mirren did. Randa liked to watch them together.

Aidan lowered his voice. "One reason I don't want you going solo is, well, it's hard for you to blend in. I don't mean this to sound sexist, but Matthias got a good look at you the night of the fires and there aren't that many female vampires with red hair running around in the woods. You haven't been turned that long, Randa. It's no reflection on you. If I didn't trust your skills and respect both you and your training, I'd have never made you a lieutenant. I came to you, remember? You didn't ask me for the job."

Well, that made Randa feel about three inches tall. He was right. Aidan had never made her feel second-rate. She'd done that to herself. What was that quote from Eleanor Roosevelt? *No one can make you feel inferior without your consent.*

"You said there was another reason you paired me with Will. What is it?" She'd put her combat skills up against his any day and beat him. Well, if she could learn not to let him distract her.

"Will's coming into his own as a vampire." Aidan looked down the now empty hallway toward the rooms where all the lieutenants bunked. "Do you know the difference between a regular vampire and a master vampire?"

Huh? "I know you and Mirren are the only masters here. You have stronger sensory skills, mental communication, stamina." Hell, they were better at everything. "What does that have to do with Will Ludlam?"

"I'm not even sure how master vampires are formed; it's one more step on the evolutionary scale, and most vampires don't reach it. But Will's going to. He's mentally tougher than he lets people think he is. He might already be developing some of the master skills; I sense that he is. You can learn from him, if you'll just find a way to get past the armor you two put up when you're together."

Randa stared down the hallway, imagining the arrogance billowing like a mushroom cloud outside Will's door. That spoiled clown was a master vampire in the making? Oh, hell no. Life couldn't be that cruel.

Aidan laughed. "Daysleep time. Try not to think about it."

Easy for him to say. Randa scuffled her boot heels on the tile floor on the way to her room and flipped the bird at Will's door on principle. Just like magic, the door opened and out came Liv, his fam.

She had a glazed-over, orgasmic expression on her face, and Randa dropped her gaze to the woman's neck. She didn't see his mark, but that didn't mean it wasn't there. Had to have been a quickie, though. "Have fun?"

Liv was five ten, with perfect skin, full lips, and hair and eyes almost the same color of dark chocolate. Just Will's type, in other words. She could be a model.

The lips were in the midst of some serious pouting, though. "I hate being down here." Liv opened the door, and Randa followed her into their room. "Will's too distracted by everything that's going on. He's no fun anymore."

"He's..." Randa had been about to say Will was too self-absorbed to be distracted by anything beyond what he could see in a mirror, but she stopped herself. Aidan considered him strong going on stronger, and Cage had thought the cocky attitude was an act. She needed to keep an open mind. "What's bothering him?"

"I don't know—he doesn't talk much, and he's been all quiet and broody. I can't make him laugh anymore." Liv yawned. "You need to feed before you sleep?"

Randa gritted her teeth. It wasn't just feeding from another woman she hated. The whole act of feeding was gross. Gross, but necessary if she was going to stay strong enough to keep up with her soon-to-be master vampire partner, who'd sure enjoyed himself tonight when he flipped her, disarmed her, and landed on top of her. "Sure, if you're up to it."

The vamps worried about having their humans feeding two vampires each, but they'd lost a disproportionate number of their bonded humans as it started looking more likely they'd have to move into Omega. Randa didn't blame them, just as she didn't blame her fam, Gary, for leaving. She'd encouraged him. They had no emotional attachment to each other beyond a polite friendship. He'd been assigned to her; she fed from him. Now she shared a feeder with Will.

Liv sat on the edge of the bed and rolled up her sleeve. Randa sat next to her and lifted the woman's arm to her lips, then stopped. Will's scent was all over her, and Randa saw two small bruises where he'd bitten—on the arm, the least intimate place from which to feed. By morning, the marks would be gone.

"I thought Will fed from...other places." Randa winced. That question had come out before she could stop it. She didn't need to know Will Ludlam's feeding habits or to have anyone think she was interested. "Never mind. TMI."

Liv huffed. "He used to feed from other places, and he used to be a good lover. I thought it would be cool to be his mate. Now he's all grumpy, and I'm sort of wishing Cage would—" She flinched as Randa bit into her arm, an inch away from Will's marks. "Well, Cage is sexy."

She chattered on as Randa fed, sharing her views on Cage's accent, Cage's wardrobe, which leaned toward a lot of black and white, and Cage's ass.

Randa finished, licked the wounds, and considered their newest lieutenant. Did he have a nice ass? She'd never noticed it.

She had noticed Will's, though. And that was just wrong.

⚜ CHAPTER 6 ⚜

Cage started talking before Will had even opened his eyes the next evening at dusk. Now that the man had been outed as a shrink, they'd never shut him up.

"What do I need to know about Matthias? I want to infiltrate his scathe as soon as possible."

Will groaned and rolled over. Cage had pulled on black pants and was already lacing up his boots. His chest was all hard planes with a light dusting of hair, but he was kind of scrawny—chicks liked that? He wasn't as heavily muscled as Will, who'd never bulk up to Mirren proportions but worked at keeping enough muscle to maximize his strength—but not enough to cost him speed.

"I just don't get it." Will swung his legs over the side of the twin-size bed and raked his hands through his hair.

"Don't get what?" Cage pulled a black sweater over his head and clamped his hands on his hips. "Why I need to know about Matthias? That should be obvious."

"No, why all the women have the hots for you. Must be the accent." Will rifled through the few clothes he had in

Omega—they'd all brought minimal wardrobes down here several weeks ago in case they ever had the need to go underground in a hurry. Damned insightful of them, in retrospect. He found a copper-colored shirt that wasn't too wrinkled and tugged it over his head.

He had one leg in his jeans before glancing up to see a perplexed look on Cage's face. "What?"

"Women have the hots for me?"

"Pffft." Will jerked up the jeans and zipped them. "Yeah, don't let it go to your head."

Cage laughed. "Well, Randa Thomas is pretty hot. Can't believe she's not with anyone—doesn't even have a real fam."

A flash of anger shot through Will's veins and settled somewhere in his gut. "Stay away from..." He straightened up and looked at Cage, who wore a broad, annoying smile. Where had this possessive shit come from? It had to stop. "Good luck to you. Randa's a hard-ass."

Cage chuckled in a way Will didn't much like. He couldn't tell if the guy was laughing with him or at him—it felt like the latter. He needed to watch his tongue around the shrink. And change the subject.

"So, back to Matthias. Let's talk about my paternal paragon."

Cage followed him into the hallway, and they sat down in the same small conference room from the previous night. "Anything that will help me not just fit in but earn his trust?"

Will looked at Cage—really looked at him, with a clinical eye. He was handsome enough, with long brown hair and eyes a funny color of green. He looked too damned healthy, although he was kind of skinny. "First thing, you have to do without food a few days after you first infiltrate his camp. Don't feed any more often than they do, maybe less at first. His followers are all hungry as hell. I think it's how he gets them to do his dirty work."

Cage nodded slowly. "I've been doing that already, been limiting to feeding every other day. Even Matthias looks half-starved. They're probably sharing humans like we are, only with a higher vamp-to-human ratio."

"Not only that, but my guess is that they're intentionally eating light so the humans won't get used up as fast," Will said. His father was nothing if not practical, and at least now he knew why his roomie looked so scrawny. If he'd been starving himself awhile, he'd been planning this even before they were all forced into Omega.

Cage tilted his chair back and propped his crossed ankles on the edge of the table. "What else?"

Will took a mental step back from Matthias the father to look at Matthias the vampire. "He's a master vamp but not a really strong one. He just has a lot of political muscle, a lot of smarts, and no conscience to get in his way. He was turned in the mid-1960s when he was forty-five years old. He can do some mental tricks but nothing like Aidan and Mirren—I think because he doesn't get close enough to anyone to strengthen his bonds. He's smart and he's ruthless; don't let your guard down around him, ever."

Will stood up and began pacing around the table, staring at the floor. "He doesn't reward creativity or out-of-the-box thinking—unless you can somehow make it look like it was his idea and it's proven successful." Another corner, another turn, more pacing. "He wants yes-men, but only insofar as they're able to say yes and then complete tasks on their own. Never show weakness. Never show uncertainty. Never ask for help. He'll exploit it."

He stopped in front of Cage. "And unless you're into rough sex play with sadistic bastards, stay away from Shelton Porterfield. I saw him in town last night, panting after Matthias like a dog in heat. He's second-in-command now. You're a little too old for his taste, but keep things professional with him, and don't give him anything to use against you."

Cage's voice was soft, calm, maddening. "Sounds like you speak from experience."

Will stopped, remembering the summer after he'd been turned, when he was still reeling from his mom's death, from having to kill Cathy, from the rapid changes to his own body. He hadn't toed the line to Matthias's satisfaction and had been sent to spend the summer "training" under Shelton. And Matthias knew exactly what Shelton's training entailed.

He'd see that bastard Shelton dead before all this was over. "Yeah, well, don't expect me to lie on the couch and reminisce, Doc. But don't kill Shelton. He's mine." He'd had a shot at Shelton when he'd gone to Virginia to rescue Mirren a couple of months ago, but he'd let the SOB live so he could stay focused on his mission. He wouldn't let that opportunity pass again.

Will left the room before Cage could respond. Something about these close quarters was playing serious games with his mouth. As in, he kept running it, talking his way into deeper and deeper holes. He'd never had this problem when he was living alone.

He walked to the end of the hallway leading to the church exit, pulled a key from his pocket, and opened the heavy steel door. Beyond it was a narrow tunnel, then a wider exit room where the drop ladder to the church hatch hung. The tunnel and exit-room walls consisted of tightly packed dirt. They'd hoped to concrete them in eventually, just as they'd already done with the outlying exit, but time had caught up with them.

Will studied the exit and saw nothing amiss, but a snuffling sound from the top of the hatch halted him. He cocked his head and inhaled. Vampires directly overhead. And something else. Not vampire or human, but...

He looked up sharply at the sound of a long, baying bark, followed by more snuffling and yips. Matthias had brought in fucking dogs, and if they hadn't found the hatch yet, they were close. Scanning the exit room, Will's gaze lit on a can of paint, left over from some of the interior work.

He pried open the lid and looked around but saw no sign of a paintbrush. *Shit.* He climbed halfway up the ladder, dipped his hand in the can, and lifted out a palmful of "Satiny Sage." It had just the strong paint odor he wanted, and he spread a thick coat of it around the hatch entrance. He didn't know if it would be strong enough to throw off a scent, but God knew Matthias had access to enough of the town's clothing and personal items to give the hounds a boost.

Scraping off as much paint as he could along the rungs of the ladder, he descended. The noises of the dogs had disappeared, and he no longer scented their presence beneath the cloying odor of the paint.

One thing was clear, though. Matthias was close. They needed two heavily armed guards in this exit room around-the-clock. Vampires couldn't stage a raid during daylight hours, but humans could, and Matthias had plenty of money to make it worth their time.

Finally satisfied that the immediate threat had ended, Will reentered Omega and locked the steel door behind him.

The entrance to Randa and Liv's room stood ajar, and he paused in the hallway. His first instinct was to keep walking; he didn't want a confrontation. Talking about Shelton had brought up a lot of heavy baggage he'd been ignoring for a long time, and he wanted to discuss security with Mirren. But after last night, he'd at least progressed enough with Randa that he didn't want to go on solo patrol and leave her behind. Asking her to join him in talking to Mirren might help make up for previous bad behavior.

And if Randa wasn't in there, maybe Liv was. His feeder was another problem he needed to handle. He'd never led her on, never made her think there was a chance for them being mated, but he knew she wanted it. And he'd been a real asshole lately. Time to suck it up and be honest with her.

Truth was, this whole business with his father had dealt him all he could handle, and Liv would never be more than a casual feeder. She was an enthusiastic lover, but she bored him outside the sheets. Lately, even under the sheets. Maybe it was time for them to have "the talk," the one where he gave her the *we'll-always-have-Penton* speech.

He pushed the door open wider, but Liv and Randa were nowhere in sight, only a brunette with one of those short, choppy haircuts, sitting at a small table with her back to the door. A pretty brunette staring into a mirror with a horrified look on her face. Will had thought he knew all the Penton residents at least by sight, especially the ones who'd gone into Omega. This one, he didn't know.

"Oh!" The woman spotted him in the mirror and turned a wide-eyed face to his.

Holy shit. "Randa?"

❦CHAPTER 7❦

Randa's new haircut had been nothing more than an impulsive whack of scissors. The dye job had been courtesy of Liv, whose natural hair color turned out to be a mousy light brown, and she'd had the foresight, or vanity, to move a box of hair dye into Omega with her clothing.

It was a girly kind of fun Randa had seen others have but had never enjoyed herself. Her mom died when she was a kid, and with a military dad and four brothers, *girly* didn't play well in the Thomas household. She and Liv had made a mess and giggled, and it had been a big release of stress and pressure.

Until Liv went off in search of dinner and Randa looked at herself in the mirror and realized what she'd done. She'd lost herself. When she was turned vampire, she'd lost her humanity. All that had been left of the old Randa Thomas was her hair, and now that was gone. After the laughter died, only the hurt and directionless feeling remained.

And now she had to endure the humiliation of Will standing in the door with his mouth hanging open.

She looked at the floor. "Go ahead, laugh. Everybody else is going to."

He cleared his throat. "Actually, it's pretty." When she looked up, he smiled, and it was such a sweet expression she almost smiled back. Almost. This was Will, after all. It wouldn't last.

"Why'd you do it?" He walked around her, taking in all sides. "It makes your eyes look greener."

She hazarded another look at his face, but saw no sign of the jester.

She swiveled to study her image in the mirror again. Her hazel eyes did look a deeper green beside the dark hair, and her skin, always fair, more porcelain. "I did it on impulse, because of something Aidan said last night, about Matthias recognizing me by my hair if I got caught while I was on patrol."

Will sat on the edge of the bed. "Maybe. But if he got close enough, Matthias would scent Mirren's bond on you no matter what your hair looked like." Aidan required all his scathe members to be blood-bonded to either Mirren or himself, partly so they could use their mental connection to find anyone who was in trouble. But Randa knew a big part of the reason also was so that they'd know if anyone tried to defect or betray them. Since they'd been sold out by a former human in January—a big screwup that ended up with Krys getting turned to save her life—they'd also required all humans to be blood-bonded to a master vampire whether they were fams or not.

She sighed. "Well, it's done. And, uh, why are you turning green?"

He held up his paint-covered right hand. "It's a fashion statement. Like it?"

"About as much as I like my hair. What's planned for tonight—more patrols? Or are you taking some people to Opelika?"

Will told her what happened in the exit room, including how he got his hand covered in green paint, and all thoughts of silly things like hair fled. Dogs were bad, bad news. Randa didn't know how canine noses compared with those of master vampires, but she'd put money on the dogs. Guess it was time for her new look to make its debut.

"We need to convince Mirren to fill in that space." And she'd smelled enough food scents wafting from the kitchen area to know exactly where he was. Glory had taken charge of the kitchen. She also ate about an hour before Mirren woke from daysleep and wanted to feed so her blood would carry traces of whatever she'd consumed. Randa thought it was kind of gross, but it seemed to work for them.

She followed Will into the hall, and they walked side by side toward the kitchen wing. He kept turning to look at her.

"What? If you're going to laugh at me, go ahead and do it."

He held up his hands in self-defense. "I didn't say a word." But he grinned so broadly his fangs showed. Damned vampire. She'd known the kinder, gentler Will would be a short-lived thing. He'd shown amazing self-restraint so far.

Sure enough, Mirren was sitting at one of the tables in the community dining room outside the kitchen, with Glory on his lap. God, what would it feel like to have a man look at her the way Mirren looked at his mate? He was the biggest badass Randa had met—and she'd met a lot of them on military bases—but his features grew almost soft when he looked at Glory. And the way he was looking at her now, they'd have been off doing something more intimate if Will and Randa had arrived any later.

Will coughed, a bit too loud and obvious to be natural, and Randa could've sworn Mirren growled at him. Then the big man's gaze landed on Randa and his annoyed frown gave way to a surprised frown. "What the fuck did you do to your hair?"

Glory thumped Mirren on the head, slid off his lap, and stood with her hands on her hips, studying Randa and ignoring her mate's grumbling. "I like it. Turn around."

The couple dozen people sitting in the big dining room swiveled to look as well.

Terrific. She turned slowly, letting everyone get an eyeful.

"I think it was a good move." Glory picked some dishes off the table next to Mirren and took them to the sink. "I mean, your red hair is gorgeous, but it's such an unusual color it drew attention to you, even when you stuck it under a cap. You can blend in better now, and once all this crap is over, you can always strip the dye out and grow it back out. Or you might decide you want to keep it this way so you can—"

Mirren interrupted. "Glory, st—"

"Yeah, yeah, vampire. 'Stop,' he always tells me. He thinks I talk too much."

Mirren raised an eyebrow, but he looked more amused than angry. "You guys patrolling downtown tonight, or you want the Opelika run?"

"We need to talk first." Will put an arm around Glory and hugged her. Randa had seen them together a couple of times before Matthias's attack had driven everyone underground, and they seemed close. Not close enough for Mirren to get jealous— even Will wasn't that much of a playboy. He just had an easy way with people, except her.

Had that been her fault? Maybe so. But he'd done his part too.

Cage and Hannah were already in the conference room— Hannah had known they needed to meet. Aidan was talking to Mark, she said in her solemn, adult-child way, and would be there soon.

"Mark thinks he wants to leave, but he will die if he does." Hannah fiddled with a tassle on her pink boots, still a little girl in so many ways. "He will use drugs again, like he did before he met Aidan. He has to stay here even though his future..." She stopped and shook her head, a frown wrinkling her smooth forehead.

Cage leaned toward Hannah. "What do you see in his future?"

"I don't know." Her voice rose on the last word, and she threw her Hello Kitty purse across the room. It hit the concrete wall and spilled little girl purse things on the floor: a tube of lip gloss, a pen, a notebook, a mirror. Randa slipped out of her chair and began gathering the items and putting them back in the bag. Will leaned over and handed her a pink cell phone that had skidded near his foot. Not that they could get signals down here, but they all still carried phones. She and Will exchanged uneasy glances.

Cage spoke softly to Hannah. Her adult familiars, who'd acted as her parents for the past three years, had reluctantly left her behind to return to Atlanta. She was using a substitute feeder she shared with Cage, and Randa wondered how much of her frustration was not being able to control her psychic abilities and how much was losing the fams she'd come to think of as more family than familiar. Maybe Cage could help her.

Being a vampire might give you immortality—as long as no one chopped off your head, scrambled your brains, tore out your heart, or threw you into a sunlit field—but it exacted a terrible toll on family. For a few moments, Randa let her mind go to a dangerous place, to her twin brother, Rory. Until last month, she'd been able to keep up with her dad and brothers by following Rory's blog. She knew their next-oldest brother, Robbie, was engaged and that the eldest had his first baby on the way. Rory was unsettled after his army discharge, playing in a band and trying to find himself.

They all thought Randa had died, and life inevitably had gone on.

A month ago, Rory had stopped blogging for no reason she could discern. Before Matthias had invaded Penton, Randa had hoped to take some time off, drive to Tennessee where he was living, and try to spot him. Just to make sure he was OK. Now that wasn't going to happen, not for a while.

The Penton scathe was her family now, and she wouldn't leave them.

She shook off the worry and returned to her seat, sliding the Hello Kitty bag across the table to Hannah. The girl was staring at the clasped hands resting in her lap and seemed still and closed off. Cage looked at Randa and shook his head.

"What's up?" Aidan came into the room but stood in the doorway instead of sitting. Things with Mark must have been bad. His injury during the attack on Penton had at least spared him the sight of watching Melissa die. Things were grim for Penton, and she wasn't sure Aidan could convince Mark that living here was worth slogging through.

Like quite a few of Penton's humans, Mark had struggled with drug addiction before meeting Aidan. The scathe leader took hard cases from the Atlanta shelters, many of whom were unvaccinated, and helped them through withdrawal with a combination of enthrallment and counseling. They were clean by the time he told them what he was and gave them the option of coming to Penton or trying to forge their old lives back together on their own. There was a no-relapse policy, though. Anyone who slipped got their memories wiped and a trip back to Atlanta.

Randa was pretty sure Aidan wouldn't let Mark return to that life, even if he didn't believe in keeping people in Penton against their will. If he had doubts, Hannah's insight into Mark's future would convince him.

After a quick update on Mark, Aidan turned his attention to Will. "Tell me what's going on." Will gave a concise account of the dogs and what he'd tried to do to mask the scents, but Aidan was frowning by the time he finished.

"Closing up that exit has to be first priority. Mirren, I know you don't like leaving us with a single exit, so get to work figuring out how to get the manpower to create a new one."

Mirren leaned against the wall with his arms crossed over his chest. "I'm on it. Until we do fill that exit in, we need to keep armed guards there night and day. I'll round up human guards for tomorrow's day shift."

Randa saw the opening she'd wanted. "I'll take tonight's watch."

Aidan nodded. "You and Will both guard the church exit, I'll take the back hatch. Cage, you ready to meet Matthias? The sooner we can get info on what he knows and what he has planned, the better. We'll have to break your bonds to me so Matthias won't scent you as mine."

Cage was laser focused, and Randa wondered if she'd ever see him again. Even the least suspicion that he was a plant and Matthias would kill him.

He gave a grim nod. "Ready and steady."

❧CHAPTER 8❧

Cage slung his hastily stuffed backpack over his shoulder, took a deep breath, and walked into downtown Penton. He'd approached from the east side, as if hiking all the way in from Atlanta with nothing to hide.

He'd been doing patrols outside of town, so this was his first postattack look at the little community he'd come to love. Now it reminded him of the bombed European villages he'd seen after World War II, piles of rubble alongside burned shells of buildings, punctuated by an occasional storefront left inexplicably whole and untouched but for broken windows. Looking at it hurt. Everything these people built had been honest and good.

He made himself a promise. If he survived this, he'd help rebuild Penton. He had an obligation to go back to England and try to replicate this place, but not until the original town was whole again.

He'd hoped to take a look in the Baptist church before being spotted, but no such luck. The door to the church opened, and a tall, thin man stood in dark silhouette against the interior lantern light. Cage could feel the weight of examination from a block away. He lifted his arm in a wave and angled toward the church. Time for his opening performance.

From Will's description, Cage thought the vampire he was about to meet had to be the infamous Shelton Porterfield. Tall, thin, with washed-out blue eyes silvered in hunger, an oversized beak of a nose, and stringy white-blond hair that fell over his forehead in the shape of a comma. Definitely Matthias's second-in-command.

"You better have a good reason for being here." Shelton's drawl carried authority, but Cage recalled Will's account of how cowed the man had been when Will had arrived at Matthias's Virginia estate to rescue Mirren and Glory six weeks ago. Will had easily gotten the jump on him. Mr. Porterfield could be intimidated.

"I'm here to see Matthias Ludlam." Shelton assumed his most formal upper-class accent and stiff-upper-lip demeanor. "As an envoy from the Tribunal's UK representative, Edward Simmons." He and Edward had come up with the alibi in case he ever ran into trouble. He figured if this situation wasn't trouble, nothing qualified.

Shelton frowned and looked him over. Cage assumed a casual stance but threw his shoulders back and never dropped his gaze. He studied Shelton for telltale body language and was satisfied. Shelton had lost his swagger. He wet his lips, jiggled his hands, frowned, and looked down the street. The man was trying to decide what to do with his sudden, unexpected visitor.

"Stay here while I talk to Matthias and see when he's available. Mr. Ludlam's a busy man; he can't just talk to anyone who wanders up."

Cage shrugged. "No problem. I'll ring up Edward at his New York office and tell him Matthias will see me *when he has time*. Pity, that. The United Kingdom organization has been a supporter of Matthias's work here in Penton. Edward will be disappointed that Matthias doesn't have time for one of his staunchest allies."

He turned back in the direction from which he'd entered town and walked away. When Shelton called after him, he allowed himself a brief smile before turning to respond.

"Wait." Shelton's voice rose with a quiver. "No sense in running off. Matthias is here. Come on, we'll find him. But"— Shelton wet his lips again, a nervous tell—"I…Well, how do I know you're who you say? You might be one of Aidan Murphy's scathe."

What an idiot. Cage gave him a level look. "Do you scent Murphy's scathe on me? Come a little closer, Mr. Porterfield."

The fool actually took a step backward. "How'd you know my name? Mr. Simmons wouldn't know me."

"Edward makes it his business to know the major players. We know that Shelton Porterfield, formerly of Virginia, is Matthias's second here. I had your description and, in fact, knew you were the perfect man to expedite my meeting with Matthias. You have a reputation for being very efficient." And he had some swampland in the Scottish Highlands to sell if the man bought that lie.

Cage reached in his pack and pulled out a forged British passport with his photo and a real letter of introduction from Edward, including the leader's personal seal and the stamped insignia of the Vampire Tribunal. All quite legitimate, except, of course, for his real business here and Edward's true allegiance.

He handed the papers to Shelton, who read the letter with a gradual relaxation of tense shoulders. "Sorry for doubting you. We've got to be careful around here—these goddamned rebels are ruthless. They'd not hesitate to take Matthias down, and the Tribunal is relying on him to take care of Penton so they can focus on how to meet this pandemic vaccine crisis."

Yeah, more likely so they could continue their graft and corruption and, judging from his last conversation with Edward, formalize a policy that would allow the black market sale of unvaccinated humans. If the vampire ruling body was seriously considering sanctioned human trafficking, they were all beyond fucked. Edward thought if they could get Aidan on the Tribunal, he'd have enough charisma and persuasion skills to turn them around. But first, Aidan had to survive and they had to turn enough Tribunal members to get him a fair hearing.

Which meant this had to work. He had to find out what Matthias was doing and figure out a way to give Aidan the upper hand.

"No problem, Shelton. I'm sure Matthias appreciates your thoroughness. Shall we see him, then?"

Shelton bobbed his head and started walking in the same direction from which Cage had come. "Matthias has taken the office at the old clinic. Part of it was damaged in an explosion, but the office is still usable and has electricity."

Cage knew he had to not appear too well informed, especially of the last few days' events. "I noticed a lot of damage around town. Fire damage, rubble. What happened?"

Shelton shook his head. "Might not want to ask Mr. Ludlam that. We almost had all of them, with some careful planning, the bombs, the fires. A lot of 'em died, but some managed to get away. Not only Murphy, but Kincaid—you heard of the Slayer?"

"I'd heard Mirren Kincaid had joined forces with Murphy, yes." Cage looked ahead, avoiding eye contact with Shelton lest he start laughing at Will's description of how frightened the man had gotten in his only close encounter with Mirren. Now that he'd met Shelton, he could visualize it. "I also hear Kincaid is quite a swordsman, that he still has his original battle sword, in fact." A downtown battle against a small army of starving vampires, who had been led to Penton by Matthias's people, had already become the stuff of legend among the Penton residents. Some said Mirren took off twenty heads; some said forty.

"He fucking lops heads off with that sword of his—you've never seen anything like it." Shelton practically shivered. "He's a monster."

Given what Will had told him about Shelton—he'd at least hinted that Shelton had tried to sexually molest him—this son of a bitch was a bigger monster than Mirren Kincaid could ever hope to be.

If Cage's long life had taught him anything, it was that *monster* wasn't measured in size or physical strength, but in blackness of heart and soul.

Cage remained quiet the rest of the walk to the clinic, while Shelton chattered more than any second-in-command should. As a result, Cage now realized Matthias knew the Penton scathe and their humans had escaped into something called Omega, that he knew it was underground and accessed beneath the church, and that Shelton was virtually living in the church sanctuary in case any of them tried to come out. In other words, Matthias was too damned close to finding them all, just as they'd feared. He hoped Mirren would get the exit plugged before that happened.

They reached the clinic entrance, and Cage followed Shelton into the brightly lit lobby. He understood why Matthias had picked it for his headquarters—it was one of the few buildings in town that still seemed to have electricity and be mostly intact. The overhead fluorescents shot their painful glare into his dark-adjusted retinas, and he squinted against the light.

At the end of the long central hallway, Shelton stopped and knocked on a door to his left. He waited a few seconds, then tentatively opened it. "Matthias? We have a visitor from the Tribunal."

Matthias came into view through the doorway, his face compressed in a frown and mouth open, probably to give Shelton a good tongue-lashing. He recovered quickly upon spotting Cage, however, and his face smoothed into a practiced smile. A politician's face, whose pleasant expression never reached the shrewd brown eyes peering cautiously from beneath dark brows and salt-and-pepper hair.

So this is the boogeyman. "Cage Reynolds." He stuck a hand out for Matthias to shake, which he did after a second's pause. "Edward Simmons sends his regards—and he sends me, his most trusted lieutenant, if I might say so myself, to be of service. He's most sympathetic with your cause and wishes to support your efforts to eliminate the Penton rogues in any way he can."

Matthias stared at him a moment, and Cage remained still while under scrutiny. If Matthias was a master vampire—even if a weak one, as Will had said—he'd have an arsenal of means to detect fraud: scent, light mental invasions, the ability to gauge whether Cage's heartbeat sped up with a lie.

Finally, Matthias smiled and motioned Cage inside. "My apologies. These are dangerous times, and we must be cautious."

"I understand, of course." Cage produced his papers and handed them to Matthias. "Your man Shelton here was very diligent in examining my credentials before bringing me to you, but I'd like you to see them as well." The fool beside him practically preened.

"Shelton's a good man. Have a seat, please. Brandy? I hope you don't mind, but I need to send Shelton on an errand."

"Not at all, and brandy sounds excellent." Cage poured himself a drink and took a seat facing the desk. He crossed his legs in a relaxed posture, but his gaze roved around the room. The office had some damage in one corner, and a buckle in the wooden flooring had exposed the hatch to the subbasement suites. That definitely would have told Matthias how adept the Pentonites were at creating underground living spaces. Correction: how adept his son Will was at engineering them.

Matthias finished his discussion with Shelton and came to sit behind the broad desk—Aidan's desk. This was where Cage had first met with the Penton scathe leader, in this very seating arrangement. The two men—Aidan and Matthias—couldn't be more different.

Cage couldn't help but look for signs of Will in his father. Their eyes were the same color of golden brown, but where Will's held an almost sweetness when he wasn't on his guard or being a sarcastic asshole, Matthias's were hard as amber. Maybe the same jawline, but otherwise, Will must have resembled his mother.

"Let's see what we have here." Matthias unfolded the letter from Edward and read it. "Very impressive credentials. A psychiatrist. Do you find that helpful as a member of Edward's inner circle?"

Cage pretended to think about the question. "Yes, and I think it can be helpful to you. I've had many years to study behavior during wartime, both vampire and human. Edward thought I might be able to advise you on different avenues the Penton scathe might have considered or taken. Maybe help anticipate their moves."

For the next hour, they talked about the scathe, and Cage was able to learn a lot about what Matthias knew and didn't know. He could identify all the lieutenants by sight except for Cage himself and knew all the others' names except for "the redhead," Randa. Matthias wanted revenge on Glory almost as much as Aidan and Mirren, blaming her telekinesis for ruining his original takedown of Penton.

There was one thing he hadn't mentioned, however, and Cage decided to tackle it directly. "I'm sorry if this is a sensitive subject, Matthias, but I have to ask about your son. Where does he fit into your plans to destroy Penton? Are you hoping to save him? It's Edward's understanding that he's been with Aidan Murphy for quite a number of years."

Matthias's glare pierced him like an ice pick before the man reassumed his politician demeanor. "I have to admit I would like William back in my own scathe, but there must be repercussions for his betrayal. If he survives, he'll be sent to work for Shelton in Virginia until he comes to his senses. He was always slow to learn—the boy didn't even pass first grade, much to my shame. It takes harsh measures to teach him, and I can only blame myself that he didn't learn his place the first time I sent him to Shelton."

Matthias gave a great put-upon sigh and leaned back in his chair. "If William doesn't survive, well, of course I'll be deeply saddened, but the needs of the Tribunal must come before my own. You may reassure Edward of that."

What an absolute slime bucket. Cage forced his fingers to relax. As Matthias had talked, he'd gripped the arms of his chair hard enough that the wood had cracked. It was a miracle Will had ended up even halfway normal.

Plus, the comment about Will being a slow learner confused him. He was one of the smartest people Cage had met— quick to grasp problems, find solutions, and able to change directions on the fly.

"I'm sorry if I'm being nosy, but it's an occupational hazard. Why did William fail first grade? How is he a slow learner? It might be something we could exploit to find the rebels or force your son into helping us."

Matthias laughed, but it sounded more bitter than amused. "It wasn't just first grade. He's slow-witted, I'm afraid. The boy simply could not learn to read. And obviously doesn't follow orders very well, either. It's a bad combination of traits."

As they continued to talk, Cage tucked away the information about Will to think about later, because it definitely didn't compute with what he'd seen.

Matthias kept glancing at his watch. What was he up to? Was it the task he'd sent Shelton to do? Cage had strained to hear their conversation earlier, but hadn't been able to detect anything beyond the word *church*.

Might as well let him get to it and not arouse suspicion. "I'm sure you have things to attend to, but please know that I'm at your disposal." Cage stood and reached across the desk to shake hands with Matthias. "Are there houses in town with safe daysleep spaces one might use?"

Matthias looked at him over steepled fingers, and Cage got the feeling he was being judged yet again. Finally, Matthias nodded and rose from his chair. "No need for that. I discovered some very nice spaces in a subbasement underneath the clinic. You're welcome to a room there as long as you want, and this end of the building still has electricity. One room appears to be locked—not sure what Murphy used it for—but the rest are open. In the meantime, I'll be thinking about how best to put your skills to use."

"Is this where you're taking your daysleep as well?" Might as well know how guarded he needed to be during his most vulnerable time of day.

Matthias closed and locked the desk, tucking the small key in his pocket. "No, I found a house with electricity across the street from where Murphy used to live—his place was burned, of course, but I wanted to be there in case he tried to retrieve anything."

Will had burned not only his own house, but also those of Aidan, Mirren, Hannah, Randa, and Cage, and had set off explosives in their subbasement spaces. Matthias could dig through the soot and ash all he wanted but wouldn't find anything.

Cage followed him to the hatch in the corner. From the story Glory and Mirren had told about their escape from Penton, at least part of the sub-suite corridor had collapsed. The day before they'd gone into Omega, Mirren and his mate had spent a daysleep on the side of the tunnel nearest Aidan's house, which meant this was the only way in and out of this end of the corridor.

If Matthias ever suspected him, it would be easy to seal off the hatch, and Cage would truly be caged. Maybe he'd spend one daysleep here and find other accommodations tomorrow. He'd come up with some excuse. Mirren wasn't the only one who didn't like being limited to one means of escape.

Once they'd climbed down the second drop ladder into the sub-suite corridor, he could see the damage at the end of the hallway, near the steel door that had led into the tunnel to Aidan's backyard. There were probably still two suites on the far side of the collapse, then the concrete tunnel that opened into Aidan's greenhouse.

All but one of the six suite doors on this side stood open, and Matthias stopped at the one nearest the hatch. "This one's in the best shape—the others have some loose plaster, although nothing seems to be structurally unsound, and only these first two still have electricity. You're welcome to take your pick, however."

Cage walked into the suite. A king-size bed with carved oak posts filled one side of the room, and everything was coordinated in warm earth tones that helped counteract the natural chill from being so far underground. "Nice digs." He set his backpack on the bed, noting the fireplace, the attached bath, and the comfortable furnishings in the sitting area and bedroom. "They're all this elaborate?"

Matthias laughed on his way out the door. "Yes, Murphy had quite the setup. Too bad he won't see it again. Have a good daysleep, Mr. Reynolds. We will talk more tomorrow evening."

As soon as he heard Matthias climb the ladder and cross the basement level above him, Cage returned to the hallway, waiting for the sound of the clinic office hatch sliding into place. Then he went room to room, checking them out. Nothing had been left behind, and all the suites were identical.

At the end of the hall, he tapped his knuckles against pieces of rubble, trying to gauge how thick the collapse was between his end of the hall and the other side. Impossible to tell. He didn't want to start pulling out pieces at random and risk further collapse, but he studied the configuration of crumbled concrete, wooden supports, and dirt to determine which pieces, when removed, would cause those around them to fall. If he needed to get out fast, it might be the only way.

Cage looked at his watch. Less than two hours left until dawn—he'd talked to Matthias longer than he'd realized, but he'd accomplished what he'd wanted from the night. So far, he'd been accepted. He'd learned a little, with hopes of learning more. Tomorrow night, he'd scope out the church before meeting Aidan in the automotive-plant parking lot—if he could safely get away without arousing suspicion.

On the way back to his suite, he stopped outside the locked door. Something seemed wrong about it. He looked at the other doors and realized what it was. All the doors except this one had no visible locks on the outside—they all locked from within. This one had a key plate and outer dead bolt lock.

Cage had heard the story about how Aidan had met his mate, Krys, how he'd kept her locked in a room beneath the clinic when the town had first come under siege. This must have been the room.

But why would it be locked now?

He held his ear to the door, but heard nothing. He knocked on it, then listened again. *There! Were those movements inside?*

"Hello? Who's in there?" He pressed his ear to the door.

He sensed movement again, maybe a muffled trace of sound. Damn it, someone was in there. Question was, who? And was opening that door akin to opening Pandora's box? No Penton scathe members or their fams were unaccounted for. They'd either died in the attack, opted to have their memories blotted, or were in Omega.

What was it the modern sports announcers said? *Go big or go home.*

Cage was going big.

He returned to his suite and retrieved a small kit of tools—one never knew when a lock might need picking. Returning to the closed door, he knelt and began the meticulous work of tripping a dead bolt.

It was a good lock, and he had to work a good half hour to coax the bolt into turning. Finally, it clicked, and he rose to his feet. Time to see what he'd decided to unleash. With only an hour left until dawn, it could prove disastrous.

He grasped the doorknob, twisted it, and pushed the door ajar, standing to the side of the opening lest anyone have a gun trained on him. When no bullets whizzed past, he cautiously looked inside.

A woman lay tied to the bed with what looked like silver-laced rope. She was gagged. He could tell she was vampire and had strawberry blonde hair, but he couldn't see her face.

He cleared his throat. "Hello?"

The woman raised her head. Green eyes widened above the gag, and her nostrils flared as she began to struggle against her bonds.

Bloody hell, but this was impossible. "Melissa?"

❧ CHAPTER 9 ❧

Will had probably been more bored during the last sixty-plus years, but he couldn't remember when. He and Randa had been sitting on the ground in the earthen exit room beneath the church hatch for—he glanced at his watch for the umpteenth time—six hours and twenty-three minutes. Two hours until daysleep and it couldn't come soon enough.

They'd played blackjack until she'd caught him cheating. The woman really couldn't take a joke.

They'd argued about the pros and cons of different hand-guns. Even Mirren hadn't been able to convince her to abandon the military-issue pistol her father had brainwashed her into considering God's gift to weaponry, so Will didn't try too hard. He much preferred blades to bullets, anyway.

They'd clashed over whether music from Will's era, the late 1960s, was preferable to Randa's country-and-western drivel from the last decade. Led Zeppelin could still rock the house, and Brad Paisley sounded like something that should be used to make a shirt, no matter what she said.

He knew they'd hit rock bottom when he realized they'd been arguing about the Civil War for twenty minutes. Good Lord, this woman would argue with a potato.

And look sexy as hell doing it. Not that he had any plans of going there. They obviously had absolutely nothing in common, since she'd just called him a damned Yankee.

"OK, let's agree to disagree about the cruel bastardry of Ulysses S. Grant. Want to play strip poker?"

"Oh, that's going to happen. Not." Randa raised an arched eyebrow at him, and he stared at it. The eyebrow was dark—she must have dyed it too. How the hell did women do that without having big smudges on their foreheads?

"You dyed your eyebrows."

She glared at him, lowering those dyed eyebrows into an upside-down chevron above her nose. Cute nose. "Gee, thanks for noticing, since I'm not self-conscious about this ridiculous hair or anything. Want to play more blackjack?"

Will groaned and leaned against the hard-packed dirt wall. "I'm sick of cards. Would you rather play cards or computer games?"

Randa looked around. "Your computer isn't even in here."

"I wasn't talking about doing it. I was starting a game of Would You Rather."

"Great. I used to play that in middle school." Randa groaned and stretched her back, which showed off an interesting figure beneath those jeans and khaki shirts she liked to wear. Will could come up with some fascinating Would You Rather questions for her. This could be fun.

"So, answer—cards or computer games?"

"Um...computer games, especially if I'm playing against you. Harder for you to cheat."

Sore loser. "OK, your turn."

Randa thought a few seconds. "OK, would you rather be in a fight with Mirren or...Attila the Hun?"

Will laughed. "How serious is Mirren about beating my ass?"

"Oh, he's dead serious. And he has his sword."

"Easy one, then. Attila in a heartbeat."

"Yeah, me too." They smiled at each other. Then Will looked away. That had been too close to sharing a moment. "OK, my turn."

What did Will want to know about Randa? "What do you miss most from your human life—food or sunlight?"

Oh man, I am such an asshole. The flicker of pain that crossed her face hit him like a slap. She hadn't been turned that long, and she missed her family. "Never mind. I shouldn't have asked that."

She gave him a searching look, then shrugged. "Food. Real food. I don't like the way we have to feed. I think it's gross."

Will pondered this revelation. He found feeding very pleasant. With the right person, it could be downright...stimulating. "You haven't found the right feeder. You feed from the forearm? Because that's, like, the most impersonal, unfulfilling spot."

She propped her elbows on her knees and covered her face. "God, I can't believe we're even talking about this. It's embarrassing."

Will dusted some dirt off his boot and pondered Randa's dilemma. She hated being a vampire. Well, hell, didn't they all? At least on some level, all the Penton vamps did. They hung on to their humanity with a fierce grip, determined not to become a political monster like Matthias or a predatory monster like Aidan's brother, Owen, had been. Now, *those* were two men who loved being vampires. Owen was the son Matthias had wanted Will to be—ruthless, sadistic, no conscience.

"None of us really asked for this life, you know?" He fiddled with his boot buckle, not wanting to meet her gaze. "Different eras, different circumstances, but we all had this existence forced on us. If we can't adapt and find some kind of happiness within what we've been handed, we're facing a long, long time to be miserable. And I don't like being miserable."

It took her a while to answer. "How do you do that—find happiness, I mean? Are you happy? Does Olivia make you happy?"

He met her gaze, startled. "Liv? Oh man. Olivia." He shook his head. "I don't want to hurt her, but we aren't going where she wants us to go. I was going in to talk to her last night when I found you and your...hair."

Randa laughed. "Well, she won't be surprised if you're ending things with her. In fact, she's already got an eye on your roommate."

"Yeah, the ladies like the shrink, apparently, and he thinks... What is that?"

Shuffling above them, then a heavy thump against the hatch.

He dropped his voice to a whisper. "Shit, they're moving the pew right above us. Lock the door back into Omega in case they get us. Shove the key in the dirt so they won't find it on our bodies—it'll buy the guys inside some time."

"Got it."

While Randa scrambled to shut the steel door and bury the key, Will checked the clip on his gun, made sure Randa had hers, and then turned the fluorescent lantern to its lowest setting. Vampires had enhanced vision but couldn't see much better in pitch-black than humans. Turning down the lantern would give Randa and him enough light to see but would give them plenty of shadows to hide in.

"You want to pick them off as they come down the ladder?" Randa's whisper sliced through the tension.

Another thump from above and shouting voices. He recognized his old buddy Shelton. Any body part of Shelton Porterfield's that came down the ladder was getting blasted to hell. Too bad he probably wouldn't come down headfirst.

"Pick them off. No point in firing blindly. They can only come down one at a time, and that's our advantage." He was surprised they'd stage a raid this close to dawn. Less than an hour and they'd all be going into daysleep. There was some part of this picture he wasn't seeing, and it made him nervous.

The hatch lid made a wrenching noise as it was peeled back, leaving a square of soft light in its place. Will gritted his teeth at the sight of Shelton's rat face looking down, then caught his breath as Matthias came into view. He'd expected his father to be preoccupied with Cage all evening. Had Cage made it in?

No time to worry about that. He stayed in the shadows, silent and still as only a vampire could be, and was glad to see the vague outline of Randa's shirt across the exit room from him. They were crouched in almost identical stances, one knee to the ground and the other foot crooked to bring them to a quick standing position if needed. Their guns were cocked and ready.

Time seemed to hang in suspension until, finally, Matthias said, "Throw it, close the hatch, and then move aside quickly."

His pinched face disappeared, to be replaced by Shelton's. He held out a hand and dropped something through the hatch, then clapped the hatch back in place, plunging the exit room into near darkness.

"What was that? Where is it?" Will grabbed the light and turned it up, pivoting to see Randa feeling around on the ground between them. They both froze for an instant as the light illuminated the small object lying on the ground between them.

"Grenade!" Randa barreled into Will's midsection, knocking him backward as the room exploded around them. The last things he saw before the world went black were her green eyes, fierce with anger, and a mountain of dirt and steel projectiles raining down on them like missiles from an angry god.

☜ CHAPTER 10 ☞

Cage couldn't believe Melissa was alive. Alive but changed. Aidan Murphy's much-loved familiar was a vampire. And Mark Calvert was grieving a wife who wasn't dead, but wasn't alive in the same way, either.

It changed everything.

He remained in his suite a half hour after sundown, indecisive for one of the few moments in his life. He'd barely had enough time to convince Melissa he wasn't working for Matthias when daysleep fell upon them. He'd rushed to get her door relocked and return to his own room before the lethargy of dawn overtook him.

Matthias had been torturing her, telling her Aidan was dead, taunting her that Mark was being held in another room. He'd been starving her, and even though Cage had been turned a good seventy-five years, he remembered the hunger after first being turned. It was fierce, brutal, consuming. When Cage told her Aidan and Mark were safe, as were Krys, Glory, Mirren, Hannah. Melissa had slumped in relief, but her eyes remained silver with hunger.

Then they'd heard the explosion, and Melissa admitted she'd told Matthias about the church entrance to Omega as he withheld her feeding and insisted everyone she loved was dead. She'd been ashamed, beating herself up about it ever since, thinking herself weak for believing him, for being so, so hungry that it wiped out every rational thought.

Now Cage faced a dilemma. Should he give up on the idea of infiltrating Matthias's organization and get Melissa out of here and back to Omega—if Omega was even still there? Or should he let Matthias keep abusing her in order to continue his ruse and see if he could keep the man from doing more damage to whatever was left of Aidan's scathe?

Shit. Even a shrink couldn't make that decision come out right for everyone.

He dressed quickly. While stuffing everything back in his pack, he tried to imagine what Aidan would say, and that was easy. Aidan would want Melissa out of Matthias's hands, no matter what, and they'd figure out another way to deal with the Tribunal.

Mirren? He'd probably go for the big picture, tell Cage to stay put and help Melissa when he could. Will would be with Aidan; he'd suffered enough of Matthias's abuse on his own that he wouldn't want Melissa going through it.

Cage ran his hands through his hair and snapped a rubber band around it to form a short ponytail. The man looking back at him from the mirror looked haunted and gaunt. Wasn't a good look for him.

He left the suite, walked down the hall to Melissa's door, and let himself inside.

He'd retied and gagged her when he'd left just before dawn, although with much softer bonds than those in which he'd found her. He eased the cloth from her mouth. "How're you doing?"

"Better now that I know everyone's OK, or at least they were before last night. Did you find out about the explosion?"

Cage untied her wrists and rubbed them to get the blood flowing. Even vampires could get muscle cramps and numbness. "Not yet. I wanted to see you first."

Melissa's voice was no more than a rasp. "You have to leave me here; go and find out what happened. If you take me out of here, Matthias will know you aren't legit. Go back and make sure Mark is OK, that Aidan and Krys are OK. Glory. Mirren. Will."

She doubled over with a dry, rasping cough that Cage didn't think would ever stop. She was too near transition to be going through this. The first few months were hard enough; she still might not survive it.

"When's the last time you fed?" He began rolling up his sleeve. A vampire couldn't survive forever feeding only from another vamp, but it would keep her going for as much as a week if he could feed her twice a day, which meant he had to feed himself, somehow.

"I don't know. I've lost track of days. How many days since I...since I died?"

"Five. Here, drink from me."

She hesitated, so he took a knife from his pocket, sliced into his forearm just above the wrist, and held the wound in front of her face. She moved fast, grasping the arm and biting hard without anesthetizing.

He couldn't help his sharp intake of air. "Easy there."

She looked up at him, tears sliding down her cheeks. God, he'd forgotten how human new vampires were. "I'm sorry. I've seen Aidan do it a million times. I know better."

Cage smiled and got a wavery smile in return. "Try again."

This time she licked a spot on his arm an inch from the fast-healing cut and bit softly. Cage closed his eyes as she pulled on the wound, enjoying a rare feeder's high. He'd only ever fed another vampire twice, both times in emergency battlefield situations. It had been nothing like these sensual waves of pleasure.

But he hadn't fed in two days himself, so he couldn't let her take too much. Plus, if she looked too rosy cheeked, Matthias would know something was amiss. "Stop now, love."

She pulled away and licked the small wounds. Collapsing back on the pillows, she smiled—the first one he'd seen from her. He'd never before noticed how pretty she was. "Thank you."

"Not a problem." He cocked his head and listened for motion in the hallway, but it was still quiet. "Now, you're right that my mission here will be over if you suddenly disappear, but I can't in good conscience leave you here. It goes against everything Penton stands for."

She was too fragile, and too many people loved her. Matthias would either kill her or mentally break her. Cage didn't think he could live with either of those outcomes, not if he could have prevented it.

"Tie me up, and lock me back in." Melissa took his hand, spoke rapidly. "I need to know they're OK. If they are, come back and tell me. We'll figure out what to do then. I can handle Matthias as long as I know everyone's safe. Between the two of us, we might learn more. Do you have plans to meet Aidan and tell him what you've learned?"

Yes, and Cage now understood why Aidan cared so much for her. Melissa was fierce and stubborn and maybe not nearly as fragile as he'd thought. Vampires were forever underestimating the loyalty and inner strength of the humans around them, to their own detriment.

"Very well. I'm to meet Aidan later tonight. I'll talk to him, see what the explosion was, and then I'll come back to you before daysleep and let you feed." He massaged her wrists again before retying them with the silver-threaded rope and gently raising the gag. "Remember to act hungry—however you were behaving with Matthias before I came. Don't do anything to make him think you're less desperate than before."

She nodded and the skin around her eyes crinkled as she tried to smile around the gag.

Cage leaned over and kissed her forehead. "Be strong, love. I'll be back."

He locked her door, wiped off any prints or scents he might have left, and climbed the ladder, first into the basement level and then to the clinic office. The hatch lid had been set back in place but wasn't locked.

"Hello?" he called out before sticking his head through the hatch. Surprising a volatile vampire was a good way to lose a scalp.

"Ah, thought you should be rising soon." Shelton Porterfield sat on the sofa beneath the clinic windows fiddling with a cell phone. There was no sign of Matthias.

"Sorry, I hope waiting for me hasn't kept you from your duties."

Shelton grinned. "No, we struck a blow for the cause last night. Now we're letting our victims think about their situation, whoever's left to think. Hopefully, there were a lot of casualties."

Cage worked to keep his own smile in place. "How's that?"

"First, do you need to feed? I kept my feeder here at the clinic in case. Happy to share."

Cage found the thought of feeding from anything Shelton Porterfield's mouth had touched revolting, but he needed the strength, especially if he were going to keep helping Melissa. "That would be brilliant. Thank you."

He followed Shelton down the hall and into what had been a small office.

Good God. Cage stopped, dumbstruck at the sight of a young boy, who looked no older than fourteen or fifteen, curled up on a love seat. He opened sleepy blue eyes that widened a fraction at the sight of Shelton, then settled on Cage.

"You have a problem with young men?" Shelton watched him closely, and Cage shuttered his expression with some effort. Where had he gotten this child?

"I think *young* is the operative word here, Shelton. He can't be of legal age." Even the Tribunal, corrupt as it was, drew the line at anything to do with children. But there were always those whose tastes couldn't be satisfied otherwise, and he'd already heard about Shelton's tastes.

"I'm eighteen," the boy said, sitting up, his tone defiant. He gave Cage a blatant once-over, sending a shiver down his spine and shriveling his balls. "You can feed from me; I like it."

The kid's fucking voice hadn't even changed. If he was eighteen, Cage was a member of the House of Lords. "Sorry, son. I prefer the ladies."

With what he hoped was a convincing smile, Cage clapped Shelton on the shoulder. "Thanks, man. I'll just round up someone a little older if you don't mind."

Shelton oozed lust as he looked at the boy, who gave him a coy expression in return. "No problem. I'll be back soon, Evan. Wait here."

"Yes, sir." The boy curled up on the love seat again and closed his eyes.

Cage would swear the kid was drugged, but he had to abandon him, at least for now. He was beginning to wish he hadn't promised to leave Shelton Porterfield for Will to finish off.

Shelton accompanied him to the front door of the clinic. Cage had to get the man talking again. "I thought I heard an explosion just before daysleep. Anything I can help with?"

Shelton pointed toward downtown. "Let's go this way. I want to show you something."

They walked in silence for a block before Cage decided to try again. "I promised Edward I'd call him tonight and give him an update. Is there anything Matthias would like to share with the Tribunal?"

Shelton's teeth gleamed in the moonlight. "Yes, indeed. Tell Edward we found a hatch into what we believe is an underground bunker the Penton group used to escape, or at least a tunnel leading out of town. It was built beneath the church up here"—he pointed at the Baptist church, whose front door hung askew—"so we threw in a grenade just before dawn, collapsed the whole thing."

Bloody hell. "Why collapse the entrance instead of going in after them?"

They'd reached the front of the church. Shelton went ahead, turning on a couple of fluorescent lanterns inside the sanctuary door. The pews had been tossed aside, and a blackened hole filled the center of the floor. Cage felt his heart stutter. How many had been hurt? Killed? They'd done it just before dawn so the vampires wouldn't be able to retaliate or tend to any of their wounded.

"Matthias felt that if we went down one at a time, they could pick us off too easily. This way we might have trapped them, or at least forced them to use another exit. The plan was perfect." Shelton clearly idolized his boss. "He said Mirren Kincaid would never leave himself without options. So he had our people fan out all over this godforsaken county at twilight. If they come out another way, we'll catch them."

Cage walked to the center of the sanctuary and stared down into the explosion site. Dirt, concrete, rebar, wiring—it all looked like a solid mass that filled up the hatch. He knelt and picked up an X-shaped piece of metal, each corner of the X in sharp points.

"How'd you like a few dozen of those flying at you at thirty miles an hour?" Shelton knelt beside him and looked into the hole.

Cage didn't ask what it was. He'd seen enough projectile grenades to last a lifetime. Probably an M67, which would thrust little steel spikes for a kill radius of five meters and an injury radius of a lot more. If the steel door into Omega had been open, anyone in the hallway would be hurt. Aidan had been planning on assigning all-night guards in the exit room. Whoever they were, he didn't see how they could have survived.

❧ CHAPTER 11 ❧

Randa awoke with a start, instinctively knowing she'd somehow slept past sundown, something that happened only when a vampire's body was trying to heal an injury. It was black as obsidian, the air around her close and damp. Something light touched her face with a feathery tickle. Where was she?

She tried to move her legs, to sit up, but she was immobile below the waist.

"Stop wiggling."

She froze, suddenly aware of a heart beating directly beneath hers, the male voice coming from just north of her ear.

"Will?" Why was she lying on top of him? Why couldn't she move?

Then it finally came back to her. She had recognized the grenade right away. Military issue, the same type the army bought by the gross. When it hit the floor of the exit room, she hadn't stopped to think. She'd plowed into Will and knocked him on his back, away from the grenade. Then it blew.

"Are you OK?" He ran his hands along her back, and she flinched at the pain of his probing fingers on her skin—her shirt must have been in tatters. "Damn it. I think some kind of projectiles came out of that thing and hit you in the back. Your skin must have healed over them during daysleep. I have one on my face."

She returned her head to rest on his chest, letting his hands stroke her hair. "Don't feel any here," he said. "Are you in pain?"

"Not too bad. How much trouble are we in? I can't move my legs."

"Me either. I think we're pinned. And I can't even feel my left foot." Will coughed, and Randa felt another feathery touch on her face. "Concrete dust and dirt keeps sifting down. We have to be in some kind of air pocket—I'm afraid if we try to pull free, it'll bring everything down on top of us." He shifted his upper body slightly, causing another shower of dust. "Don't guess you have a cell phone on you?"

"Planning to call nine-one-one?" She regretted the words before they were out of her mouth. She had to stop being such a smart-ass. If she lived through this, *nicer* would be her goal. "Sorry. Being bitchy is a habit I'm trying to break."

"It's hard to stop something when you're so damned good at it."

She bit back a retort, then realized he was laughing. His upper body shook with it. An embarrassing giggle-snort escaped her before she could stop it, which made him laugh harder. She fought to control the giggles. They were both on the verge of hysteria, just happy to be alive, but if they didn't quit laughing, the whole damned tunnel was going to bury them. "I think my phone's in my pocket—why?"

"You got a flashlight app on it?" Smart man. Randa tried to move her right arm, but it was pinned beneath Will's body. She was afraid to reposition enough to retrieve it. "It's in my right pocket, and my right arm's pinned."

"Let me try." His left hand was warm as it slid slowly down her side and eased between their bodies. Fingers explored the waistband of her pants and slid straight down with a pressure that sped her heart rate. Her left hand was free, and she pinched his side. Hard. "Watch it, buddy. My pocket isn't over my... crotch."

"Sorry." Will's voice didn't sound the least bit sorry. In fact, it sounded as if he might start laughing again. "I was afraid it might be my only chance to get my hand in your pants."

"Just get the damned phone." She ground the words through her teeth, thinking of mountains of dirt over their heads, whether they could run out of air, anything except Will's wandering fingers and how this was not the time to flirt.

His hand found the opening to her pocket and slid inside, scrambling for the phone. Finally, he pulled it out. "Where's the power button? Oh, never mind. Found it."

The little screen cast a greenish light over Will's face, and Randa gasped. His left cheek was red and swollen where a projectile had hit him and he'd healed over it. Her back probably looked the same way.

He was frowning at the screen, punching buttons. "You have it password protected?"

"The password is..." She paused. Damn, she hated to admit she'd used his pet name for her as a password since she'd spent so much time pretending it pissed her off. Really, she thought it was funny. It was the first nickname she'd ever had. "The password is *veranda*."

The phone's glow caught his smile, then his scowl. "Here, you type it in."

"But you've got both hands free and I only have my left— try again."

He closed his eyes, and his chest rose and fell beneath her. "I can't. Here, I'll hold it, and you can punch in the letters."

Weird. Maneuvering her left hand, she did as he asked, then scrolled to the flashlight app and clicked on the icon. A brilliant light came off the back of the phone. "Take it," she said. "I can't see anything but your pretty face."

"Yeah, I'm sure it's a dirty shade of gorgeousness right now." He turned the phone over, and Randa watched his eyes as he followed the beam of light above them. Shifting his head an inch to the left, he squinted past her shoulder toward their legs. "Hm."

Not helpful. "What do you mean, *hm*? What's the situation?"

He laid the phone on his chest, and she was glad he hadn't turned the light off yet. They needed to save the battery, but she didn't feel as panicked when she could see him.

"One end of a support beam's wedged across our legs, and the other end's propped against a part of a broken beam above us. We probably have enough vampire power between us to shove the beam off our legs, but it would bring everything down. We're gonna have to wait until the cavalry arrives."

Randa felt panic bloom in her gut like an unfolding flower. "Which 'cavalry' will find us first—our people or Matthias's?"

Will didn't answer. His gaze had grown distant, and she badly wanted to know what he was thinking. The only way to get him to open up might be for her to do it first. She would not be taken hostage.

She rested her cheek on his chest again. "If Matthias finds us, I'm going to make sure he kills me—just warning you." Her voice was little more than a whisper, but she knew he could hear her. "I hate being a vampire. I'm not good at it. I don't know what I'm doing half the time or how to gauge what I can do. Feeding grosses me out. I'm intimidated around you guys who are so good at everything. I felt that way growing up around all my brothers, trying to be as good as them, trying to be a good little soldier like them. And now I have to do it for eternity. So if it isn't Aidan coming through the cave-in first, don't try to save me from Matthias."

Will didn't say anything, so Randa shifted her head to see his face. His eyebrows were bunched so tightly he had crinkles between them, and the muscles in his jaw clenched and released. "None of us knows how to be a vampire the first few years; give yourself time." His voice dropped, grew hard. "If you think I'll let Matthias touch you, forget it. He'll have to tear me to pieces to get to you, and I don't think he will. If he finds us first, I'll go with him peacefully on the condition you go free. He'd consider that a good deal."

It was Randa's turn to stare. Will had obviously been abused by his father and, at least on some level, was afraid of him—with good reason, as near as she could tell. "Why? You don't know me that well. You don't even like me—and don't get me wrong, I know I haven't given you any reason."

Will finally lowered his gaze to look at her, and the fierce light in his eyes softened. "I like you, Randa. I...You intimidate me with all your training—look how you pushed me away from that grenade when I hadn't even figured out what it was. When I feel threatened, I get competitive and act like an asshole."

She intimidated him? Randa searched his face for a twinkle in his eye or an upturn of his lips, but they weren't there. "So

I've been a bitch because you intimidate me, and you've been an asshole because I intimidate you?"

He grinned, then winced when the gesture stretched the reddened skin on his cheek. "We are a couple of pathetic losers."

"Damn straight." Randa knew she shouldn't be smiling. The world was literally about to cave in on them, and they had a fifty-fifty chance of rescue by a murderous sociopath. And yet, here she was, smiling.

Will clicked the flashlight app off, and they rested in the soft light from the illuminated phone screen.

"If you go to settings and type in the password again, you can set that light to stay on. It won't drain the battery too fast, and I don't think I can stand the dark again."

Will moved the phone toward her left hand, which was resting on his shoulder. "Here, you do it."

"I don't think I can maneuver it left-handed." She'd always been hopeless with her left hand. Ambidextrous, not so much. "You have both hands free."

Another big sigh. "I can't."

He was Mr. Computer Wiz, architect, engineer, good at everything. Why was he being so pigheaded about her stupid cell phone? "What do you mean, you can't? What's the—"

"I can't spell without sounding it out, and I didn't want you to think I was stupid, OK? Shit." His voice dropped so low she had to strain to hear. "Don't tell Aidan. Please don't tell Aidan."

The exit room was silent but for the soft thud of earth hitting earth. Another piece of the matchstick palace had fallen somewhere.

Randa tried to process the admission, but couldn't. It made no sense. "Will, you are the smartest person I've ever met, but you know that. Help me understand." And if he was pulling some joking crap, she was going to forget her vow to be nicer.

He didn't answer for a while, and she settled back down, with her head tucked under his chin. He ran his hand up and down her left arm, shoulder to elbow and back up to shoulder, but she didn't think he even realized he was touching her. He was a million miles away from this cave. She wanted to understand him, but he had to let her in, and she didn't know how to make him. "Talk to me, Will."

"I flunked first grade—how stupid was that?"

Randa held her breath, willing him to go on.

"I couldn't learn to read. Dad tried to beat it into me. Mom tried to defend me. They fought all the time. He'd lock me in the basement—this was all before he was turned vampire. I didn't see words the same way the other kids did."

Understanding finally dawned. "You're dyslexic?"

Will looked at her finally, a long, steady gaze before he nodded. "I know that now. I heard something about it on the news and started doing some research. But I was a kid in the 1950s from an upper-class family, the son of a prominent New York attorney. Nobody knew what dyslexia was. I gradually learned to cope, to fake my way around things, to get by enough so my father only made fun of me instead of beating the shit out of me. I like computers because they're so graphic intense."

Randa thought of her own childhood, growing up with a by-the-rules father whose only way of raising five children by himself was to treat them as another army unit. She'd always beaten herself up over not being as strong or fast as her brothers, but her dad had never made her feel that way. He'd never belittled her. She never felt as if she measured up, but now, listening to Will, she realized she'd done that to herself. Blaming her dad had been easier than seeing the flaw in herself.

"Thank you for telling me. I won't tell Aidan, but you should."

He gave a bitter chuckle. "Not so intimidated by me now, are you?"

God, how could his self-image be so totally wrong? And how could she have misjudged him so badly?

She hated Matthias Ludlam. If she got a chance, she'd kill him herself for screwing up his beautiful son so badly.

"Will, I'm in awe of your strength. I mean"—she lifted her head to look at him, willing him to meet her gaze—"you are an amazing person, and I always thought it was because you had everything handed to you. Now I realize it's because you made yourself what you are, through strength and smarts and determination. I'm sorry I've been such a bitch."

He gave her his old cocky eyebrow lift, but it was shaky around the edges. "And I'm sorry I knocked you out and left you on the sofa before I went to rescue Mirren."

OK, so he'd had enough soul-searching and was ready to hide behind his humor again. Now that she knew it was his defense mechanism, she could deal with it. Aidan had been right when he'd paired them up to...

"Holy shit."

"What?"

Their rescue was within reach, and neither of them had realized it. "Call Aidan. You need to call Aidan." Randa's heart rate sped up. They could get out of here!

Will stared at her. "Do you have a concussion or something? What the hell are you talking about? There's no cell service this far underground."

Randa's mouth dropped open. He honestly had no idea what she meant. "You really don't know, do you?"

❦ CHAPTER 12 ❦

"You're becoming a master vampire." Just like that—she'd said it twice. Then he made her repeat it, just to make sure he didn't have dirt and concrete dust plugging his ears.

She must've misunderstood Aidan. "Why didn't he tell me this big news? I mean, shouldn't I know if I was turning into some kind of supervampire?" It was ridiculous. Except the more Randa tried to explain, the more he thought about a couple of nights ago when he'd been able to alter Ethan's memories, and the kid at the ice-cream shop. Later, he'd been able to not only scent vampires in the woods from greater distances, but also to tell what scathe they were from.

Shit.

Randa's eyes were so bright they practically glowed in the semidarkness. "You should be able to communicate mentally with Aidan—you're blood-bonded to him already. Try it. Try talking to him."

Will frowned and tried to send out a mental *yoo-hoo* to Aidan, but he couldn't concentrate with Randa lying on top of him, staring at him all disheveled and sexy and, well, excited. Her lips were parted, and in the gloom, he could imagine that tousled brown hair was a deep, sexy red. Plus, she was waiting for him to perform like some kind of trained seal with fangs, and he didn't have a clue how to do it.

"Stop looking at me. I can't do this if you're watching me."

She rolled her eyes. "Meet Will, the self-conscious master vampire." But she tucked her head under his chin and closed her eyes, smiling.

He took a deep breath and still couldn't concentrate. "Turn the phone off for a minute to help me focus."

Randa slid the Off arrow, and in a few seconds, they were plunged back into darkness. Will cleared his mind and visualized Aidan. *Can you hear me? Aidan? It's Will.*

He waited a few seconds, tried it again, and was so startled to hear an answering voice he moved enough to send a new flurry of dirt down on them.

Will? Where are you? Are you both OK?

"Man, this is some weird shit."

Randa shifted on top of him. "You hear him?"

"Yeah." Will closed his eyes and focused again. *We're pinned under a support beam. It's holding on by a thread, so you'll have to be careful coming in. We're to the left of the tunnel from the steel doors, just inside the exit room.*

Aidan's voice came in and out like a bad radio signal— probably because Will wasn't very good at this yet. Or hell, who knew? Maybe this was normal. Will's knowledge of master vampires was rudimentary, at best; he'd never expected to be one. He wasn't even sure how one became a master vampire—only that Matthias bragged about being one.

We're already digging from this end but have been going slow so we don't dislodge too much. Hang in there. Any sign of Matthias?

Sharp pains shot through Will's skull, but he focused. *No, it's caved in at the top. We can't see the hatch.*

I'll warn you when we're close. We might have to collapse it on you and dig you out. Randa OK? You hurt?

Shrapnel for two, plus something was wrong with his lower leg—as in, he wasn't sure it was still there since he couldn't feel it. No point in sharing that. They'd deal with it when they dealt with it. *Minor injuries, both of us. We'll need Krys.*

OK, you're going to have a headache from this—too much talk, too soon. But good job, Will.

Aidan's presence disappeared, like a soft whisper that left a vacant spot in his skull—a vacant spot quickly filled with pain.

"OK, you can turn the phone back on." Aidan had been right. A jackhammer was beating into his skull, shooting shards of pain into the back of his eye sockets.

"What did he say?" Randa's eager face shone in the cell phone light. "What did it feel like?"

"Like Michelangelo's sculpting a new masterpiece on the inside of my eyeballs." Will closed his eyes and tried to convince the pain to recede. "They're already digging. I was able to tell him where we are. Now, we wait."

He pondered whether or not to tell her they might have to be buried for a while since the darkness freaked her out a little, but she needed to know. "When they break through, they might have to let everything come down on us. Be prepared."

Her heart sped up, vibrating against his chest. "I can't do that. I can't be buried under—" She tried to move, and a rain of dirt came down on them.

Will shook his head to dislodge the latest rain of debris and locked both arms around her waist. He had to calm her down, or she really would bury them. "It will be OK. Can you imagine how much dirt Mirren can move and how fast? Maybe he'll get Glory to lift the whole mess off us in a second or two."

"But we"—her breath came in sharp gasps—"we won't be able to breathe. Oh God, I can't do this." She tried to move again, but Will tightened his grip.

"Shh…" He held her in place with one hand and stroked her back with the other, avoiding the sore spots. "Randa, we don't have to breathe."

She raised her head, a look of confusion on her face. "What?"

Good, he'd gotten her attention. "Vampires have to breathe to stay up and moving, but it won't kill us if we get buried. We'll just go unconscious until they dig us out, kind of like daysleep, and then we'll wake up." Or at least that's what Mirren had told him in the two years it had taken the scathe to excavate this nest of tunnels and safe spaces in the red clay–laden soil beneath Penton. And Mirren wasn't prone to making jokes, so it had to be true.

"Are you sure?" Randa's eyes were wide, on the verge of panic again.

"I wouldn't lie about impending death." On impulse, Will cupped her jaw in his palm and lifted his head to brush her lips with his, just a feather of touch. Their gazes met, and Will knew they'd turned another corner tonight. She knew the worst about him and hadn't judged him harshly.

Well, not the worst. She'd never know he'd been sodomized by force with what amounted to his father's approval, had been forced to beg for it. Although, he'd as much as admitted it to

Cage. Surely there was some sort of implied rule about shrink confidentiality.

"Kiss me again. Take my mind off being buried." Randa shifted a little higher on his chest and twined the fingers of her free hand into his hair.

"You sure are a bossy woman." He slanted his mouth on hers, and the force of her response rocked his head back against the ground. Her lips were hot and wet, her mouth open to his. Their warm tangle of tongues slowed and deepened. His fang nicked her lip, and she pulled away, her pink tongue slipping out to touch the blood.

Will turned his head to the side, exposing his neck. "Feed from me, Ran. Try it this way."

"I don't...I can't..."

"Try it. Do it now."

Her lips hovered over his throat, her heart pounded against his chest, and she'd have to be totally clueless if she didn't feel his cock pressing hot and hard against her thigh.

"Are you sure?" Her breath sent hot puffs over his neck. The woman was going to drive him crazy.

"Stop stalling, Randa. Do it."

Her tongue swept a small path across the side of his neck, and he sighed as she finally bit. Damn, but it felt good to be a feeder. He'd never fed anyone before and had only heard how it was the next best thing to an orgasm. As she pulled at his throat, a fiery tingle shot through his veins, heating him from the inside out and settling in his groin.

When Randa groaned against his throat, he had to visualize computer diagrams to keep from coming. If Mirren Kincaid dug him out with a wet spot on the front of his pants, he'd never hear the end of it.

She pulled away, licking the punctures to heal them. When she looked back at him, her eyes were slightly unfocused. "Damn."

He grinned. "Ditto that. We'll have to—"

A crash to Will's right, the caved-in spot nearest Omega, killed any thoughts of sex, although it was a subject he planned to revisit. Another crash sent a rain of debris on them.

"Will, I can't do this."

Yeah, well, he wasn't wild about the idea, either, but it was going to happen regardless.

Another crash and the support beam on their legs nudged to the right.

He grasped her tightly as the beam across their legs fell with crushing pain. "Tuck your head and hold on. This baby's coming down."

❧CHAPTER 13☙

A idan lifted a chunk of rebar and threw it aside. The hallway of Omega was lined with piles of dirt, broken concrete, steel cable, and more dirt. They'd been digging for two hours since the beam over Will and Randa had given way, with no sign of them so far.

"Shift excavations to the left," he told the team of scathe members and humans, who were taking turns digging and resting. Well, except Mirren. The guy was a machine, taking the heaviest debris and hauling it out of the way. He hadn't stopped. Aidan remembered a time not so long ago when Mirren had questioned his choice in putting so much faith in Will. Since Will had rescued Mirren and Glory, first from Matthias's silver-barred jail cell and then again in New Orleans, the big guy had changed his opinion. Will drove Mirren nuts, but he liked him anyway.

"You sure they're going to be alive after being buried this long?" Aidan had no experience with buried vampires, but Mirren insisted they'd live.

"Positive." Mirren hauled out another piece of a splintered support beam. "This was a favorite Tribunal torture technique back in the good old days. Didn't kill the prisoners; just freaked the shit out of them."

Aidan shook his head. He loved Mirren like a brother—hell, he loved Mirren better than the sad excuse for a man his brother had been. But he didn't want to know half of what that vampire had done in his life, first as a Scottish gallowglass warrior and later the Tribunal's best executioner—or worst, depending on which side of the torture one sat on.

"We found 'em!" One of the scathe members stuck his head out of the opening to the steel door. "We've got feet—looks like she's on top of him."

"Bloody miracle they didn't kill each other." Aidan led the way into the opening and watched while three scathe members dug furiously, gradually unearthing Will and Randa.

"Doesn't look like they were fighting." Mirren arched an eyebrow, and Aidan chuckled before moving alongside them. Will's arms were wrapped tightly around Randa's waist, but he could see angry red welts in four or five spots across her back through her shredded shirt. Will had a similar mark on his cheek, and his left leg was…Holy hell, it was bent about six inches above the ankle, in a place legs weren't supposed to bend, in a direction they weren't supposed to bend. This was no minor injury.

He sent a mental message to Krys to meet them in the makeshift medical room they'd set up and gently pulled Will's hands away from Randa's waist. He shifted her enough to get his arms underneath her knees and shoulders and roll her into his arms, avoiding her injured back.

"Mirren, get Will. Watch out for that left leg. Krys is meeting us at the med room." He pushed through the piles of debris and waiting people. Liv, Will's feeder, was standing at the edge of the group, eyes red and puffy.

"They'll be OK." He passed her, then paused, turning back. "Hang around, Liv. They'll need to feed—see if you can find another feeder too." Healing sapped a vampire's strength, even a brand-new master vampire's.

Mirren wasn't far behind him, carrying Will and barking orders. The man's idea of multitasking. "Don't leave a fucking millimeter of open air in that hole," he barked at the scathe members lined up to work. "Fill it in, and then solder the steel door closed. And do it fast."

Aidan turned the corner and saw Krys waiting in the open doorway to the med room. Her dark-auburn hair was pulled back, and she had her doctor face on, dark-brown eyes serious as her glance flicked across Randa. She stopped Aidan just inside the door and leaned over to look at Randa's back. "Put her on her stomach."

Mirren had arrived with Will. "Where you want him?"

Krys stopped in the middle of pulling on exam gloves to look at Will's leg. "That's a bad one. Put him in the bed across from Randa. I'm going to need your help setting that leg, both of you. See if Glory can do nurse duty and get them cleaned up."

Mirren stood with his hands planted on his hips. "Why can't Liv do it? She's their feeder."

Aidan had been leaning against the wall beside the door, watching the exchange with bemusement. He knew exactly what Mirren was balking at.

Krys had been gently trying to get Will's left shoe off but straightened up and narrowed her eyes at Mirren. "Liv's too emotional. Glory won't mind. What's your problem?"

"He doesn't want Glory giving Will a sponge bath, or something like that." Aidan grinned, and Krys deepened her doctor glare at Mirren.

"Aw, fuck me. I'll go and find her." Mirren strode out of the room, scowling.

"He'll probably get less possessive after they've been mated a little longer. It's all new to him." Then again, maybe not. Aidan watched Krys cut off Will's sweater and run her hands over his abdomen, feeling for internal injuries. He wanted to growl at her, but refused to act like a Neanderthal. "What do you think?"

"Will's leg was broken, obviously. Badly broken. The explosion happened right before daysleep, so I'm guessing it healed in the only way it could, given the way he was pinned down."

Holy hell. The scenario gave him the shudders. "Can you fix it?"

"He needs an orthopedic surgeon who's also savvy about the vampire world—in other words, something that probably doesn't exist." Krys took her scissors to Will's pants leg, cutting up to midthigh and pulling the fabric away from his skin. "We don't even have access to an X-ray machine down here. The only thing I know to do is to have one of you hold him down or tie him with silver while the other breaks his leg again. We'll secure it as straight as we can and pray it re-heals in some way that at least lets him walk again. Once we get out of this mess, we can break it again and set it properly."

Damn it. Matthias's latest strike against them might have maimed his only son, but Aidan found it impossible to enjoy the irony. He didn't know the details of the suffering Will had endured at his father's hand, but it had scarred him. That Will had come out of it with enough mental toughness to become a master vampire—the major prerequisite for a master—was no minor miracle.

He took a deep breath and nodded. "We'll do what we have to. What about Randa?"

"I think she's OK except for those places on her back—Will's got one on his face. What hit them?"

"My bet's on a projectile grenade." Mirren had returned and rumbled from the doorway.

Glory eased past him, eyed Randa's back, and stopped next to Krys. "What do you need me to do?"

"We need to get them out of these clothes and clean them up. Once I cut out these...projectiles, or whatever they are, the wounds will need to be sterilized. Those injuries should heal by themselves after that."

"I'm on it." Glory twisted her shoulder-length black hair and secured it in a loose pile on her head before turning to her mate. "Mirren, honey, vampire-o'-mine. You cannot stand in the door and scowl. Make yourself useful."

Aidan didn't give Mirren time to provide whatever colorful epithet he was about to spew out. "We need silver-laced rope to tie Will down when we rebreak his leg, just in case he comes to. We need a board that will work as a splint. We need regular rope to secure his leg to the splint. Can you find that?"

"Why don't you use duct tape?" Glory looked up from where she was using Krys's scissors to finish cutting off Will's pants.

There was a long silence as everyone looked at Glory. She shrugged and went back to cutting. "Just a thought."

"It's a damn good idea," Aidan said. "There should be some in the room with the generators."

Mirren gave Aidan one final heated look, grumbled something under his breath, and disappeared down the hallway.

Aidan turned to Glory, eyebrows raised. "Did he just tell me to go fuck myself?"

The skin around her black eyes crinkled with laughter. "I'm going to have to work on my mate's attitude, I think."

"Yeah, good luck with that." But Aidan smiled. Mirren was mostly hot air with the people he liked, not that anyone was going to share that with him.

By the time Mirren returned with the supplies, plus Hannah, they'd managed to get both patients undressed and modestly covered. Krys sat in a chair next to Randa's bed, leaning over her with a scalpel and pair of oversized tweezers. Glory stood beside her with a bloody cloth.

"This brings back old memories." Mirren set the supplies inside the door. During the attack by Aidan's brother back in January, he'd been shot with buckshot that had been scored and tainted with vaccinated human blood. Poison, in other words. Krys had dug it out of his back in much the same way she now worked on Randa.

Krys glanced up at him. "Yes, I cleaned you up, and you flashed fangs at me. Nothing was ever the same in my life after that."

"I do what I can." Mirren leaned against the wall next to Will's bed. After staring down at him a moment, he sat on the edge of the bed and ran his fingers along Will's misshapen calf. "I think there are three breaks in here."

Krys clinked the last of the steel projectiles from Randa's back into a metal tray and turned to look at him. "How can you tell?"

Another souvenir from his mercenary days, Aidan was sure. "Let's just say I'm guessing he's had some experience with broken bones."

Understanding dawned on Krys's face. "Ah...gotcha. Do you think you can rebreak the leg in the same places?"

Using a pillowcase to keep it from burning his hands, Aiden picked up the silver-laced rope from where Mirren had dropped it inside the door and began to uncoil it. "We're going to try."

While Glory finished cleaning Randa's back, Krys came to watch them tie Will to the steel frames of the bed. "How long you think they'll be unconscious?"

Mirren looked up. "I don't know, but since they're also trying to heal wounds, they might not wake up before daysleep. Especially Will. Which is probably a good thing. I wouldn't want to be awake for this. But we're tying him down just in case."

Once they had Will secured, Aidan took his mangled leg by the ankle and nodded at Mirren. "You're on."

Sitting in a chair beside the bed, Mirren again ran his fingers along the length of Will's leg from knee to ankle. Once. Twice. A third time. His eyes were closed, his face frozen in concentration. Finally, he stopped at a point a few inches above the ankle and quickly snapped the bone in the opposite direction from the way it had healed. Will's foot and ankle flopped loosely, secured to the rest of his leg only by skin and muscle and tissue.

Will groaned and tried to thrash, but the ropes held him.

"Oh my God." Glory turned away. "I can't even look."

"That was the worst one of the breaks—the other two aren't both leg bones, but just the smaller one."

At Mirren's direction, Aidan slid a hand underneath the new break to support it while Mirren snapped the fibula in two more places. Krys, meanwhile, had retrieved the board. "Slide it under his leg gently," Mirren directed. Aidan helped him lift Will's leg and then settled it onto the board. If they situated the top of the board behind his knee, it reached to his ankle.

While Mirren held the leg in place, Aidan used the duct tape to secure the leg to the board. "Remind me not to be around when we pull this tape off. That might hurt as much as the break."

Krys made quick work of removing the steel projectile from Will's cheek and cleaning the wound. "Now, prop the board on a pillow to elevate his leg a little, and until they wake up, that's all we can do for them."

Aidan glanced at his watch—3:00 a.m.—and they hadn't done any patrols tonight. He was supposed to meet Cage at 4:00 to see if he'd made any progress with Matthias.

Aidan looked up when he heard a light tap on the door facing and was surprised to see Mark Calvert, on his feet and out of his room for the first time. "Liv said they might need to feed. I told her I could do it."

Krys shook her head. "You don't—"

Aidan put a hand on her arm and squeezed. "Thanks, Mark. I'm sure of it. Krys will, even if Will and Randa don't wake up." The quicker he could get Mark involved in the goings-on of Omega, even in this small way, the less time he'd have to dwell on everything he'd lost.

Hell, at least Aidan had his little weird trace of a bond with Melissa that survived for some reason, and he took comfort in it even though he knew it was a shadow bond. Like he'd heard of people who'd lost limbs, yet still felt them.

He'd planned to tell Mirren about it and see if he'd ever heard of such a thing, but it would have to wait.

For now, he had to focus on Matthias and see what his British spy had to tell him.

❧CHAPTER 14❧

Cage had been walking around downtown Penton with Shelton Porterfield for five fricking hours, and the only thing
of interest he'd learned was that Matthias was on a quick trip
to New York on Tribunal business and that Shelton was a sick,
sadistic pedophile.

Oh, wait. Redundant.

Finally, Shelton had suggested a threesome with his little
teenage blood whore back at the clinic, and Cage saw an exit.

"Told you, boys don't do a bloody thing for me." Cage
stopped at the clinic parking lot. "I think I'll join the patrols,
fan around the outskirts of town, and see if I can catch wind of
some of the Penton crowd."

Shelton took a business card from his pocket and handed it
to Cage. "This has my cell number on it. If you find anything,
call me and I'll handle it."

The front of the card identified Shelton as manager of a
limited liability corporation in Virginia. No doubt one of Matthias's many fronts. The man had apparently been a successful

business attorney in his human life and kept up with all the latest loopholes.

"I will certainly do that." Cage pocketed the card and walked south, back toward downtown and the opposite direction from the remaining Omega entrance. He wanted to be well out of Shelton's scenting range before he looped around town and went to his 4:00 a.m. rendezvous with Aidan.

He turned it into a two-hour maze of a trip, arriving at the meeting point a few minutes ahead of schedule. He didn't want to risk Aidan being caught outside, so he located the hatch, unlocked it, and climbed down the long drop ladder into the exit room.

"You get the hatch closed and locked behind you?" Aidan stepped out of the tunnel from Omega just as Cage reached the bottom ladder rung.

"Yeah, I didn't want to take a chance on having you caught outside."

Aidan turned on two of the fluorescent lanterns, setting the concrete-and-steel-lined room awash in soft light and shadows. If Matthias found this hatch and dropped a grenade, at least its effect would be limited.

He dropped heavily to the floor and leaned against the wall. "Talk to me."

Cage sat on the ground and propped his back against the opposite wall. Aidan looked tired. "First, I heard the explosion but didn't find out what it was until afterward. Who was on guard duty? How many were killed?"

"Will and Randa were in the exit room and got the door closed before the grenade went off, so nobody in Omega was killed. They're both injured, but alive. Will was able to direct me to their location—it ended up caving on them, but we dug them out."

Cage processed that. "How was Will able to tell you where they were?"

Aidan gave him a weary smile. "Young Will is our newest master vampire in training. I think he's surprised as hell by it, but I'm not. He's stronger than he's ever given himself credit for. Probably had to be strong to survive Matthias and then have the guts to get away from him."

Cage suspected Aidan had no idea of the extent Will had suffered under Matthias, but that wasn't his story to tell, at least not right now.

What *was* his mission to reveal was what he'd seen of Penton and of Matthias's setup—before he dropped his real bombshell. Once he heard about Melissa, Aidan would have trouble focusing on anything else, or at least that's how he'd react in Aidan's place.

"I think Matthias has anywhere from twenty to forty vampires fanned out around the woods, waiting for us to make the next move." Cage cracked his knuckles. "My guess is that they're on the Tribunal payroll, at least temporarily. Not a scathe, as near as I can tell, but all hired fangs. None of the ones I came across, other than Shelton Porterfield, were blood-bonded to Matthias."

Aidan shook his head. "I'd hoped he didn't have that many with him. Any idea what his strategy is?"

The strategy least likely to get Matthias's hands dirty, as near as Cage had been able to tell. "He figures if we're all underground and they can find our other exits—he's sure we have at least one—then his people can just wait with no risk to themselves and pick us off one by one as we try to come out. So they're actively looking for the other exit hatch. So far, they haven't moved far enough out of town to get near the one we have left."

"We're working on a new exit, but it's slow going, and we had to stop work to dig Will and Randa out," Aidan said. "This soil is packed clay, and there's no place for us to put the displaced dirt. Question is, how many people can we slip out of Omega at a time without attracting attention? Do you think you can get yourself assigned to our exit area?"

"Probably." If he went back undercover. He hoped Aidan was ready for the rest of his news. "There's something else you need to know. It's about Melissa."

Aidan stilled—that lack of breath and movement only vampires could achieve. The man's blue eyes lightened with emotion. "I knew it. Damn it, I knew something was off because I could still feel my bond to her. She's alive, isn't she?"

Now it was Cage's turn to stare. He knew Melissa was Aidan's fam and had been for several years. Their bond had to be strong, or else it was a master-vampire thing. Cage wasn't sure.

"Apparently, as soon as Matthias had his guy snap her neck, he had another drag her off and turn her. She made it through the transition. She's vampire, Aidan. And Matthias has her bound and gagged in one of those suites beneath the clinic."

Aidan was on his feet and halfway up the drop ladder before Cage caught him around the ankles and jerked him back down. They both landed in a heap on the floor, and Aidan landed a punch to Cage's jaw before he got himself under control. His face was contorted in anguish and fury.

"How did I not know? I should have known." He ran his hands through his hair. "What has he done to her? I swear, if he has raped her or let that SOB Shelton Porterfield near her..."

Cage's laugh was bitter. "Oh, she's not Shelton's type. She's female and an adult."

He rubbed his jaw and felt for broken teeth. Aidan had been a powerful man as a human farmer back in early-seventeenth-century Ireland, Cage figured, and he was no lightweight as a vampire.

"Sorry about that." Aidan flexed and unflexed his fist. "I won't lose it again. Tell me about Mel."

Cage leaned against the wall. "He put me in the suite down the hall, and I got curious as to why one was locked, so I picked it open. She's hungry—he's barely fed her. I let her feed from me. And he'd been torturing her for information, telling her that you were dead, that Krys was dead. Telling her he had Mark in another suite and would kill him if she didn't talk."

"Damn it." Aidan was on his feet again, and Cage sat upright, ready to spring if he tried leaving. But Aidan simply paced the exit room.

"We talked just after daysleep," Cage continued. "She wanted me to check out the explosion, talk to you, report back to her." He thought of her fierce expression, her determination to keep his identity a secret. "She's a strong woman, as I guess you know."

Truth was, he hadn't been able to get her off his mind all night, and getting hung up on a newly fanged Melissa Calvert was in the dictionary, illustrating *exercise in futility*.

Aidan continued to pace, although he'd slowed down. "Is there any way to get her out of there without blowing your cover?"

"I've been asking myself the same question all night, and I don't think so." Cage rubbed his eyes and wished he could leave all the stress behind, just for a few days. But he saw no end to it. "I'm the only new face in Penton, and the only other one who's been in the sub-suites, or so Matthias says. He knows she isn't strong enough as a new vampire to escape and get out on her own. If she comes out, I'm going to have to come out with her."

Aidan didn't answer, only stared at the floor, deep in thought.

"Oh, and one more thing you need to know," Cage said. "Matthias had already figured out we had an underground bunker, but Mel told him about the hatch in the floor of the church. He'd been tormenting her and starving her, and she finally cracked. She's horrified, afraid she caused someone to be killed and jeopardized all of us."

Aidan sat down again. "He'd have found it eventually, and we weren't going to be able to use that exit under their noses anyway. How sure is he that we're down here and not already escaped to Atlanta or China or anywhere but here?"

Cage shook his head. "He's not positive, but he has people in Atlanta who know the Tribunal's offering big rewards for any information on the Penton scathe or its members—I mean, *really* big rewards. So far, with no word from them, he's assuming we're down here. And he's sure he can wait us out."

Aidan stared at his hands a long time, flexing and unflexing his fingers. "You know I can't leave her there. I know it's the smart thing to do for the good of the scathe, but...I just can't."

Cage had come to the same conclusion. "I agree. She's strong, but Matthias is ruthless. Eventually, he'll break her. We can't let that happen."

Aidan gave him a steady look. "You sound like you've come to care about her, Cage. Make sure it's just a friendship. Nothing good can come from it."

"I know." And he did, but it didn't keep him from admiring how strong she was to have held on this long. "You going to tell Mark she's alive?"

"Not yet." Aidan clicked off the lantern closest to him. "Let's get her out safely. Then I'll figure out the best way to tell Mark the wife whose death he's been grieving over is now a vampire."

☙CHAPTER 15❧

A whoosh of filtered air came to her first, then the sensation of lying on a pillow. Or was it still Will's chest? No, too soft. His chest had been firm, warm, not smushy. Definitely a pillow.

Randa opened her eyes to a dimly lit room she'd never seen before, and panic drove enough adrenaline through her bloodstream to wake her up fully. Had Matthias found them and locked them up? If so, she needed to find Will and get out of here. Were there guards outside the door?

She sat up, letting the sheet fall. Only then did she realize she was naked. Well, except for the granny panties the army issued to all female soldiers. Gray granny panties, white granny panties, or tan granny panties, plus matching sports bras. Those were the choices. Welcome to today's army. They'd issued so many of the damned things she'd never wear them out, and it seemed a shame to waste them. Wasn't like anyone but her ever saw them.

In a frantic glance around the room, she spotted a familiar doctor's bag—a small suitcase on wheels—on the floor near her bed. Randa relaxed as she recognized it. It belonged to Krys.

She was in Omega, then. She'd been rescued by her people. Randa closed her eyes and let the adrenaline drain from her system, replaced by a warm gratitude.

The room had four twin beds in it, and finally, she spotted Will in the bed directly across the room from hers. The room was lit by a single fluorescent lamp on its lowest setting, but Randa could make out a sink, cabinets, a rolling cart with some tools on it. The medical room.

"Psst. Will?"

No answer, no movement. He was still unconscious.

Randa climbed out of bed, wrapping a sheet around herself, wincing at the sore spots on her back. The projectile had been dug out of his cheek, and it was still red and angry, but healing. Her back probably looked the same way.

The sheet covered him to his waist, and she couldn't stop herself from looking. Couldn't help but take advantage of a rare moment when neither one of them could open their mouths and say something insulting or inappropriate. She'd like to think they had moved past that stage, but really, it was in their natures. They both ratcheted up the smart-assery to hide their insecurities. One near-death experience probably wasn't going to change that. It went all the way down to the bone.

Her fingers twitched with the urge to slide over the smooth expanse of his chest and stomach. Vampires kept whatever skin they'd had as humans, and Will might have been a sixty-plus-year-old vampire, but at his turning, he'd been a beautiful, athletic twenty-two-year-old human, with tanned skin that took its definition from layers of muscle and bone. His forever-sun-streaked blond hair spilled onto the pillow with just a hint of curl, his cheekbones a perfect slant to set off full lips.

The man was a work of art. And now she knew there was a real guy inside all that muscle and bad attitude. A decent guy. A brave guy. And despite what Matthias had brought him up to believe, a smart guy.

Randa didn't know what tomorrow would bring. She didn't know if they'd survive the assault on Omega, or if the Tribunal would kill them all, or if they'd escape and scatter to far-flung places, breaking their bonds to Aidan and each other.

But she had learned this from her close encounter with an M67 grenade: Even as a vampire, life could be shorter than you expected. If something was meaningful to you, take care of it. Respect it. Cherish it. If something you wanted was within your grasp, you shouldn't assume time was unlimited.

She wanted Will.

She seriously doubted they'd have a great romance for the ages. She wasn't a dewy-eyed teenager, and he'd never shown any inclination to even settle down with one feeder for very long. But they would be lovers. She knew that like she knew her name. She'd know the sensation of his skin against hers, his hands doing more than probing her pocket for a cell phone.

One of his legs was under the sheet, but the other was...silver? She looked more closely and realized it was wrapped in silver duct tape and attached to a board below the knee. When they'd been pinned, he'd said he couldn't feel his foot. What had happened?

The overhead lights flickered on, and Randa whirled to see Krys in the doorway. "Mirren says he'll be asleep for a while—he has a lot to heal." Krys came to stand beside her. Had she noticed Randa giving Will a visual undressing? "He's really gorgeous when he's unconscious and can't talk, isn't he?"

Oh yeah, she'd noticed. Randa considered crawling under the bed in humiliation, but why pretend? She'd been busted. "I was just thinking the same thing—maybe we should tape his mouth shut. How's his leg?"

Krys explained the break and the attempt to duplicate the injuries so he could heal properly. "We won't know whether or not it's healing until he comes out of daysleep tomorrow night and we untape it. I kind of hope he doesn't wake up before then. It'll hurt like hell. Mirren says it might even take longer to heal—another day."

After rubbing some cooling cream on Randa's back, Krys stretched and yawned. "It's almost dawn. You can go back to your room if you want. You'll heal during daysleep. Some really deep bruises have spread across the back of your legs—other than the projectile wounds, that's all the injuries you had. It's a miracle none of them hit your head."

Yeah, well, she definitely needed her head examined because she didn't want to leave. She should go to her room, put on clothes, and take her daysleep in her own bed. And yet her feet didn't move.

"Or you could stay here and keep an eye on Will. If he does regain consciousness before dawn, well, you know where I am. Might be better if he's not alone in that case so he doesn't move." Krys's voice was calm and professional, but Randa caught the glint in her eye.

Yeah, she was busted again, big-time. But as long as they were both pretending, she'd do her part. "Sure, I can stay here if you want. No problem."

"You need to feed, though. It'll help the healing. Liv's outside."

OK, in case she wasn't already embarrassed enough. "No. I, uh, fed...earlier."

"Huh?" Krys looked at Randa, then shifted her gaze down to Will. She didn't even try to keep the grin off her face. "Oh. I see. Well." She burst into a low, husky laugh—an infectious laugh. People had a hard time being around Krys when she lost it. You always wanted to laugh with her. Even if she was laughing at you.

"Please don't tell anybody you caught me ogling Will while he was unconscious." Randa bit her lower lip to keep from laughing herself. "Especially don't tell him. I'd never live it down."

Krys laughed harder. "I didn't see a thing. Not a single thing. Enjoy your daysleep."

She flipped the overhead switch on her way out, returning the room to the soft darkness of the small lamp.

❧ CHAPTER 16 ❧

Will's leg throbbed like a son of a bitch. He hadn't been able to feel the damned thing for so long it had freaked him out, but now he longed for the numbness again. Randa's head was still tucked under his chin, and he turned his head toward her scent, floral and soft even in this muck. Why had Aidan and Mirren not found them yet?

Randa stirred and he wrapped his arms around her. "Don't move, remember?"

"Will, open your eyes."

"I have dirt in them. They're..." He blinked, shifting his eyes around the shadowy room and doing a quick mental reshuffle. They were back in Omega, then, coming out of day-sleep. He slid his hands up Randa's back, and it was smooth, healed—and bare. Will had never been a praying man, but he wanted to thank someone.

"We're OK," she whispered against his cheek, then moved her lips across his jawline. "We made it."

Will wanted to ask why she was still lying on top of him, then thought better of it. The last thing he wanted was for her to get up. He liked her exactly where she was.

She hovered her mouth over his. "Say something."

Uh-uh. His mouth got him in trouble when he used it to talk. He could do other things with it, though. He raised his head and caught her lower lip between his teeth, tugging her down into a soft, warm kiss. Her breasts pressed against his chest, and he slid his hand between them. He paused before his fingers reached her. Her boundaries were a mystery to him.

"Touch me." She shifted to the side so he could take her tight nipple between his fingers while his mouth claimed hers again, his tongue promising what else he wanted to do.

He slid eager hands down to her waist, kneading soft skin with his fingertips as she deepened the kiss, her hands sliding over his shoulders and tugging at his hair. He slid his hands lower and...What the hell? Will hated to interrupt the enthusiastic assault she'd begun on his earlobe, but he couldn't help it. "What are you wearing?"

She moaned something and bit him hard on his ear.

"Ow." Laughing, he tugged on the waistband of what he swore were the kind of panties old ladies in nursing homes wore—not that he'd seen many old ladies in nursing homes, especially in their underwear, but he was pretty damned sure they wore these things. "Seriously, what are you wearing?"

"Oh hell." Randa sat astride him, and the sight of those beautiful full breasts made him want to bite off his own tongue and never open his mouth again except to make her moan. "They're granny panties. The army makes us wear them." Defiance leaked out of her every pore, and her eyes dared him to comment.

He stared at the high-waisted white monstrosities and swallowed hard. If he laughed at her, he might never get his mouth on those breasts. "Um. Well." He cleared his throat. "Are you still in the army?"

She squinted at him. "Well, no. But I don't much like to go shopping at night, you know?"

He hooked a finger on each side of the waistband and tugged the panties down as far as he could. She had a pierced belly button, and suddenly, his mouth had a new spot it wanted to visit. "You could always go commando. And I need to introduce you to this wonderful invention called the Internet. It'll rock your world. You can shop naked at three a.m."

He hiked an eyebrow at her and pulled her back onto his chest by tugging forward on the elastic of the world's ugliest panties. "Come back here and I'll help you get rid of them."

Laughing, she kissed him again, and he eased the offensive things over her hips. Randa rolled to one side to help him along, and he screamed when her right leg brushed his left.

"Goddamn! What happened? My fucking leg is on fire!" He expected to see flames erupt from his lower limb at any second. He closed his eyes and tried to move his leg to relieve the agony, but it wouldn't budge. Trying to move it made the sharp, hot pain grow hotter and sharper.

"Shit. Shit. Shit." He covered his face with his hands and tried to convince himself the pain was lessening. It was twelve on a pain scale of one to ten. OK, maybe it was down to ten now. He could breathe without wanting to cry, at least.

"Oh my God. Sorry, sorry, sorry. I've been trying to stay away from it." Randa rolled off him and got to her feet, hitching up the underwear. Will was sure at some point he'd think all this was funny, but right now, it felt like a bulldozer was laying waste to his lower leg.

He struggled to a sitting position and stared at his mangled limb. It looked like it had endured a hard night at a BDSM club. Tape was neatly wrapped around it in four or five places, and the skin had turned four funky shades of purple. The whole thing had been strapped to a freaking two-by-four and lay propped on a pillow.

He looked up at Randa. "Why?"

She'd pulled a sheet off another bed and wrapped it around her. "I'm going to get Krys."

"Wait, tell me what happened first."

"They had to—"

"It healed wrong when it was pinned under that beam, so we had to rebreak it." Aidan strode through the door, followed by Krys. They were both rosy cheeked and recently fed, which was fine for them. Didn't help his leg any.

Randa had sidled toward the door clutching her sheet, and Will caught her eye. She smiled at him, full of promise that he'd see those army panties again, and slipped into the hallway. At some point, he'd revisit that look. Now, not so much.

Will turned his attention back to Krys, who was cutting tape away from his leg. As she pulled it away, he had the pain of leg hairs being ripped out, along with the top layer of skin. "Why don't you just shoot my ass while you're at it? Shouldn't it have healed during daysleep? Why is it the color of an eggplant?"

"It has healed some, but it's slow." Krys's brow wrinkled in a frown. "I wonder why."

Great. Those were not reassuring words coming from Penton's only doctor.

"A wound this severe is probably going to take longer to heal. I think that's what Mirren said." She looked up at Aidan. "Do you know?"

Aidan shook his head and turned back toward the hallway. "I'll find Mirren. He's our expert on injuries—not many he hasn't either had himself or given to somebody else. Krys, while I'm gone, fill Will in on...you know."

You know? OK, first Will had woken up with an almost-naked woman in his bed. Then his leg had caught on fire just when things were starting to get interesting. Now his scathe master was off to consult a semiretired executioner about his injury, and they wanted him to play guessing games?

He flopped back on his pillow, gritting his teeth at the pain that shot through his leg at the movement. "Does morphine work on vampires?"

Krys pursed her lips. "That's a good question. I brought some down here. Want me to try it? I think the worst that could happen is, well, that nothing would happen."

"Please. It's more than ten hours until another daysleep, and it's throbbing like it might explode." He'd welcome an explosion. If it exploded, it couldn't throb.

"One morphine cocktail coming right up." Krys opened her medical bag, selected a vial and syringe, and turned back to him with a grin. "I always thought you had a fine ass. Now I'll get to see it."

"You can look at it all you want as long as you stick that needle in it." Will rolled toward the wall enough to give her access to his butt without jarring his leg. "That's as far as I can move, so you're gonna have to make do."

"Here it comes." A sharp pain in his ass cheek was nothing compared to the jolt of agony from his leg when he shifted back onto the pillow. Man, being a vampire turned a guy into a pansy. He'd played football in school and dislocated a shoulder. He hadn't screamed like a banshee at that. Vampires were spoiled by their quick healing.

"If the morphine works, it'll work fast, I promise." Krys crossed her arms and watched him like he was a lab experiment. "I gave you a double dose."

Will took a deep breath as the pain eased, then eased some more. It still hurt, but it was a bearable three or four. "Oh yeah. That's better. Muuuuch better." Was he slurring his words?

"A human would be laid out by that dose, but you might need another one later to get you through until another daysleep."

He had to be taped to a board for a whole night? Will studied the pattern of acoustical tiles on the ceiling and thought the dot pattern might be swirling. Then again, he might be stoned. "What was the big news Aidan wanted you to tell me?"

"Cage came back last night with his first report, and he found out something we weren't expecting." Krys pulled a chair next to the bed, leaning over and talking softly. "No one else can know this until it's done, but Melissa's alive. Matthias had her turned vampire immediately after he had the guy break her neck, and somehow—God only knows how—she made it through the transition. He has her locked up in one of the clinic sub-suites. He knows she's been Aidan's fam for a long time and is trying to force information out of her."

Will sat up and growled as the pain shot through his leg again. At least this time it quickly leveled out. He fucking loved morphine. "We have to go in and get her. You don't understand how Matthias can screw with a person's head. And a new vampire? Shit. We have to get her out of there before he does so much damage she isn't the same person we knew."

"You aren't going anywhere, junior." Mirren came in, followed by Aidan, who closed the door behind them. "What's going on with the leg?"

"It's bruised, swollen, painful." Krys pointed out the obvious. "I do think it's healing, but shouldn't it be further along by now? I gave him some morphine, and that seemed to help."

Mirren pulled up another chair and wrapped a beefy hand around Will's ankle. With his other hand, he slowly began feeling his way up the calf.

Will ground his teeth and tried to kick Mirren with his right foot. "Stop that, you sadist."

Mirren impaled him with an icy-gray glare. "Shut the fuck up and be still."

The big guy felt his way along the bones of the broken leg, fingers probing at every fiery ball of agony. Will was so going to beat the crap out of that vampire one of these days.

Mirren looked up and actually smiled. "You might try it, junior, but you'll never be able to take me."

Will looked at Aidan. Oh, this was so not good. "He can hear me too?"

Aidan's smile was faint. "Only when you're really projecting. You were really projecting."

Awesome. "Well, stop listening unless you hear me scream your name, OK?"

Mirren sat back. "It's healing. Stay off of it, and by the time you come out of another daysleep, you might be able to put weight on it. I'll come back then." He stood up and moved the chair back behind the corner desk. "If you try to walk on it too soon, it'll break again and we'll have to start over. So keep your ass where it is, or you'll have to deal with me."

Normal sick people in Penton got the gentle touch of Dr. Krys. Just Will's luck he required the prickly care of the evil Dr. Slayer.

Aidan had remained standing, leaning against the closed door. "About Melissa. We decided not to tell Mark until we've successfully gotten her out. I gave Cage until three a.m. to bring her to the Omega entrance. If he isn't there, Mirren and I are going after her."

Will swiveled his head to see Aidan, keeping his lower body still. "Why not let Cage stay put? If we go after her"—*damned leg*—"if *you* go after her, it doesn't out him as a plant, and we'd be able to find out what Matthias is up to."

Mirren sat on the bed across the room from Will's. "He's going to be outed anyway. Cage says nobody—not even that asshole Shelton—knows Melissa's down there. Other than Matthias, Cage is the only person who's been in the sub-suites since Mel was turned."

Aidan nodded. "If we take her out, Cage is still compromised. The only way to keep him in place is to leave Melissa in Matthias's hands."

Will settled back on his pillow. "I hope you don't consider that an option."

Aidan opened the door. "We'll send you a feeder. And no, leaving her there is not an option. One way or another, she's coming out tonight."

☙ CHAPTER 17 ❧

Cage had hoped to go to Melissa as soon as he awoke from daysleep, but by the time he dressed and left his room, Matthias was already descending the ladder into the sub-suite corridor. "Good, you're up early. I just got back from a meeting with the Tribunal and have a message from Edward. Let's go up to the office."

Cage avoided looking in the direction of Melissa's door and followed Matthias through the hatch and into the office. They took their seats from three nights earlier. "How is Edward doing?" Cage hoped the UK's Tribunal representative hadn't let his dislike of Matthias or support of Aidan show. He'd managed to get a call to Edward last night before returning to town and had filled him in on Matthias turning Melissa. Hopefully, Edward could use the information to turn more of the Tribunal members away from Matthias.

Actually, he'd hoped it would be enough for the Tribunal to call Matthias home and let the assault on Penton drop, but as Edward pointed out, Aidan himself had illegally turned his mate, Krys, and Mirren Kincaid had killed former Tribunal member Lorenzo Caias, no matter how justified it might have been. The Penton leaders had gotten their hands dirty, and the Tribunal wouldn't overlook it. They were too paranoid.

"Brilliant man, Edward." Matthias poured himself a whiskey and offered one to Cage. He declined. Alcohol had very little effect on vampires, but he needed to be at his sharpest if he hoped to get Melissa out of town and to the Omega hatch by 3:00 a.m. The last thing the Penton scathe needed was Aidan and Mirren putting themselves at risk.

"What was his message?" Cage settled back in his chair and wondered if Shelton was down the hall, feeding from the boy—or worse. That situation sat badly with him. He'd seen his share of blood whores, male and female, but never one that young. He couldn't save everybody, but he didn't like leaving the kid behind.

"First, Edward is certainly a fan of yours—speaks very highly of your skills, both as a fighter and as a strategist, because of your background."

Cage nodded his head in acknowledgment of the compliment. "Edward is a highly principled man." *Unlike you.*

"Yet you're not bonded to him, which I find interesting." Matthias sipped his whiskey and set it back on the desk. "Why is that?"

A partial truth would work. "I was bonded to him before coming here, actually. But we agreed that if I came in contact with Aidan Murphy by some chance, he'd know I was tied to the Tribunal—or at least that I had pledged fealty to another scathe. Being a free agent seemed safer. I could pretend to be looking over Penton as a possible place to relocate."

Matthias picked up his glass again and watched the amber liquid swirl around the glass. "Would you be willing to bond yourself to me? I'd consider it a sign of good faith, a reassurance of your loyalty. Once this operation is over, of course, I'll release you from your bond so you can return to Edward.

"That was Edward's message to you, by the way—that you should honor my request."

Bloody hell. He hadn't seen this coming, and he didn't believe for a second that Edward had recommended it. But he didn't dare hesitate. "Certainly, that seems reasonable enough. I'm unlikely to run across Aidan Murphy in downtown Penton, given the current situation. Our bonding decisions were made before we knew you'd led such an assertive attack on Murphy's scathe."

"Good." Matthias set his glass on the desk. "I'm glad you see things the way I do."

He had to think fast and buy time. What would satisfy Matthias as a plausible reason for delay? "Would you object to waiting until just before dawn? Feeding—and being fed from—makes me feel a bit lazy and complacent, I'm afraid, not being a master vampire like yourself. That's rather embarrassing to admit. But I'd like to help patrol and be on alert tonight."

Matthias smiled, a stretching and thinning of lips that made his slim face distort like a fun house mirror image. "Quite understandable. There's nothing quite like the blood exchange, is there? It's sensual even between virtual strangers."

Cage fought to keep from visibly shuddering. If the bastard thought Cage's mouth was going anywhere near his body— even a forearm—he was deluded. "Shall we meet back here about four?"

"Perfect," Matthias said. "I have some reports to file for the Tribunal and would like to go back and inspect the grenade site as well. And with any luck, you or one of my other scouts will discover the Penton scathe's hideaway tonight."

Cage nodded thoughtfully. "Are you certain they're still here and hiding underground? The most prudent thing for them to have done would be to use their escape hatch and scatter while things were still in chaos."

Even Aidan admitted this would have been the best plan, but the scathe had been in disarray when they escaped into Omega following Matthias's unexpected attack. By the time they regrouped, especially with that many humans, it wasn't safe to move a lot of people out at once.

"I can't be certain, of course." Matthias got up and refilled his whiskey glass, then returned to his seat. "But Murphy is arrogant, and he had quite a little kingdom built up here"—he looked around with a sniff—"albeit a boring one. He'll think he can wait us out or stage an offensive of his own. Now that we've destroyed one of his exits, time is on our side. Once we find the other exits, they'll be like ducks in a shooting gallery when they pop their heads up."

Cage nodded. He had to admit that, from a tactical point, it made sense. Time was on Matthias's side. "Assuming they are underground, how long do you think they can last?"

Matthias's laugh sent a shiver across Cage's shoulder blades. "Oh, not long. If it were only the vampires and a few feeders they didn't care about, they could survive quite a while. But they've made unwise emotional bonds with their humans, and I've never met a human who had much stomach for no daylight or fresh air or the ability to move around at will. I predict conditions will grow squalid quite fast if they haven't already."

Again, Cage had to acknowledge Matthias's logic. Will had designed a solid system of filtered air, steady light, fresh water, and waste disposal. They'd last longer than Matthias might think. But eventually, if nothing else went wrong, cabin fever— or bunker fever—could easily spread. All it would take would be one person to panic, run, and give away the Omega entrance.

A sharp knock sounded from the doorway, and a flush-cheeked Shelton stuck his head in the door, obviously well sated—something Cage didn't want to think too much about. "You ready to go and take a look at the grenade site?"

"I certainly am." Matthias rose from his chair. "Cage, would you like to join us? I'm anxious to see if there are any signs of movement from below. We took photos of the original cave-in, so if dirt or debris have been moved, we'll have our answer about whether or not the good citizens of Penton are belowground."

Shit. Even if the Penton scathe had been careful filling in the lower part of the grenade site, Matthias would probably find his visual proof that they were down there. Cage was torn between going with the vampires to stay abreast of their findings and getting Melissa out as soon as possible. But he'd promised Aidan. Melissa had to come first, and he had no intention of bonding with Matthias.

"I think I'll find a feeder and then help with the patrols." Cage got to his feet as well. "I thought I scented unfamiliar vampires south of town, so I might head down that way again. I'll meet you back here by four, though." Right. He'd stake himself first.

"Cage is going to become a bonded scathe member, at least for a while," Matthias told Shelton. "We'll be happy to have him officially aboard, won't we?"

Shelton nodded a little too enthusiastically. *Bastard.*

Cage accompanied the men outside, and when they headed north toward the church, he turned south. He made a broad circle around the downtown area, through the woods, and emerged behind the burned ruins of Aidan's home. Next to it, still intact, stood the greenhouse where Aidan had liked to dabble at the closest thing a vampire could come to farming. He'd raised night-blooming flowers, which had apparently helped win him over with Krys.

Mirren and Glory had fled there after Matthias's attack on Penton, spending a daysleep in the other half of the tunnel that led to the clinic. The cave-in was closer to this side. But if Cage could work his way through it, it would be the safest way to get Melissa out.

He had to dig fast.

Aidan had told him where the hatch was and how to spring it. But it was so well hidden in the dirt floor of the greenhouse that it still took him a half hour to find it and get it open.

He climbed onto the concrete steps, closed the hatch behind him, and descended into a small exit room. A concrete-floored tunnel led off of it, sloping downward. The air was damp and musty, and the tunnel was dark. No electricity on this side, so Cage knelt and pulled a flashlight from his pack. And a knife.

After twenty or thirty feet of decline, the tunnel leveled out. Ahead, Cage found a mattress and a bloody shirt—leftovers from Mirren and Glory, who'd been shot by Matthias after getting everyone else out through the church hatch. There was a couple of suites on this side of the cave-in, but they didn't look structurally sound. Their ceilings cracked and sagged.

If the suites on this end of the corridor were this shaky, he might risk bringing this whole side of the clinic down on his head by digging through the rubble that blocked the tunnel. He played the flashlight beam along the debris and paused on a spot that seemed to have a lot of loose stones and plaster beneath a collapsed support beam. No need to tear the whole thing down; he only needed an opening big enough to crawl through.

Propping the flashlight so it illuminated the spot, he knelt and used his knife to lever out a small chunk of concrete, then another. After an hour of meticulous removal, stone by stone, waiting between each piece to see if the rubble looked as if it were going to shift, he had an opening that looked wide enough to accommodate his shoulders. That was the broadest thing that would be going through it.

The tricky part would be sliding through without touching and dislodging anything else. Still, it was the best he could do.

He checked his watch: 11:00 p.m. No time to waste.

Cage slipped off his jacket, took everything from the pockets of his combat pants, and, after consideration, jerked his sweater over his head. The fewer things to get caught on pieces of debris, the better.

Carefully, he reached through the opening and laid the flashlight on the other side, then the lock-picking tools from his pack. He stuck his head and upper body through, then pushed off with his feet and tried a forward somersault through the opening.

Damn it. His heel caught the top of the hole, and a rain of stones came down. He held his breath, praying the mangled support beam would hold. If he got caught half-naked on this side of the tunnel with Matthias and Shelton roving around, it would not be pretty. Plus, Matthias was taking his daysleep in the house across the street from this greenhouse. Who knew when he might pop over there for something?

The sifting dust settled with one final groan of the beam.

Cage climbed to his feet, grabbed the flashlight and tools, and ran down the corridor to Melissa's room. The loosened dead bolt didn't turn, and he knelt to look at it. *Damn it.* The lock had been changed to a new lockset—had Matthias figured it out? Paranoia and dread settled on him as he fumbled with the new lock, finally hearing the tumbler turn. *Thank God.*

He slipped quickly into the room and closed the door behind him. Melissa was in the same place, but she'd been blindfolded. At the sound of the door, she'd begun visibly trembling. Those bastards. "It's me, Mel. It's Cage."

He made quick work of the blindfold, aware of the glassy, unfocused look in her hazel eyes. The gag came off next. "Are you OK? Can you answer me?"

She looked at him and blinked, then blinked again. The awareness seeped into her gaze, along with a look of fear. "Cage? They knew somebody had fooled with the locks, and you're the only one who's been down here. You've gotta get out."

"We're getting out of here." He fumbled with the ropes, finally got her untied, and helped her sit up. As soon as she tried to stand, however, she stumbled. She'd been tied up ever since her transition, he guessed.

Opening the door and glancing down the hallway, Cage went back and picked Melissa up. "Arms around my neck. We're getting out."

New vampires had no way to gauge their own strength, and Melissa almost choked him as they made their way down the corridor.

"Stick your head and arms through the hole and stay propped on your hands," he whispered. "I'll push you through."

She nodded, but moved slowly. Cage hadn't heard anything, but some instinct told him time was short. "Move faster if you can, love."

"I'll try." Melissa's voice was a dry rasp. She needed feeding, badly.

Finally, she got halfway through the opening, and he was able to push her through.

The sound he'd been dreading—an opening hatch—sounded down the corridor, and Cage dove toward the hole in the debris.

"You son of a bitch—stop!" Matthias's voice. Running footsteps. Not just Matthias—more than one person.

A shot echoed down the corridor, and hot pain erupted in the back of Cage's thigh as he tried to roll through the opening. The debris began raining down on his legs, and he struggled, unable to pull himself out.

"Mel, help m—" He didn't have to finish. She grasped him under the arms and tugged, pulling him through just as another shot sounded, followed by a groaning shift of debris. It wasn't just in the tunnel, but above their heads. This whole fucking side of the clinic was coming down.

"Run!" He snatched up his pack and took Melissa's hand, but he was virtually dragging her. A brick hit him on the side of his head, grazing his temple and sending a wet stream down his jaw and neck. He lifted Melissa and ran, ran like he'd never run before, up the twenty yards of inclined tunnel and into the exit room. Every time weight hit his leg it increased the hot pain, as if each step were a pile driver, jamming the bullet in deeper.

He set Melissa down and collapsed to the floor, gasping. The cave-in rumbled along the tunnel they'd just exited, spewing dust over them until he put his arms around Melissa and pulled her face against his chest to help her breathe.

Will had designed the exit rooms with a separate infrastructure, anticipating this very scenario. They couldn't stay here long, though. He had no idea if Matthias knew the other half of that tunnel exited in Aidan's greenhouse, but he couldn't gamble.

Finally, the rumbling stopped, the dust settled, and the silence pressed in on them.

"Let me go, Cage." Melissa struggled out of his grasp and looked around. "We're under Aidan's greenhouse?"

"Yeah." Cage wiped the grime off his face with his forearm. Guess he wouldn't be getting that sweater and leather jacket back. Better them buried than Melissa and him. "And we have to go. If I don't get you to Omega by three, Aidan and Mirren are going to walk into a big mess." Plus, for all he knew, Matthias and Shelton were racing toward the greenhouse with a horde of hired guns and fangs.

Melissa struggled to her feet and managed a few wobbly steps.

This would be an arduous trip. And as Cage stood up, he realized how arduous. His leg threatened to give way, but he forced himself to put weight on it. He hobbled to the stairs and turned to Melissa. You climb ahead of me. I'll catch you if you stumble. Just go slowly, and keep your balance."

Melissa nodded, shoving her hair off her face and tugging up the jeans that had grown loose over the last week as she'd gone through both transition and starvation. She placed one foot on the steps and stalled. They were steep and narrow.

"Here you go." Cage grasped her waist and lifted her, then held on while she got her feet under her. The next step she managed alone. When she'd made it to the fourth one, he started up after her, pulling his weight up each step with his good leg.

Finally, they reached the top. "Spring the hatch, wait a few seconds so we can listen and scent, then when I say so, climb out."

"OK." Melissa turned the release lever on the hatch and lifted it a few inches. A few inches more. Cage closed his eyes and scented the air, the cool dampness, the warm, sunny smell that lingered on the plants in the greenhouse. It seemed like a hundred years since Matthias had attacked and they'd fled their homes, but it had been only a week. Aidan's blooms still scented the air with sweet, heavy perfume.

What he didn't smell was vampire. "OK, crawl out. I'll be right behind you."

Melissa needed a boost to make it out of the hatch. Cage could have done with one himself.

He looked at his watch, but the face was cracked. He hoped it wasn't an omen.

❧CHAPTER 18❧

Krys had given Will the second double dose of morphine at about 1:00 a.m., along with a lot of snark about how men couldn't tolerate pain and how Dr. Slayer was going to be in charge of his drug rehab if he got addicted.

Fine with him. After the last shot, he didn't know if he even still had a fucking leg and didn't much care. Mirren could come in and twist it six ways to Sunday, and he'd just float through it.

The holes in the acoustical-tile ceiling had quit dancing in swirls, but he couldn't concentrate enough to even play games on his laptop.

His thoughts were still clear, just trapped inside the attention span of a gnat, so he lay in a drugged stupor and thought about his father, about how they might get out of this crap-pit situation, about Melissa, about how Mark would react when he saw her—and if she'd feel the same about him as before she was turned. Krys's bond to Aidan had held after she became a vampire, but it didn't always work that way.

Vampire mating bonds were some seriously weird shit. Who'd think Mirren and his battle-ax would fall for a sweet Georgia girl? Although, Glory was far from ordinary.

And then there was Randa.

Veranda.

Memoranda.

Randa-Panda.

Randa Thomas was fun to think about while stoned.

The door whispered open, and Will wrested his eyes from the acoustical tiles and looked at the woman standing in the doorway. Not Randa, which was too damn bad.

"What kind of panties you wear?" he asked Krys. "You know what kind of panties soldiers wear?"

Krys shook her head, took his pulse, and tried to shine a flashlight in his eyes—no, a damned tractor beam. "Your pupils are the size of dinner plates."

"You didn't answer me about the panties."

She laughed. "Nor will I. There are some things in life, Will Ludlam, that are just flat-out none of your business."

He pondered this, and he could see her point. Aidan probably wouldn't like Will knowing his mate's underwear secrets.

"How's the leg?" Krys uncovered it and studied it with clinical detachment, which was kind of insulting. He had great legs.

He arched his head up and took a look. The color was almost back to normal. "I think it's ready to be untaped from the board."

"I don't think so." Krys pulled the sheet back over it. "I don't want you moving until after daysleep. I just came to prepare you—you're getting a new roommate."

Will suddenly felt a lot more sober. "You got word on Melissa?"

Krys shook her head. "Not yet, but Aidan gave Cage until three a.m. to get her here. We've got another"—she looked at her cell phone—"hour. But we might need to put her in here, depending on what kind of shape she's in. Even if she's relatively healthy, Aidan won't let her and Mark stay together alone for a while—she might not have enough control not to drain him when she feeds. I think Aidan's going to ask Randa to stay with them."

Will's sobriety ratcheted up another notch, to the point where he was aware of a dull throb in his damned leg. "I don't think Randa's a good option, Krys. Be better if you stayed with her."

Randa had shown a lot of facets to her character in the last forty-eight hours, but he still wasn't sure nurturing a new vampire was the right role for her.

Krys looked surprised. "Why? I mean, I'm so new myself I don't think I could answer all her questions. I've only been turned a few months, and I thought a woman might be more comfortable for Melissa as a mentor."

Will stared up at his favorite acoustical tile for a few seconds. It had holes in the shape of a B-57 bomber if you looked hard enough. He didn't want to sell Randa down the river, but the counseling Melissa got now was too important. "Randa hates being a vampire. She didn't get a good indoctrination herself—I'm not even sure who got her through her transition."

"The asshole who turned her, I think. Still, she's been turned five years. She knows more than I do about what to expect."

Will thought about her dislike of feeding and how surprised she'd been to find feeding from him pleasurable. "I don't think she does. She only knows what she needs to stay alive. She hasn't embraced anything. I don't think she'd be a good person to counsel Melissa, and more than that, I don't think she'd want to do it."

She'd feel obligated to try. She'd want to be the good soldier and please Aidan. But it could be disastrous for both of them. Will was as concerned about the impact on Randa as on Melissa. He wanted to show her how to embrace her nature, not just tolerate it.

Krys remained quiet as she busied herself putting away the tape and bandages she'd pulled out while treating Will and Randa. Finally, she snapped her case shut. "We'll play it by ear, then. Maybe we need to move you so that Aidan and I can both stay with Melissa in here. Mark too, if Mel's in good enough shape. We can get Mirren to take you back to your room with Cage."

Will could think of no scenario where Mirren taking him anywhere was a pleasant option. "Define *take*."

Krys grinned. "How do you think you got from the cave-in to this hospital bed, macho man?"

It had never occurred to him to ask. He'd envisioned a scenario where three or four scathe members wheeled him down the hallway on...a golf cart or something. "Please don't tell me Mirren picked me up and carried me."

"Clasped in his arms like a baby."

He would never live this down. Never in his immortal life.

⊱─━━━◦◯◦━━━─⊰

Randa watched Liv stuff her few clothes into a backpack. "Who's this person you've hooked up with?"

Liv stopped packing and sat on the bed. "Jeremy? He's one of Hannah's feeders since her fam parents left. We've been spending a lot of time together down here in Omega and found out we have a lot in common. And he's cute."

Randa smiled at Liv's blush. She was happy the woman had found someone, although it seemed awfully fast. "I thought you and Will..." She shrugged. She wasn't sure what she thought Will and Liv had, or at least what Liv thought they had.

"Will's never going to settle down with somebody like me. I'm not..." The girl paused and picked up a tablet computer. "He gave me this, you know, to play with. I don't even know how to turn it on. Not that I can't learn, but I just don't care about the stuff he cares about."

She knew it was an inappropriate question, but she asked it anyway. "What does Will care about?"

Liv laughed. "If I ever figure it out, I'll let you know. He doesn't let anybody inside, which is another problem. I know more about Jeremy in two days than after six months as Will's fam. He's hot as a habanero in bed, but the man is an ice cube upstairs, if you know what I mean."

Randa didn't answer. She did know what Liv meant, although she hadn't experienced the habanero part—and was more than a little jealous that Liv had. A day ago, she would have agreed about him being an ice cube. Now she knew better. Will wasn't emotionally unavailable; he just protected a heart that had been hurt too often and too badly. She liked the man she'd been stuck with in the exit room. She wanted to see more of him. Not the face he showed the world, but the one he kept hidden.

"You've already fed, but if Will needs to feed, come and find me." Liv picked up her bag and opened the door into the hallway. "Jeremy's got a room by himself, so I'm going to be staying there and we'll see if we have something. His is the last room on the left."

After she'd gone, Randa changed into her favorite daysleep wear—a black T-shirt with ARMY stretched across the front in gold block letters—and settled into bed with the tablet computer Liv had left behind.

What had Will put on it for Liv? She'd expected mostly games, and there were a few. There was a reading app, and when she opened it, she was surprised to see more than a hundred books he'd downloaded. And not for Liv, she suspected. History, architecture, military strategy—they were the books of a man bent on learning as much as he could. Maybe for the love of learning. Or maybe to prove something to himself.

A commotion from the hallway roused her from bed, and before she got to the door, someone knocked. Maybe they'd found Melissa.

Krys stood outside the door, looking down the hallway toward the hatch. "We're having to shuffle some folks around—think you can put up with a new roommate? Has Liv already gone?"

Great, another new person to break in. "Sure—Liv's gone." She hoped it wasn't Melissa. She loved Mel to death, but Randa knew she was the last person a new vampire needed to be bunked with.

It wasn't Melissa who came through the door, but Mirren, carrying Will in his arms.

Will appeared to be unconscious. His head lolled against Mirren's shoulder, and his arms dangled at his sides. Did he have a setback? But his leg looked better, and it had been removed from the two-by-four. It had stripes of reddened skin where the tape had been jerked off.

He wore a pair of black boxer briefs and nothing else, not that Randa noticed.

"Which bed is yours?" Mirren asked, and Randa pointed to the one on the left. Mirren held Will over the other one and dropped him from a height of about four feet.

He landed with a grunt, followed by a string of curses. "What an asshole. And if you broke my damned leg again, I'm going to kick you to India and back."

Mirren looked at Randa and shook his head. "Good luck."

Before Randa could ask any questions, Mirren had gone and closed the door behind him. Will struggled to sit upright and examined his leg.

She tried not to stare at the expanse of tanned skin sprawled on the bed in front of her. He seemed a lot bigger in her little room than he had in the medical ward. "Why were you pretending to be unconscious?"

"Because it seemed..." He looked up at her, his words trailing off as he took in the T-shirt, the bare legs, and what probably looked like a bad case of bedhead since she hadn't done anything with her hair after her shower. "Damn, I like the army. Did I ever tell you how much I like the army?"

Uh-huh. "How much morphine did Krys give you?"

"Not enough. But I won't be whining for more. Only a couple of hours before daysleep."

Randa sat on her bed and tried to figure out why Will was here. "What's going on?"

"They're bringing Melissa in, and Cage was injured, so they need all the beds in the ward. Krys wants me to stay off the leg until after daysleep, but other than that, I'm off medical care."

Randa sprang to her feet. "Is Melissa OK? What happened to Cage? Has anyone told Mark?"

She started toward the door, but Will grabbed her wrist on her way past and pulled her back, almost falling off the bed in the process. "They want as few people as possible right now, which is why they kicked me out. Cage hadn't made it back by his deadline, so Aidan and Mirren slipped out and went into town, dodging Matthias's vampires all the way." He shook his head. "So damned risky."

Randa agreed. If either of those two were killed, the rest of them might as well march down Main Street and turn themselves over to Matthias. Aidan was Penton's heart, and although he'd chafe at the title, Mirren was its soul.

And Will, she realized with a start, was its mind. So much of what they'd accomplished here had been done because he'd figured out a way to make it happen.

"So they rescued Melissa and found Cage hurt?"

Will bunched the pillow up and lay back down. "No, they intercepted Cage and Mel coming from Penton. Cage was shot in the leg trying to get them out of the tunnel from the clinic, and Mel's weak from being tied down so long. She needs to feed."

"What about you? Do you need to feed?" Randa's heart sped up before the question was out of her mouth. She wanted Will to feed from her, to know what it was like to feel his mouth at her vein.

Will grew still. "Only if you're not talking about Liv."

Randa kept her eyes focused on his. Neither of them blinked. Neither looked away. "She moved in with her new boyfriend."

"Good."

Randa walked slowly toward the bed. He didn't answer, but slid toward the wall to make room for her.

She stretched out beside him. "How should we do this? You don't need to move your leg."

"I don't need my leg." Will cradled her face in his hands and pulled her toward him, touching his lips lightly to hers. He slid a hand to the back of her neck and turned the kiss into a military assault, straight down the front lines, thrust and counterthrust. Randa felt a foreign heat wash across her skin as his hands traveled into enemy territory—or created friendly fire. She wasn't sure which.

Oh yeah, definitely friendly fire. She trailed low, slow kisses along his jaw, then eased her body on top of his.

"This position's starting to feel familiar." Will smiled as she kissed him again, then tilted her head, baring her throat to him. Thanks to her tonsorial experiment, she didn't have to push her hair out of the way.

He gripped her waist with warm fingers and pulled her higher on his chest. Randa's heart pounded as he slid a hand through her hair and grasped a fistful of curls, holding her head taut. He swept his tongue along her shoulder, paused to nibble on her collarbone, then her earlobe.

His left hand still held her head fast while his right slid around her waist and clamped tight. Her breath grew ragged as he sent his tongue on a leisurely route across her neck. "Are you ready?"

"Please..." Good grief, had she just begged him to—

The sharp pain of the bite disappeared in waves of pleasure as he drew from her vein, each soft pull killing any rational thought. It was all sensation now, sweeping from her neck to pool between her thighs.

As if following her thoughts, Will slid a hand between them and found her hot and wet and ready for his fingers to dip inside her, using her own body's arousal to spread in and out and around her until she cried out for him.

He withdrew his fangs and she turned to kiss him, but he jerked her head back into place, leaning in to bite a second time, then a third, a fourth. Each bite sent an almost physical thrust of pleasure through her core. Each time he pulled away, it was a withdrawal. The rhythm sent her spinning.

He stopped feeding, replacing his teeth with tongue and lips. His breath puffed against her ear, his voice rough. "Come for me, Ran. Now."

With wicked, agile fingers, he took her over the edge. She cried out against his neck as he bit a final time.

Shuddering, she lay in his arms, kissed him, took the skin of his throat between her teeth.

"Don't feed from me. Not now." He worked his hands up to the tail of her T-shirt and began sliding it up. She pulled away and sat up.

Will's eyes were glassy, his lips red from her blood, his breathing as heavy as hers. He'd never looked more beautiful.

"Why don't you want me to feed from you?" He'd enjoyed it before; she'd felt him grow hard beneath her, even in the less-than-romantic confines of the caved-in exit room.

Slowly, he ran the tip of his tongue over his lips, capturing the last drops of her lifeblood. Then those lips lifted in a smile. "Oh, I do, believe me. But do you know how much morphine Krys pumped into me tonight? I don't know what it would do to you."

Randa arched a brow at him, slipped her fingers beneath the sheet, and cupped him in her hand with a slight squeeze. "Anything else off-limits?"

His body arched beneath her. "Ah...no. Although, Krys said I couldn't get it up until the morphine wore...ahh."

She pumped him once, twice, three times. "I think Krys was wrong. How about you?"

He held her hand in place over his shaft, making her fingers curve around it as he slowly thrust against her hand. "Uh-huh."

Randa leaned over him and nipped his lower lip as she worked him with her hand. She wanted him inside her, and badly, but not enough to risk reinjuring that leg. Tonight was foreplay.

❧CHAPTER 19❧

Cage's leg hurt, and he was bored. A normal bullet wound should already have healed, but when Krys ha'd dug the plug out of his thigh, they'd discovered it was silver. Whatever else Matthias Ludlam was, he was cunning. Had to give him credit for that. And sadistic.

So instead of being back to normal in a couple of hours, he'd be useless until after his daysleep—maybe two daysleeps. He wouldn't heal human slow, but it wouldn't be vampire fast, either.

They'd first taken him into the medical ward with Melissa, but as soon as Krys dug out the bullet and offered something for the pain, Aidan had ushered him back into his room. Aidan and Krys wanted to spend time alone with Melissa, a good idea. New vampires needed mentoring to understand the changes in their bodies and how to control their impulses. Without that mentoring, some vampires turned out OK, but most turned into predators. It was their nature, after all, and Melissa was getting a late start.

Cage also didn't want to be there when Melissa saw Mark again. He hoped for both their sakes that their love and their bond could withstand her being turned. For his own sake, he wished he hadn't started to care so much. Her selflessness, even when she was in pain from her transition and facing a possible eternity with Matthias, had touched him like nothing he could remember.

Aidan had sensed his attraction to her that first night, and he'd be on the alert for any inappropriate attention from his British lieutenant.

No worries. Cage was the consummate professional. Which sometimes royally sucked.

The door to the hallway opened after a soft knock, and Aidan stuck his head in. "Can I talk to you a minute?"

"Sure." Cage maneuvered to a seated position on the bed and propped his back against the wall. He had nothing but time and a boring novel that probably should never have been published.

"How's the leg?"

"We need to get some of those bullets—they're damned effective. Hurts like hell."

Aidan smiled. "Already put them on Will's shopping list for tomorrow night—he should be able to travel by then. That was my first question—is it safe to send anyone out of Omega?"

Cage thought about the areas he knew Matthias's men were searching. "So far, as long as he's careful. They haven't fanned out as far as the Omega entrance. But are you sure you want to send Will on these runs? If Matthias captures you or me, he'll eventually kill us. Will's future would be worse than death."

Aidan took a seat on the other bed. "I picked him because he's fast and can think on his feet. I know he hates Matthias.

Is there something I need to know from Matthias's side of the story?"

Cage pondered his suspicions about Shelton, weighing Aidan's need to know against Will's right to privacy.

Aidan leaned forward, propping his elbows on his knees. "If it's something that might impact his ability to do his job, you need to tell me. It won't leave this room. If it's not, just say so and I won't ask again."

It could impact his ability to do the job. If he were confronted with Shelton again, how would Will react? He knew Will had seen Shelton briefly when he went on the successful raid to free Mirren and Glory in Virginia the month before last. He had even spared Shelton's life, mostly because he was focused on Mirren.

Cage didn't think that would happen again. If he got caught and Shelton pushed him enough, Will might snap. That could backfire on Matthias—or it could backfire on his friends in Omega.

"I'll tell you this," Cage said. "There were things done to Will when he was young, just after he was turned, that might impact how he'd react if his father caught him."

Aidan nodded slowly. "I know Matthias killed Will's mother and sister, trying to turn them, that he strong-armed Will into going along with it. I know he's been verbally abusive Will's whole life."

"Not just verbally, Aidan. Sexually. Not Matthias himself, but his man Shelton, with Matthias's knowledge and permission. I'm pretty sure it's how they got Will under control—well, until he ran away. Will hinted as much, and I saw Shelton in action with a kid he's got up there who can't be more than fourteen or fifteen. Will was older, but he looks young and he'd only been turned a few months, so he wouldn't have known how to defend himself."

"Shit." Aidan ran his hands through his hair. "It's a goddamn miracle he even survived. I need to give it some thought. If I pull him off patrols, he'll want to know why. He'll see it as punishment, not us trying to protect him."

"Understandable." Cage sighed. There were no easy paths in this new world of theirs. "Just know that if Will gets caught, there are worse things Matthias can do than kill him. He still wants him as an acolyte, however he achieves it."

Aidan nodded. "I'll give it some more thought. In the meantime, there's something else I need to ask you. About Melissa."

Cage tensed. "What about her?"

"She's asking for you. I think it's because you fed her, yes? She's formed an emotional bond to you."

"I did feed her, a couple of times." Cage's tone came out defensive, but he wouldn't apologize for his actions. It had kept her from falling even more under Matthias's influence.

"Don't get me wrong—I'm glad you kept her as strong as you could. But I want to bring Mark to her to feed. She's nervous about it, afraid she'll hurt him. We can keep that from happening, but it might help if you were there."

Cage closed his eyes. God help him, he wished Mark wasn't in the picture or wasn't such a good guy. But Mark and Melissa had a solid marriage before she'd been turned. Since she died— or he thought she died—he'd been shuffling around Omega like a wraith. There wasn't a person here, vampire or human, who hadn't agonized over his pain and wanted to help him.

"The faster Mark and Melissa get together, the better their chances of reforming their bonds to each other." Ten points for Cage. Shouldn't doing the right thing feel better? "I think you really need to prepare him, though. He can't go in without knowing what to expect. And it might not just be Mel who has some adjustments to make."

"I'm going to talk to him now." Aidan stood and looked down at Cage. "I know you care about her, and whatever happens, happens. Just give them a chance first."

Cage met Aidan's gaze and held it. "Agreed. Do you still want me in there, to help ease her way to Mark? If she has formed some attachment to me, it might make things worse."

"I trust you to help her."

While Aidan headed down the hall to tell Mark that Melissa was alive—and thank God it wasn't his job—Cage hobbled back to the medical ward. He knocked and waited for Krys to open the door.

"I'm glad you're here." She moved aside and let him in the room.

Melissa looked paler than before, if possible, but she wore a clean sweater and jeans, and her hair was damp and pulled back in a ponytail. Cage had barely cleared the door before she ran to him and threw her arms around his waist. "I wanted to make sure you were OK."

He met Krys's worried look over Melissa's head, but wrapped his arms around her and pulled her close. "It's OK, love. You're safe now. We're both safe now."

Cage wasn't sure they'd ever truly be safe again, but safety was relative.

He gently extricated her arms from around him and stepped back to look at her. So fragile and yet strong. He smiled at her and received a tentative one in return. "You're looking like yourself again. How do you feel?"

The good doctor Cage, that was him.

"Better. Aidan's bringing Mark." She lowered her voice. "I'm afraid to see him."

Cage took her hand and enveloped it in both of his. "You won't hurt him."

She shook her head and fought back tears, still looking very human and vulnerable. Her voice came out in a whisper even Cage, standing next to her, struggled to hear. "I can't remember loving him. I remember it in my head, but not in my heart."

Something alien and predatory unfurled in Cage's chest, something that met her pronouncement with rejoicing. He beat it down with self-control forged of iron. "When you see him, you'll remember. Your heart will remember."

"That's what I told her," Krys said. She'd been standing near the door, giving them privacy, but now joined them in the middle of the room. "Aidan and I went through this, remember, Mel? It took us a couple of weeks, but we found our way back to each other."

Melissa nodded. "How long do you think it'll be before they come?"

"Soon." Cage led her to the bed and sat beside her. Krys took one of the chairs. "It's only an hour until dawn, so it can't be long."

He'd thought it might take at least a half hour for Aidan to explain things to Mark, but fewer than ten minutes elapsed before Mark came bursting into the room, with Aidan following close behind, his brows lowered in a frown. "Where's Mel?"

As soon as Mark spotted her, he froze. He'd probably lost half a stone's worth of weight since they'd been in Omega, and the bruises from his injuries hadn't finished healing. Mark, in his own way, had had just as rough a time as Melissa. Shame filled Cage's heart that part of him wanted this man's wife, wanted her to reject the man she'd loved so deeply.

Melissa's hand still rested in his, but she pulled it away and walked to meet Mark. Anticipation, dread, excitement, fear—they all swirled in this room with an almost physical presence.

Mark tried to smile at her, but the tears overwhelmed him as soon they made eye contact. Cage wished it was possible to give them privacy. They couldn't, though. Not yet. But he walked to the desk at the far end of the room and pretended to study a roll of athletic tape. Krys and Aidan stayed near the door to the hallway. It was the most privacy they could give them while still keeping Mark safe.

Whispers, crying, soft words. Cage tried to shut them all out until Mark yelped in pain, and he whirled to see Melissa with her mouth at her husband's neck. They'd expected this. He and Aidan reached them at the same time. Cage put an arm around Melissa's waist from behind and lowered his mouth to her ear.

"Go easy, love. You know what to do. Remember when you fed from me? Remember Aidan feeding from you? You know how to keep it from hurting."

Melissa shoved Mark away and crumpled to the floor with her head in her hands, Mark's blood streaming down her chin. Krys put her mouth to Mark's wound and stopped the bleeding. It took him a few seconds to stop shaking.

"Mel, it's OK." Mark knelt in front of Melissa, but she wouldn't look at him. He looked up at Aidan, desperation widening his eyes.

"It's almost dawn," Cage said. "Maybe Melissa needs to get through a daysleep. It's been a long night for everyone." He wanted to sit on the floor next to her, take her in his arms, tell her everything would be good after a day of rest. But for one thing, with his bum leg, if he ever got on the floor, he'd need help getting up.

Plus, he wasn't sure it was true.

❧CHAPTER 20❧

Damn, but it felt good to stand upright. Will had spent the first two hours after daysleep walking back and forth across the length of Omega, taking occasional breaks to stop and chat with the small groups that had settled into chairs or wandered aimlessly around the facility. The evil Dr. Slayer had ordered him to stay on his feet awhile before going on shopping patrol, to make sure the leg would hold his weight. So far, so good.

The people of Omega were bored, and Will couldn't blame them. Mirren was working with Glory, hoping she could use her telekinesis to clear a new exit, but there was nowhere for her to move the dirt. Will had little hope for that project. Aidan, Krys, and Cage were sequestered with Mark and Melissa—whose arrival had spread around Omega like a brush fire and cheered everyone up, at least temporarily. People smiled more and argued less.

But they were all restless and unsettled. Before he'd escorted Mark back to the medical ward, Aidan had asked Hannah and Randa to sit down and develop work schedules in different parts of Omega to keep everyone busy and to come up with ways for the humans, especially, to entertain themselves during the vampires' daysleep. Those plans would determine part of his shopping trip.

So far, as he'd passed them on his Omega walkabouts, he'd heard discussions about a karaoke night, a puzzle contest, and art classes.

"I have an idea." He smiled at Randa as he sat next to Hannah and slipped an arm around her thin shoulders. "We could talk to Mirren about drawing lessons. You know, turn the meeting room into an art studio and let him teach."

Hannah giggled. "He could wear a beret and hold a palette."

Randa was grinning now too. "He could *model* for people. Whoever draws the best likeness wins a prize."

"Maybe a—"

"A what, junior? Finish that fucking sentence." A ham-sized hand landed on Will's shoulder, hard enough to knock him off balance.

It was worth Mirren's wrath to see Hannah laughing again. "You really shouldn't curse around women and children, big guy."

"Shut it." Mirren upended Will's chair on his way out of the room, causing him to do some fancy balancing maneuvers to keep his ass off the floor.

Might be a good time to leave. "Like I was saying, gotta run some errands. Tell me what you guys need besides art supplies."

"Can I talk to you a minute before you go?" Randa stood and pointed toward the hallway toward their room.

"You bet." Will leaned over and kissed Hannah on the cheek. "You need anything, sweetie? A new cat purse?"

Her dark eyes turned solemn, and she shook her head. Will gave her a squeeze before following Randa into the room.

Things had been a little awkward between them when they woke from daysleep, half-dressed, their limbs tangled together. He didn't plan to let the awkwardness move them backward, so he closed the door behind him and pulled her into a kiss before she could start telling him all the reasons why it was a bad idea.

To his surprise, she didn't fight him. Instead, she met him with an aggressive assault of lips and tongue that slowed and softened as he figured out she wasn't running from him and vice versa.

He smoothed a curl behind her ear. "I was afraid you wanted to tell me last night couldn't happen again."

"Oh, last night's not going to happen again." Randa arched a brow at him. "Next time, you're going to be a more active participant, minus the morphine buzz. Got that, soldier?"

Oh yeah, he definitely got that. "I might have to come back from Opelika a little early." Cage hadn't mentioned moving back into their room, and Randa hadn't mentioned throwing him out of hers. Which meant he had his pick of sleeping spots. Not that he planned to sleep.

Randa turned away from him and walked to the bookshelf that functioned as dressing table, nightstand, and storage for the small room. She pulled down a backpack and drew a sheet of paper from it.

"Think you can find a Wi-Fi hot spot in Opelika?"

He took the paper. "Sure. I can take my laptop with me. What am I looking for?"

"Read it."

He unfolded the sheet, which had been printed off a website, and sounded out the words. "Rory's Ramblings? It's a blog?"

"Notice anything familiar about the guy?"

He looked at the grainy ink-jet print job, at a smiling soldier in uniform, with red hair cut military short, a straight nose, eyes that crinkled just like...

"He's your brother?"

"My twin brother, Rory. We were the youngest of the five kids—I'm the only girl—and when our mom died, Rory and I shared everything. It tore him up when I...when I died." She wouldn't meet his eye, but seemed to be examining her shoes. "He blogged about it."

"What's wrong, Ran?" Will led her to the bed, and they sat side by side. "You want to try and make contact with him?" He wasn't sure how he felt about that. He'd heard of very few vampires who'd been able to form any kind of relationship with human family members. For one thing, families aged and vampires didn't. Plus, it was dicey with the Tribunal, who, for all their dithering and hypocrisy, had been consistent in advising vampires to be very careful in letting humans know of their existence. Aidan had the Penton fams bonded or erased memories to prevent people from talking, for their own protection as well as the vampires'.

"I've been keeping up with the family through Rory's blog since I got back to the States after being turned. He stuck with it until last month, when he suddenly stopped. Until then, he'd posted a blog at least three or four times a week." She looked down at their intertwined fingers and squeezed Will's hand. "I have a feeling something bad has happened."

"You want me to see what I can find out?"

Randa nodded and finally looked up at him. "I hear you can hack into anything."

Her eyes were haunted, maybe even a little frightened, and Will wanted nothing more than to protect her. "If there's anything to be found, I'll find it."

⊱•──•◦•──•⊰

He'd found it all right, and he wasn't sure how he was going to break the news to Randa.

Will struggled to keep his mind on the road as he drove back from Opelika. He'd blown through a Dollar Tree and a Walmart, grabbing only the essentials he could carry.

After Cage's report on how close Matthias was to finding them, Aidan had decided Will could take only three people out at a time and only bring back what he and Mirren could take by hand. It was too risky for the other scathe members to be going in and out of the only Omega exit, too risky to use the Gator for bigger hauls, and too risky to take more people out at a time.

What Aidan hadn't said, and Will didn't want to think too hard about, was how the ratio of vampires to humans was dropping. Their numbers were down to forty vampires and fifteen humans. From now on, they'd be asking vampires to leave with their fams.

Will parked in a dark spot of the automotive-plant lot and sat in the pickup a few minutes, both watching for activity in the woods and deciding how much to tell Randa of what he'd learned.

Will was tired, and it wasn't just that his left leg had started throbbing; three more hours and he'd have another daysleep to finish healing. The stress of the last few months, after evading Matthias for years, had exhausted him. He wanted more than anything to spend a few weeks with nothing more pressing than taking nighttime swims and making love to a beautiful woman. Correction: making love to Randa Thomas, whose heart he was about to break.

Will exited the truck and gathered the bags of supplies, walking toward the tree line. He was within twenty yards of the Omega hatch when he scented another vampire nearby. Not just another vampire. Shelton.

And right on cue, his old friends returned: the panic, the shakes, and the rage. His usual reaction to Shelton, in other words. He fought back the onslaught of memories, of being restrained while Shelton taunted and touched. The pain, physical and mental, of being violated. Humiliation that Matthias knew and not only let it happen but put him there, in that cage at the Virginia estate where he'd rescued Mirren.

Shit. This was no time for a stroll through happy valley. Will returned to the truck and unloaded all but the most essential of his purchases—medicines and food that would fit into a backpack. The rest he covered in the bed of the pickup. Aidan had wanted to avoid it, but Will thought they were going to have to start sending one or two of the most reliable humans out to retrieve this stuff. Nighttime was getting too dangerous.

Ignoring the ache that had set up in his left calf, Will ran into the woods far west of the Omega entrance and made a big loop. When he approached the hatch again, Shelton had moved on.

Until he was securely inside the exit room with the hatch closed and locked behind him, Will didn't relax and let the tension drain out of his muscles.

"See anything?" Cage sat near the exit room opening into the tunnel, smoking a small cigar, a makeshift crutch and a shotgun propped against the wall next to him and a book open in his lap. The single fluorescent lantern barely gave off enough light to read. "We're a fine pair of gimps, aren't we?"

Will shed the backpack and flexed his left calf. "That's the truth. As for seeing anything, no. I scented Shelton close to the hatch, though, so I laid a false scent trail before coming back. They're getting too close. I had to leave most of the supplies in the truck."

"Maybe Mark can slip out during the day and retrieve them." Cage pinched the end of his cigar to kill the flame and stuck it in his pocket. "Can't waste these."

"Can you fill Aidan in on Shelton? I need to talk to Randa before daysleep." Will wanted to stay and ask about Mark and Melissa, but that would have to come later.

"I'll tell him. Everything OK?"

"No problem." *Liar, liar, calf on fire.*

Will knocked on Randa's door, and she must have been sitting right by it—she had it open before he'd lowered his hand.

Wide green eyes betrayed her fear—that and the nervous way she clenched her hands together. "Did you find anything?"

"I did. Let's sit down."

He closed the door behind him and led her to the bed, but she balked.

"I don't want to sit down. Will, people only tell you to sit down when it's bad news. What's going on with Rory?"

He pushed aside memories of his sister Cathy's wasted body and took Randa's hands in his. "He died a week ago, Ran. Cancer."

❧ CHAPTER 21 ❧

Randa did sit, after all. Her legs gave way, and she found herself on the bed, sitting with Will at her side, looking as if he expected her to scream and go hysterical on him.

On some level, she'd known. When Rory quit posting, she'd known something was wrong. Maybe it was a twin thing. If part of her had realized he was gone, did he still feel her presence after she'd been turned? She'd never know the answer to that. "Are you absolutely sure?"

Will retrieved his backpack, which he'd thrown to the floor when her legs had folded like an accordion, and took out a folded sheaf of papers. "Your older brother...His name's Rob?"

She nodded. Robbie was next in age to Rory and her, three years older. Classic middle child: loud, bossy, a risk-taker, always looking for attention so he wouldn't get lost in the shuffle of Colonel Thomas's kids, whose names all started with *R*. She'd always hated her name, Randalynn, her grandmother's name.

Will handed her the papers. "I found Rory's obituary first, but then came across a Facebook page Rob set up as Rory went through treatments. He went fast, like five or six weeks after he was diagnosed. I printed out as much as I could find."

Randa's hands shook as she unfolded the sheets. The obituary was on top, and her eyes zeroed in on the last sentence: *He was preceded in death by his mother, Alicia, and his beloved sister, Randalynn.* Her voice was little more than a whisper. "What kind of cancer?"

"It's on Rob's sheet—some kind of aggressive thing I can't sound out."

Randa stared at the photo of her brother. They hadn't been anything near identical twins, but definitely shared their coloring and facial structure. "Our mom died of leukemia really young. I don't even remember her." Her expression turned fierce. "Will, if I'd known, if I had tried to turn him vampire, would it have wiped out the cancer? Could I have saved him?"

"I'm not..." Will stopped and considered the question. "I've never thought about it, but maybe. I don't know. His illness might have made it impossible for him to get through his transition."

"If we could actually help somebody, it would make this"— she pointed at herself, then at him—"mean something."

A hard look crossed his face that she couldn't interpret. But he slid closer to her and took her restless hands in his, long fingers stroking along her knuckles. "Ran, we'll find out the answer to that question—Cage might be able to tell us if turning someone could cure an illness, and maybe we can find a way to do that once all this shit with the Tribunal is over and it isn't illegal to turn willing people again. But no matter what that answer is, you can't bring your brother back."

Her eyes closed, and a knife's edge of pain shot through her chest. "I know." Thinking she might have saved him if she'd known would get her nowhere, but those what-ifs kept scrolling through her mind.

"But here's the thing." He stroked a hand down her cheek and turned her face toward his. "The thing you can do for Rory is to live the second life you were given."

How could she, when she couldn't see anything ahead but years of fighting? She grew up a soldier, trying to prove herself, but she hadn't thought about having to do it forever. Literally forever, fighting for respect, fighting for food, fighting for survival.

But if she had a goal…

"Would you help me?" She shifted on the bed to look at Will, hope rising like a baby phoenix. "You know how Aidan's done with the drug rehab in Atlanta? We could do something like that with cancer patients."

As soon as she said the words, the reasons why it wouldn't work popped up without Will having to say anything. Helping addicts shake their cravings for drugs or alcohol was far different than intentionally making new vampires to help people survive diseases.

Once a new generation of humans grew up, the ones born after the pandemic vaccine, most vampires believed the feeding shortages would be over. But those were hopeful guesses, not a sure thing. It was a belief full of ifs: if the blood-chemistry change wrought by the vaccine wasn't passed on to babies, for example, and if the whole vampire world didn't implode from starvation and civil war by then.

Will nodded slowly. "I think it's a great idea, but not yet. Once we get through this pandemic stuff, I will help you. We'll see how we can make it work. I promise."

Randa closed her eyes and nodded. "I know—that idea has a lot of holes in it."

"You can make your vampire life worthwhile without trying to save the world."

Her laugh was as bitter as her heart felt. "How?"

God, she hated sounding so lost in front of Will. How had the jester of the vampire world suddenly become her confidant, the closest thing she'd had to a friend since she'd been turned? Even before then. She'd always kept people at a distance, but the cave-in had forced them to open up, and she found she didn't want to go back to where they'd been.

Will squeezed her hands. "First, accept this scathe as your family. It doesn't mean they're better than your human family, or even replacing your human family. But even as humans, families get redefined all the time. You marry someone and take on new members. People move in and out of each other's lives, and we take them in and then let them go when it's time."

Randa looked down at the folded sheets of paper, then reached over to place them on the bookshelf. How had she ever thought Will was shallow and unfeeling? "I'm not sure I'm ready to let them go. But I understand what you're saying. It's why I've stayed in Penton, why I've tried so hard to prove myself so Aidan would let me stay."

Will pulled her into a hug. "You don't have to prove anything."

The arms she reached around him were tentative at first, then tightened. "Make me forget, Will, just for a while. Love me." Had she just said that? She knew he didn't *love* her. Not love with a capital *L*. Neither of them was ready for that.

She just wanted to forget, to stop thinking.

Randa had spent a lot of time in the past few days imagining what her first time with Will—their real first time together—would be like. In her mind, sex with him was always playful, aggressive, teasing, high octane. This fragile need scared her, and probably scared him. She wouldn't blame him if he went running back across the hall to his room with Cage.

Cupping the back of her neck, he gently pulled her to him. He smelled of the night air, clean skin, a trace of pine.

He dug his fingers into her hair and met her frantic, open-mouthed kisses with a slow, steady pressure. He was holding back, and she didn't want him to.

When the tip of her tongue touched his, tentative and searching, he took that as an invitation, sucking her in as if he could inhale her.

"Oh." She pulled back, wide-eyed, her gaze settling on his lip, where a drop of blood oozed and spread. "I cut you. I've never...I mean, you're my first..." *Damned fangs.*

He stilled, looking equal parts alarmed and confused. "You're a virgin?"

She smiled, then laughed, the stress of the last week—the last hour—escaping in giggles. People could probably hear her all the way down in the common room. "I'm not a virgin, Will. You can get that deer-in-headlights look off your face."

But she was, sort of. "I haven't...you know...since I've been turned, and I'm afraid I'm going to slice you to ribbons." She ran a fingertip across his lower lip and lifted her blood-covered index finger to her mouth, tasting his sweet essence. "Too bad we can't remove these things except when we feed."

He grabbed her wrist and pulled her against him. "Taste me."

Randa twined her fingers through his hair, pushed it away from his face, and kissed him again, scooting closer until her knees hit his thighs. He slid his hands underneath her and pulled her onto his lap, turning her so she sat astride him. She felt how much he wanted her, and rocked against him slowly. He pulled her tightly against his chest, lifting his thighs to position her on him. "Move against me," he whispered. "Show me what you like."

His need hit her like a jolt of electricity as she opened her knees wider, slid forward, and ground against him until she thought she'd explode.

He groaned into her neck. "Ran, you're killing me."

"Good."

She let him roll her over, cursing at the tight fit. "Damned twin beds," he muttered. "Whoever ordered these things should be shot."

She laughed. "I thought *you* ordered them for all the rooms that weren't assigned to couples."

"I did, so if I fall on the floor, it'll be my own damned fault." He stood up, grabbed the hem of his sweater, and tore it off, the heat in his eyes turning them a molten gold. Most vampire eyes turned silvery, but not Will's. One of the fun things about arguing with him and getting him agitated was watching his eyes turn this beautiful shade of amber.

Turns out it didn't take an argument.

She stood up and began unbuttoning her shirt.

"I think that's something I'd like to do." He took over the task, easing each button slowly through the buttonhole, spreading the fabric away from her skin, trailing the whole process with his mouth.

"Yes." She half whimpered, half groaned as he eased the straps of her bra down and then ripped it off. Some primal need invaded her heart, wanted him inside her even as he sucked and licked his way down her body. Was this just vampire stuff, or was it this ridiculous chemistry?

"You OK?" They stood chest to chest, breathing ragged. His eyes were slightly unfocused as he tugged the front of her jeans, popping the button.

She helped him push them down, and while he shucked his own jeans, she shimmied hers off and kicked them aside, smiling as the grin spread across his face.

"Sweet." He hooked his fingers in the band of the red bikini panties—the only "sexy" pair she owned.

"If you tear those, I'll have to bring you up for court-martial."

He ran a thumb over her lips and dropped his mouth over hers in a hungry kiss. The force of it stole her breath and wiped out all feeling except for the throbbing that had set up deep inside her as he pulled her hips against his and lowered her back onto the little bed. He ran hot fingers between her thighs, spreading her open, cradling his body against hers, his erection a sweet pressure against her.

Her mouth opened, gasping for air, as he cupped her breasts, dragged his nails across their tips, and following them with teeth and tongue. Each nip sent waves of pleasure down her spine. Her hands tangled in his thick hair, pulling and clutching until he groaned and returned for a demanding kiss.

"Still going to have me court-martialed?" He waited until she looked him in the eye, then slowly lowered his mouth back to her breast, bared his fangs, and bit, sucking her blood and her tender skin into his mouth at the same time.

"That's not...omigod...fair." She arched against him and lost track of time for a few seconds, or minutes. Who knew? When she finally quit trembling and opened her eyes, he was propped on his elbows, watching her.

He gave her the cocky Will Ludlam smile, the one she used to find annoying. All of a sudden, it was amazingly sexy. "Did you like that, maybe just a little? That look on your face said you did."

"You are evil."

"I'm not evil. I'm in pain. I'm feeling neglected." He pointed downward. His erection was straining the front of his boxer briefs in a serious way.

"Yeah, you are kind of overdressed and standing at attention. Guess we better take care of that."

He rolled onto his back, and she eased the briefs off him. He was long, thick, heavy with need. He gripped himself and stroked, her eyes following the motion. "Taste me."

She dragged long, hard licks along his length, tracing the veins with her tongue, pressing his thighs down with her elbows so she controlled his movement.

"No, wait, wait, wait. God." He grabbed a fistful of her hair and pulled her up his body, then rolled her over, cracking his elbow against the wall, leaving a small indentation in the Sheetrock. "Fuck."

They both laughed until their gazes locked and the heat rose again, hard and fast. He lowered himself onto her, gasping as he brushed against her wet heat. She reached between them and grasped him, guiding him in.

He pushed forward, sinking into her body inch by inch in a slow rhythm. His cheeks were flushed, his body hot and trembling with the effort to remain still, moving slowly. He was going to drive her insane.

"Move it, soldier."

He kissed her and smiled, his forehead an inch from hers, moving in short thrusts. "Half march?"

"Double time."

She didn't have to order him twice. He drove in with deep, dragging strokes, his arms curled under her shoulders.

The world reduced to a single hot ball of nerves set afire by friction and fanned by desire, and as Randa went over, giving in to the tingling pressure, she felt him come with her, pulsing inside her and clenching his thighs as he threw his head back with a feral groan.

Only afterward, when she lay with her cheek resting on his chest, his fingers tracing circles on her back, did Randa think again of Rory. She should feel ashamed of that, but somehow she thought her brother would approve.

❧CHAPTER 22❧

Matthias paced the office of the Penton clinic, avoiding the back corner where the ceiling was cracked and on the verge of collapse after that damned Cage Reynolds had duped him and dragged Melissa Calvert out of Penton.

It wasn't the loss of the woman that bothered him so much—she'd proven annoyingly strong-minded for a new vampire and had told him very little after accidentally spilling the location to the Penton scathe's underground hiding-place entrance. He'd come to the conclusion she honestly didn't know where the other exits were and had decided to kill her. He didn't need another pair of fangs to feed. And she hadn't seen enough of Matthias's operation to tell Aidan Murphy anything helpful.

Nor had Cage Reynolds, but what really pissed Matthias off was the duplicity of Edward Simmons, the UK Tribunal chief. Matthias had called him in a fury after Cage escaped, and had to listen while that maddeningly calm voice expressed shock that his trusted lieutenant "would behave so egregiously. So sorry, old chap."

Old chap, my ass. Matthias didn't buy it for a second. Simmons had thrown in his lot with Murphy; Matthias's only consolation was that vampire law was on his side this time. His second call had been to Tribunal director Frank Greisser. The Austrian vampire, ancient and powerful despite looking like a thirtysomething ski instructor, had promised disciplinary action against the UK delegate.

A knock on the clinic door interrupted Matthias midpace. "What?"

Shelton stuck his ugly head in the door. "I have some news, sir."

Matthias sat behind the desk and waited for the man to sidle in. His face and neck were scored with raw, seeping wounds, and he wore a loose shirt that wouldn't touch his torso more than necessary. A little punishment with a silver-laced whip had been administered to remind Shelton that keeping tabs on Tribunal representatives was more important than playing with that little boy he kept locked up in the other clinic office.

"What do you want? I'm busy." He had to get busier. Frank Greisser was an ally, but he'd told Matthias a lot of the Tribunal members were growing restless. The way he'd come into Penton by force and by fire, causing so many deaths, hadn't sat well with a lot of their delicate sensibilities. The sympathy for Murphy and discontent with Matthias was growing. It would limit how hard Frank could be with Edward Simmons, and it meant if Matthias didn't produce results soon, the Tribunal could pull its support.

"We caught a couple of breaks." Shelton sat in the chair facing the desk, gasped when his back touched the chair, and scooted up to sit on the edge of the seat. Matthias smiled. Nice new invention, that silver whip. He hoped to be trying it out on William very soon. Or maybe he'd let Shelton do it.

"Go on."

"One of our scouts scented Cage Reynolds last night, using his backpack we found in the collapsed tunnel under the greenhouse. He was farther away from Penton than where we've been looking. We didn't find a hatch to their hiding place yet, but maybe we should fan our patrols farther out?"

Matthias smiled. *Finally.* "I'll take care of it. Anything else?"

Shelton pulled a sheet of paper from his shirt pocket. "The man from Atlanta you hired to track down Aidan Murphy's financial holdings finally found some activity at a small bank in southern Georgia. Place called Whigham. There's a sizable account under a corporation name headed by a Mark Calvert—that was one of the names on your list."

Matthias leaned forward. Melissa Calvert had never identified her relationship to the Penton resident named Mark, but his intelligence had identified him as Murphy's business manager. "Excellent news. You have the account numbers and the name of the bank?"

Shelton nodded, wincing as he reached out to lay the report on Matthias's desk. "Need me to handle it?"

Other than patrolling the woods, Matthias wouldn't give Shelton Porterfield more than a janitorial job to handle at this point. "I'll do it myself. Go back on patrol."

"May I...May I feed first?"

Oh, poor Shelton was missing his little boy. "Not today, Shelton. Maybe tomorrow. Maybe not. And you don't want me to find you cheating."

As soon as Shelton shuffled back into the hallway, Matthias made three calls.

The first was to the human security guy he'd hired to bring in a search dog earlier. They'd let the mutt get a whiff of Cage Reynolds's backpack and see where it led.

The second call went to a colleague in California with ties to the farming community. Farmers knew about pesticides. Matthias's patrols also had uncovered a spring not too far from where the men had scented Cage. He'd thought it was too far away from the Penton scathe to be used as a water source, but maybe not. A little poison in the spring might make things unpleasant for the humans if they were drinking from it. Sick humans would have to be brought out for treatment.

The final call went to a man at the Securities and Exchange Commission who'd become a bit of a blood junkie. He was a prime candidate for blackmail, and Matthias had been waiting for just the right situation. He could have that bank account frozen due to a pending SEC investigation by close of business tomorrow.

The next time one of the Penton crew tried to go shopping—and they would, because humans were needy creatures who needed much in the way of food and shelter—they'd be in for a surprise.

❧ CHAPTER 23 ❧

Another daysleep gone, and as he drove the latest soon-to-be ex-Penton citizens out of town, Will reflected that his leg finally felt normal again, except for a slight limp. Dr. Slayer said he'd be doing the gimp routine until they broke his bones yet again and reset them properly. A limp wasn't such a bad thing.

He stopped the pickup at the corner of Eighth and Orchid in a suburb of Opelika. "Welcome home, such as it is." The wooden house, painted white with black shutters, screamed generic. Which made it a perfect safe house. It blended with every other white house on this block, which sat among other blocks full of white houses, all full of indifferent neighbors.

Still, he slid from behind the wheel and scented the air before escorting his vampire companion and the young couple who were his familiars to the door. Will had taken several humans out of Omega because they wanted to leave, but this was the first scathe member who'd been asked to leave, and it weighed on him. Why should they have to abandon the home they'd made in Penton when all they'd done was try to live peacefully?

The Tribunal needed taking down. The way of life that had worked for vampires since...well, since eternity...didn't work in this postpandemic world. Men like his father couldn't accept that they no longer sat at the top of the food chain. If someone reasonable—someone like Aidan—didn't prevail with a better way to live, they all were going to starve or gradually kill each other off in a war of attrition.

Jeff Jackson had managed the superette in Penton almost from the beginning, and his wife, Leslie, had helped out at the office that kept the public services up and running. They'd been fams for an older vampire named Alexander for years. Even if the remaining Penton scathe remained intact, they were losing three valuable members of the community. But Leslie's health had never been great, and Will couldn't blame them for wanting out of Omega.

"I know you have to do it, Will. Let's go inside and get it over with." Alexander clapped him on the shoulder and led the Jacksons inside the house.

"It" was a memory wipe. Once he'd proven to Aidan he could do them, it left Aidan free to work on other things, and Will could wait until his charges were in a safe place before altering their memories. Alexander would remember his fams, and they would know him. But none of them would remember Penton, which was just a freaking shame. Nor would they know the tired young vampire who was bidding them good-bye.

Before heading back to Penton, he made another stop for supplies at the big-box building supply in Opelika, searching the aisles for something to patch a leak in the air-filtration system. It was probably their most important system. Unless the air pumps kept chugging, they'd have bigger problems than Matthias.

The same girl as before, Cindy, worked his checkout line, and she gave him a flirtatious smile while running his items through the scanner. Will found himself comparing her to Randa, who suddenly had become the standard by which he judged women. He suspected they'd all fall short, but he didn't want to think about the reasons too closely.

"That'll be forty-five dollars even." Cindy nodded at him. "I remember you from before. How'd that project go?"

"It's a work in progress." Will swiped his card through the machine and stared at the word DECLINED blinking on the little screen.

Cindy shrugged. "No big deal. Try it again—sometimes it's fussy."

Same thing. Will had a bad feeling about this. He also had a problem. They'd all shut down their private accounts when the issues with the Tribunal began, figuring Matthias eventually might strike at the Penton scathe financially.

"Do you have a check or cash with you, or another card?" Cindy looked as embarrassed as Will felt.

"Sorry, Cindy." He reached across the counter and grasped her wrist, smiling broadly so the guy behind him in line, fidgeting over the delay, would only think Will was a guy slowing down the checkout line by flirting with the clerk. As soon as Cindy made eye contact, Will rolled her mind. He'd paid her; she'd given him his receipt already; the cash register had malfunctioned; she was about to wish him a good evening.

He released her hand, and she blinked a couple of times before handing him the bags. "Thank you, sir. Come back and see us."

Probably not.

Will drove to a Starbucks a few blocks away and settled into a far corner with his laptop. He'd brought it to see if Randa's brother had updated his Facebook page, but now he had other business.

He needed to talk to Aidan, but he'd never figured out a way to get a cell signal in Omega. It was too far underground.

You're an idiot for a master vampire. Talk to him in your head. There were geographic limitations, and Will was a good forty miles from Penton, but he closed his eyes and focused on his connection to Aidan. He felt it—like an invisible cord running between them. But his attempts to talk to the man went unanswered.

Gonna have to do this the hard way. He accessed the bank where the Penton finances had been moved to, a tiny little independent in Whigham, Georgia, where Glory had been born. Matthias must have hired some tech wizard to track this down, because he couldn't imagine his father taking the time to learn how to use a computer, much less learn how to hack into financial information.

No surprises. He couldn't access the account. If Matthias had managed to get it frozen, no way he'd be able to hack in without a lot of time, which he didn't have.

Will sat back, watching people drink overpriced coffee, chatting, laughing, without a care. Damn it, they needed money. Not a lot, but enough for emergency supplies and, especially, gasoline for the generators. If the generators went down, the lights went out. If the lights went out, the humans wouldn't be the only ones in a panic.

Will looked at his watch: 11:00 p.m., still early. He'd left Omega shortly after rising, wanting to get his errands run so he could get back to Omega and help with the new activities. Well, OK, and see Randa again. He could still smell her on his skin, and waking from daysleep next to her was beyond sexy.

It might have to wait, though. He needed to pay a visit to Penton.

Ninety minutes later, he parked the truck in its usual spot but headed away from the Omega entrance. He moved fast, stopping to scent every few minutes. He'd learned from patrolling with Randa that his new master skills had given him an enhanced sense of smell, so he had to assume he had an advantage over most of the hired fangs out here.

Which is why he wasn't going after Matthias for money. His father was a master vampire, but Will would bet none of his minions were—Matthias wouldn't risk anyone being stronger than him.

Most vampires were old-school. They didn't want the hassle of trying to mainstream their businesses with humans, so they kept a lot of cash on them. In this case, the Penton scathe's ability to mainstream had backfired on them and tied up their funds.

Will had always wanted to be Robin Hood.

Whenever he scented a vampire, he began tracking. The first one he came across was walking down the long street where the mill village had stood. The fool stopped at the burned-out shell of every house, probably looking for any signs of Aidan or his scathe. Most of the village was in ruins, though. Their own people had burned it in an attempt to flush out Aidan's psychopath brother.

The vampire looked about forty in human years but didn't strike Will as having been turned very long—or maybe he was just an idiot. For one thing, he walked down the middle of the street, not trying to stay in shadows. True, the streetlights were out, but the moon illuminated enough for a vampire to see. For another, when he stopped to look at a house, he stayed in place and didn't check the basement spaces, which is where a vampire who wanted to hide would go.

If this was the caliber of Matthias's help, Will had more hope for the future. Too bad he and Aidan and the other scathe members couldn't just kill them all, but it would bring the Tribunal down on them in a big way. Mirren had been right about that.

Will moved faster than Dumbo the Vampire and caught up with him on the fourth house. When the guy stopped to look for lights, he missed Will slipping up behind him, slicing his throat with a silver-coated blade, and lifting his wallet. The guy would heal, but he'd hurt. And it would be a few hours before he'd be talking or singing.

In two hours, Will had collected more than a dozen wallets. He didn't stop to look at them, but stuffed them in every available pocket.

At 3:00 a.m., he headed back to the parking lot and threw the wallets in the bags with his air-filtration supplies. He'd gotten to the edge of the tree line nearest the Omega entrance when he scented another vampire. No, make that two.

In a few minutes, he got a visual. The guys were armed with what looked like assault rifles, and Will would bet some of his stolen money that they had silver bullets in them.

He didn't dare take down these guys so near the Omega entrance unless he planned to kill them, and they didn't seem to have scented him. So he moved restlessly, setting his leg to aching again, watching them. They'd have to go back to town, or wherever their lighttight space was, before dawn, and he'd slip into Omega.

Thirty minutes before sunrise, they finally walked away in the direction of Penton. Will waited until they were well out of scenting range before opening the hatch and climbing down.

"Where the hell have you been?" Randa stood guard in the exit room, her gun trained on him.

"Are you going to shoot me?" Will held his hands up in surrender, the building-supply bags dangling from his fingers.

"Maybe." But Randa lowered the pistol. "I'm not sure I like it that we're...whatever we are. Before, I could just get pissed off at you. Now I have to get pissed off *and* worried. What took so long?"

Will dangled the bag. "I've been playing Robin Hood. Want to see what I took from the big bad vampires?"

~CHAPTER 24~

Randa counted wallets spread on the conference table in the meeting room. None had driver's licenses—not surprising since vampires couldn't exactly spend a morning standing in line at the Department of Motor Vehicles and sign up to take a driving test. All had cash, however, as Will had expected. Although even he had been surprised to have gathered more than eight grand. Not bad for two hours' work; the Tribunal must have been paying these guards well. At least it would keep the generators running for a while.

She could punch Will's lights out for taking that kind of risk. Plus, it was clear from his account of his exploits he'd thoroughly enjoyed himself. *Idiot*.

The lieutenants had gathered to wait for Aidan, who had risked a trip out of Omega to call Margaret Lindstrom, the US Tribunal representative and an ally—or at least she had been an ally the last time they talked. Since Cage hadn't been able to stay undercover, they needed to know what the Tribunal was up to, what Meg knew about the financial freeze, and if sympathies still lay with Matthias or had begun to shift their way.

Mirren paced around the four walls of the room so many times Randa had lost count. "It's taking him too long. Too fucking long." Just as well, Mirren was muttering to himself. No one had the nerve to try engaging him in conversation.

Cage watched him awhile before turning to Will. "Can't you hack into the bank account and unfreeze it?"

Will shrugged his shoulders. "Maybe, if I had unlimited computer time with Internet access. But not from down here, and not in the time I have when I go out in the evenings. If we could get Mark outside to make phone calls during business hours, he could probably work around it faster through normal channels since he set the account up. Is he stable enough to be doing something like that?"

Cage thought about it. "It might do him good to—"

"No, he can't go." Hannah had been slumped down in her seat and was staring at the floor. She sat forward so quickly Randa feared she'd overturn her chair. "Mark has to stay here, in Omega. He's in danger if he leaves."

Will reached over to grab her hand. Randa loved that he was so comfortable with the girl, even though half the time what she said had a high creep factor.

"Sweetie, do you know how he'll be in danger?" Randa asked. Earlier, she'd said Mark would relapse into drug addiction if he left, but that was before Melissa came back. Randa wasn't sure how well things were going between Mark and Melissa. They'd stayed away from everyone except Krys and Aidan, and Will was afraid their human bond wouldn't survive her transition.

Hannah turned to look at Will and grasped his hand with both of hers. Randa's gaze met Will's, and he shook his head.

"What is it, Hannah?" Cage leaned forward. "Do you see something that has to do with Will?"

The girl squeezed Will's hand so hard that Randa half expected blood and broken bones to seep through her fingers. "I can't quite see it. Almost." She gritted her teeth in anger or frustration—Randa wasn't sure which. Maybe both.

Cage leaned closer to Hannah, who hadn't taken her intent gaze off Will's face. "Close your eyes," he whispered. "Close your eyes and stop trying so hard. Relax your mind. Hold on to Will's hands, but open your mind and don't think. Try it."

Hannah remained still for what seemed like a day and a half, although Randa figured it was more like thirty or forty seconds. Then a gasp and her eyes sprang open. "Will can get us out of this. Will and Randa together. And a human named Richard."

Randa stared at Will, and she saw her own confusion mirrored in his raised eyebrows and slightly parted lips. Mirren stopped pacing to watch.

"Who the hell is Richard?" Will pulled his hand away from Hannah.

She smiled up at Cage. "It worked! Do you think it'll work every time?"

He ruffled her hair and laughed. "I don't know, love. But it's worth a try. I imagine it's one of those things that will get easier as you do it more."

Randa gave them an exasperated look. "Uh, excuse me, but who is Richard?"

Hannah wrinkled her brows, which would have been cute if she hadn't just laid the salvation of Penton at her and Will's feet. Plus Richard's, whoever the hell he was. "I don't know," she said, then smiled. "But Aidan's back."

The mystery of Richard was forgotten for a while as Aidan filled them in. "It's a mixed bag," he said. "Good news, bad news."

"First, the money. Matthias has pulled in favors and had the SEC freeze the Georgia account. But Meg is going to get some of her tech people to pull funds out of one of our overseas accounts. So we should have money"—he looked at the cash spread out on the table—"make that *more* money, in a couple of days. We might have to risk sending a human out to pick up a card she'll leave for us in an Atlanta lockbox to access the funds."

Mirren finally settled into a chair. "What about Matthias?"

Aidan looked at Cage. "As soon as you got Melissa out, Matthias came down like a brick shithouse on Edward Simmons."

"Figured as much," Cage said. "Edward and I knew that was a possibility. I doubt he's intimidated."

Aidan chuckled. "Far from it. He seems to have become our most open supporter, which has given Meg the balls to step up as well. Matthias still has the overt support of the Tribunal, mostly because so many are afraid of Frank Greisser, but it's starting to turn our way. We just have to hold on."

⊱─◈─⊰

Aidan had no ideas about Hannah's vision, either, but as if by unspoken agreement, Randa remained in the conference room with Will after everyone else had left. Mirren returned to his work on a new exit, still hoping to use Glory's telekinesis to move the dirt. Cage stood watch in the exit room. Aidan went to talk with Mark, trying to decide if they dared send him out during the day to help with the finances.

Will closed the door and sat across the table from her. "What do you think?"

Randa didn't have a clue. "What is it we can do that the others can't? Why would we be able to come up with a solution to this whole mess?"

She had been raking it over in her mind while Aidan filled them in on the Tribunal. "Obviously, your claim to fame is that you're Matthias's son, but I don't see how to use that in any way that would involve you and some guy named Richard. I don't have any direct ties to Matthias or the Tribunal—he's only seen me that one time, right before everything fell apart and we had to go into Omega."

Randa rubbed her eyes. The air-filtration system had gotten dust in it, and Will had been planning to fix it tonight. The common room sounded like a TB ward, what with all the rattling coughs from humans and vampires alike.

Will channeled his inner Mirren and started pacing. "I think the key to whatever Hannah thinks is supposed to happen centers on this Richard person, but I swear to God, I don't know anybody with that name. Do you? A Rick or a Rich or a Ricky or a Dick? And if you tell me I'm a dick, I'll be highly insulted."

Randa barked out a laugh. She knew one Rick, but there was no way it was him. "The only Richard I know is my father, and no way is he the answer to our problems." Her smile faded at Will's thoughtful look. "What?"

"Tell me about your father, Ran. I know he's a military guy—a colonel, right?"

"Right. He's a retired colonel. He still keeps his finger in the military, but he does it through a private security firm." She held her fingers up like quotation marks when she said *private security firm*. It had been a running joke between Rory and her. Dad would go missing for weeks at a time after they'd been grown and out of the house, then make up nebulous business excuses for his absence. "Why? What could he have to do with this?"

She could practically see Will's brain sorting, cataloging, and testing theories. "Think about it. If your dad's the only human either of us knows named Richard, it has to be him. We're in Omega virtually all the time now, so we aren't likely to meet any new humans."

Randa was getting a bad, bad feeling about this. She missed her dad and her brothers. She'd always wished she could let them know she wasn't dead, even though she couldn't imagine them in her life on any regular basis. But how could a retired army colonel help them?

Will continued to pace and repeated his request. "Tell me about your father."

"Will, what are you thinking?" She picked up a sheet of paper off the table and began shredding it, just to give her something to do with her hands besides wring them. "How could my dad have anything to do with this?"

"I don't know, but I've learned to trust Hannah's visions. They're usually half-formed but rarely wrong. Don't forget, she was the one who forced me to focus on how to get Mirren away from Matthias month before last."

Yeah, Randa remembered—Will had knocked her unconscious long enough to get out of town without her tagging along or following. That had been a real low in their relationship, and a month ago, if anyone had told her Will Ludlam would be the last person she thought of before daysleep and the first upon awakening, she'd have decked them.

"What do you want to know?"

Will took the seat across from her again. "You said your dad runs a private security firm. What does that mean?"

Good question. "Once all of us kids grew up and either enlisted or moved away from home, Dad retired from the army and started hunting down some of the guys he'd commanded over the years, mostly Army Rangers. Real hard-asses. They all teamed up." She pushed away the pile of shredded paper she'd amassed in front of her. "They spend a lot of time in Europe and the Middle East doing special missions—or at least that's my interpretation of it."

Will scratched his chin, drawing Randa's attention to that talented mouth. She'd sure rather be doing something besides discussing her father. "So they're kind of like one of those special-ops teams in the movies?"

She laughed. "I think so. That's my guess, anyway. He and his buddies—talk about a pile of alpha males. Although, by the time I was turned, he'd already gotten old enough that he seemed to stay more on the strategic end of things, not running actual missions, or at least he was home more. Remember, I've been gone five years, and Dad certainly never confided in me or Rory—we were the babies. My older brothers might know, especially Robbie since he was a Ranger, but maybe not. It's Dad's MO to keep his business locked up tight. He'd say it was to protect us, but…" She shrugged. "Maybe he really is doing private security in Brunei, but I'm thinking not so much. My guess is he's doing contract work for the military."

"I have a little experience with military guys," Will said. "A vampire can't exactly go through boot camp, but I've taken evening training classes with some guys who had military backgrounds."

Randa hadn't known that, but it explained a lot about how Will handled himself under fire and knew how to move undercover. She tried to imagine her father and Will having a conversation and couldn't do it, but it might be interesting. Or ridiculous. Or deadly.

"What does your dad believe in?"

She had to think about that one. Randa and Rory had been toddlers when their mom died, so the only household she remembered was the one with Rick Thomas in charge. Everything was a drill. Chores. Activities. Every minute accounted for. *Spur of the moment* was a foreign concept to be beaten down and annihilated.

She resented it when she was young, chafed against it as a teen, and strived to earn his respect as a young adult. Now, with some forced perspective, she realized he'd simply been using the only coping methods he knew when suddenly faced with raising a bunch of kids as a single father with a demanding career. Not the duty he signed up for, but also not one he'd ever tried to avoid. He'd send them away to live with their grandparents when he was deployed, but he'd always collect them and take them home, wherever home was, as soon as he returned.

"Well, the thing he always preached to us growing up was personal responsibility—you know, own what you do. Go to bed every night without regrets. Defend those who can't defend themselves, even if it's hard. You know, the usual stuff."

Will smiled and reached across the table to twine his fingers through hers. "It doesn't sound that usual to me. In fact, he kind of sounds like the anti-Matthias. You know, screw whoever you can before they screw you first, blame others whenever possible, and exploit a weakness when you see it."

"Will, what are you think—"

A disturbance in the hall interrupted, and Krys stuck her head in the door, her voice higher than normal and definitely on the shaky side. "Do you know where Aidan is?"

Will was on his feet before the words were out, and Randa was right behind him. She'd never seen Krys anything but cool and in control. "What's wrong?"

"I'm not sure. Two of the fams were sick yesterday, now it's eight. I mean, really sick. Whatever it is, I think it's spreading."

☙CHAPTER 25☙

While Aidan talked to the sick humans who'd filled up the medical ward, forcing Melissa and Mark into a regular room, Will pulled Mirren and Randa into a corner of the common area.

"We need to cover Omega—every inch of it," Will said quietly. "Scent every room. See if anything comes up funky."

Mirren's gaze traveled across the people sitting around the open space, relaxing on sofas, playing cards, watching videos, not yet aware that they could be in trouble. "Don't be a drama queen, junior. Might be a cold or virus or something."

"Not possible." Will lowered his voice when one of the fams gave them a curious look. "We've been down here long enough that any kind of virus would have already shown up. None of the humans have been outside, and vampires can't carry human viruses. I guess it's possible that I brought in some bug on my clothes, but I'm guessing it's environmental. I'm hoping it's nothing more exotic than mold in the air ducts, but we need to be sure."

They split up, and Will first went to the room where the air-filtration system had been built. It pulled air from the outside through a long underground pipe that, if found, wouldn't lead anyone back to Omega without a lot of digging. He went ahead and repaired the filter, but couldn't scent anything wrong with it.

Same with waste management. All systems working.

As soon as he opened the door to the water-filtration room, the fumes hit him. His eyes stung and the insides of his nostrils burned. He'd set up the system to feed from a spring he'd found not too far from the Omega entrance, pumping it in, then running it through a filter similar to the ones people put on their faucets, only bigger.

The filter was still operating, but the water intake from the spring gave off some kind of noxious aura. Will stuck his hand in the reservoir and brought a palm full of water to his nose. Didn't smell different, and if he hadn't shut himself in with the big reservoir tank, he probably wouldn't have noticed it. He shut the water system down and stuck his head back into the hallway.

"Randa!" He saw her at the end of the storage corridor and motioned for her to come, then moved aside to let her inside the water room.

"Gah. What is that?" She blinked rapidly and walked to the reservoir.

"Don't know. Didn't you say one time you took courses on biological weapons?" The last thing Will wanted to do was spread panic. A simple contamination from animal shit would be less alarming than what he feared.

"Yeah." Randa stuck her finger in the water, rubbed her fingers together, and lifted them to her nose. "Turn down the lantern a minute."

Will reached to where he'd set the fluorescent lantern on a shelf and turned it to half-light. The water in the reservoir glowed an eerie blue-green, as if one of Will's hippie high school friends had put a black light or lava lamp in the bottom. "What the hell is it?"

"Not sure." Randa propped her hands on her hips and stared at the reservoir, her lips pursed. "There's a class of chemicals that have a luminescent effect in water, and they're all very poisonous. Some are pesticides that are highly regulated, which would be my guess." She turned back to Will, frowning. "They don't occur in nature."

Back in the meeting room again, behind closed doors, only Krys had joined the lieutenants this time. Will thought she looked mad enough to spit.

"We have eight people who are extremely sick," she said. "They're all heavy water drinkers. Another dozen are showing symptoms. There's not much I can do for them other than treat the nausea and diarrhea and give them plenty of water—bottled, of course. Can they survive? I don't know."

Cage and Hannah had stayed in the common room with the fams and other scathe members, trying to maintain the facade that everything was fine except for a pesky virus making the rounds. So far, no one had realized there was no way to introduce a virus into a closed community like Omega.

Will looked out the door to make sure everything remained calm. Melissa and Mark had come into the common room together for the first time and were being treated like celebrities. Everyone in Penton loved both of the Calverts, and people's genuine excitement over seeing her again would probably do Melissa as much good as her presence was doing for them.

Inside the meeting room, attitudes ranged from angry to grim. Mirren leaned against the wall in his favorite spot, looking like a human grenade. Aidan was as pale as the sick people.

Will sat at the table next to his open laptop. He'd been scrolling through lists of files stored on his hard drive, pretending to look for some type of chemical database. Just to use up nervous energy.

"Is there any way to filter this stuff out?" Aidan asked.

Will stopped scrolling and dropped his hands into his lap. "Short answer? No. Whatever it is, it's getting through our filter system. We can try running it through a second or third time by hand, but I don't think it'll help. If the chemical goes through the first time, why wouldn't it go a second or third?"

Aidan nodded, his expression unreadable. "What about a different kind of filter?"

Will shrugged. "We already have the top-of-the-line commercial filters. There are probably specialized ones, but without some kind of water testing, we don't know what we're looking for."

Aidan pushed his chair back, drumming his fingers on the padded arms. "That means it's strictly bottled water for bathing and drinking. How long can we hold out?"

"We have enough for a couple of weeks if people are conservative."

Krys cleared her throat. "Another thing to think about. We can't feed from these people who are sick. Even if we're immune to it, which I assume we are, they need all their strength to fight it. I'd say we feed every other day, at most, from the ones who aren't sick. We can take some nourishment from each other between times."

"Mirren, come with me to talk to the patients." Aidan stood and wrenched open the door into the hallway. Krys got up to follow him, but he turned to stop her. "Stay here, *mo run*," he whispered, and kissed her.

Will watched them leave, his eyes narrowed. They were up to something. No one took Mirren Kincaid on a visit to cheer the troops.

Randa began gathering the wallets that were still spread across the table, throwing them back inside the plastic bag from the home-improvement store. "Throw these away?"

"Maybe you should save them." Krys sat in the chair Aidan had vacated. "A few have IDs, and you never know if we might need them with the Tribunal down the road."

Will had started thinking about Randa's father again. What would the man do if he found out his daughter was alive, but had been turned into something he believed didn't exist? Would he kill her? Try to protect her? Shut her down before she could even explain? He wondered...

The door flew open, and Glory slipped inside, gasping for air as she tried to cry and talk at the same time. The woman was practically hyperventilating. Will slammed the computer lid and stood up. "What's wrong? Are you sick?"

"You have to stop them." She looked from Will to Randa before grabbing Krys's hand. "Aidan and Mirren are going after Matthias just after daysleep. I overheard them planning it. They're too outnumbered, and if they kill him, the Tribunal will come after us."

"What?" Krys propelled herself from the chair, headed for the door. Will stopped her.

Shit. Will knew they were up to something, but this was nuts. "Wait, Krys. Slow down, Glory. Do they know you heard them?"

"N...no. They're in one of the supply rooms."

Damn it. They hadn't gone through all of this just to have Aidan and Mirren go down the for-the-greater-good highway. Taking out Matthias would do nothing but buy them a little time, get help for the sick humans, and make things worse in the long run. At best. "Hold on a minute. Let me think."

He walked to the entrance of the common room and got Cage's attention, then motioned for him to join them. They were going to need his smarts and maybe his muscle.

Once Cage and Will were both inside the closed meeting room, Will turned back to Glory. "Tell us exactly what you heard."

She sat next to Krys and swallowed hard. Will was struck again by what an odd thing love was. This sweet-natured little human had tamed the big, bad former Tribunal executioner, and Mirren didn't seem to mind a bit.

Only, now that he looked at her closely, she looked...damn. "Glory, truth now. Are you sick?"

Krys wrapped an arm around her when she closed her eyes and nodded. "How bad is it?"

"Just a little nausea, but Mirren walked in when I was throwing up. God, you should have seen his face. I've never seen him scared before. He got Aidan, and they shut themselves in one of the storage rooms to talk. I followed them."

The tears started again. "He and Aidan think if they kill Matthias, the Tribunal will arrest them and let the rest of us go. Or at least they'll buy us enough time to get help for the people who are sick. Will, you've got to stop them."

Damn it. They had worked too hard for this—all of them—to have Aidan and Mirren do something without thinking it through. "OK, let's stop and think. If they go after Matthias, what will happen?"

"He'll kill them and make it look like it was self-defense or they were trying to escape." Cage leaned forward, propping his elbows on the table, his shoulders hunched. "Or they succeed, and the Tribunal tracks them down. They won't overlook another Tribunal member being killed. At best, they'd have to go through a trial, and there are still too many against them right now."

"They're also wrong about it ending with them." Randa absently rubbed Krys's arm, but she was looking at Will. "Matthias wants Will. He wants revenge against you, Cage. He'll be after Melissa and Glory and Krys because all of them know too many of his dirty dealings. He'd kill Hannah and me because we're loyal to Aidan and know too much. If Krys is right and this illness is something we just have to wait out, they're throwing everything away for what—the ability to get antinausea medication?"

"Agreed." Will looked at Cage, who nodded. "Then we have to stop them until they've had time to think." He could believe Mirren was going off half-cocked—he'd think he was saving Glory. Aidan surprised him, though. Through this whole ordeal, for four months now, he'd been patient, calculating, careful.

Maybe he didn't see any other way to end it. Not just the water contamination, but the whole siege. Time had been on Matthias's side from the beginning, and it still was.

Not acceptable. "Glory, would you be willing to be locked in the silver cell with them?" The room had a small bathroom and a slot in the door to push food through. Krys could probably get

Aidan to go into the room on some fabrication, but the only way they could wrangle Mirren was to dangle Glory as bait.

"But she's sick." Krys brushed Glory's hair away from her face and felt her forehead.

"The only way you'll get Mirren in that room is if I'm there." Glory had a strong practical streak, one reason Will had always admired her. The woman never flinched. "And if they're as stubborn as I think they'll be, Aidan and Mirren might have to stay in that room awhile and might need to feed. I'm the only one who can do it, sick or not." She looked apologetically at Krys, who nodded.

Will needed strategic help on this one. "Randa, you and Cage are our military experts. How should we play this?"

Randa didn't hesitate. Her straight posture was rigid, her eyes bright and alert. She loved this stuff, and Will felt badly that he'd spent so long being threatened by her instead of learning from her.

"We need to get them in the room just before daysleep, when their guard is down," she said. "Our energy levels will be down as well, so we have to make sure everything's in place. Who has a key to the room?"

"I do," Will said. "The only one—I never had time to have duplicates made before we came into Omega."

Randa nodded. "Then you make sure the door is unlocked and be waiting in the storage room across the hall to lock it once Mirren and Aidan are both in there. Krys, tell Aidan that Glory is in the silver cell and she's upset and wants to talk to you about Mirren. He'll want to do damage control."

Krys frowned. "I hate tricking him. After all the lies he told me when we first met, we promised we'd never lie to each other again."

"Would you rather have him honest and dead or tell a lie to save his life?" Will knew he sounded harsh, but time was short and everything was at stake. "With any luck, you'll have plenty of time to apologize."

She looked at the floor with a slight nod.

Randa watched her for a moment, then turned to Glory. "As soon as we see Aidan go in the room with you, Cage can tell Mirren that Glory's in there."

Better Cage than Will. "Tell Mirren that Glory's crying or sick," he said. "It will get him moving faster."

That earned a weak smile from Glory.

"Which leaves me." Randa looked at each of them in turn. "I'll run interference in the common room and make sure no one else goes down that hallway."

Cage had been listening quietly with his arms crossed and a bemused expression. "What think you, Doc?" Will asked. "Will this work?"

"It's a good plan," he said, smiling at Randa. "But I hope that's a soundproof room, because Mirren Kincaid is gonna make some noise."

❧CHAPTER 26❧

Randa checked her watch—4:30 a.m.—and sat in the chair at the edge of the common room nearest the corridor to the hallway. Most of the fams were asleep, and the vampires were already in their rooms or on their way. Four still played cards, seated around a game table against the far wall.

Glory, looking a little wobbly and pale, held up crossed fingers as she passed Randa on her way to the silver-lined room. Randa prayed she'd be able to talk some sense into Mirren and Aidan before she got sicker. Krys had already put bottled water, crackers, aspirin, and instant ice packs for fever in the room.

Will had taken his place inside the doorway of the storage area across the hallway from the silver cell, key in hand. On the other side of the common room, Cage sat, ostensibly reading. But his shoulders were rigid, his feet on the floor, ready to move in an instant. He scanned the room over the top of his book.

Randa couldn't believe she'd finally gotten to plan an operation for the scathe and it involved locking up Aidan and Mirren.

She should have felt ashamed, but her adrenaline was pumping; her body hummed with it. She'd missed this kind of rush.

Krys emerged from the medical ward, nodded at Randa, and headed toward the room she shared with Aidan. She must have done a good acting job; Aidan passed Randa less than a minute later, headed toward the silver cell with purpose in his stride and a grim set to his jaw.

So far, so good.

As soon as Aidan passed him, Cage tossed his book onto the side table and headed for the generator room, where their advance scouting told them Mirren was tinkering with the machinery.

Tears worked every time. Mirren barreled past Randa without looking at her. She gave a thumbs-up to Cage, rose to her feet, and followed Mirren at a distance, Cage close behind her.

The only thing they hadn't counted on was Mirren's fast reflexes. Before Will got the door shut, Randa saw a scuffle, and Will flew across the hallway and crashed into the wall, crumpling to the floor and leaving a chipped place in the concrete.

Cage looked at her and grinned. "Plan B," he said, and started running. As Randa reached the doorway, she scooped up the key Will had dropped and turned just as Cage gave Mirren a hard shove back into the room.

Will climbed to his feet and helped Cage hold the door shut by propping his feet against the wall. Randa slid the key into the lock and turned it.

Then the yelling, cursing, and threats began, and it wasn't just Mirren.

Damn, but Mirren Kincaid could pack a punch. Will sat on the edge of his bed in the room he now officially shared with Randa, massaging his swollen jaw. It felt like he'd had a face-first collision with a freight train. Melissa and Mark had moved into his old room with Cage since Mel was treating the vampire like a security blanket anyway, which was probably beyond awkward for all three of them.

Randa came into the room with a towel wrapped around an instant ice pack from Krys's medical kit. "You'll heal that in daysleep, but this will help the swelling. Lie back."

Funny how Randa's bossy qualities didn't bother him nearly as much as they used to. Will stretched out on the bed, and she reclined beside him, holding the makeshift compress to his face.

"You do know Mirren will probably beat the crap out of me when this over, right?" He set the compress aside—it was cold, and ice reminded him of their poisoned water supply, which pissed him off all over again. He fingered his jaw, making sure no bones had been broken. "Cage too. We did all the dirty work. Mirren doesn't even know you're involved. Aidan and Mirren have both been cursing and calling me names inside my head that I can't repeat in polite company."

"Oh, you poor little soldier." She kissed his jaw. "It was my turn to be general. I devised the strategy, so it was my job to watch my minions carry it out. Big, bad Glory will protect you."

He turned to face her. She had been pretty spectacular tonight, and the two other master vampires had finally fallen silent, so he could think. He needed to get some tips on how to shut them out. Later.

"Yeah, I'll show you what a minion can do to a general." He buried his face in the curve of her shoulder and neck, tasting his way down. "Got those sexy bikinis on tonight?"

Randa's heartbeat sped up as his teeth found her hard little nipple through her T-shirt and bit. "Uh. Not exactly."

He raised his head. "You're wearing army-general panties, aren't you?" Before she could wriggle out of his grasp, he had her jeans unbuttoned and a hand inside. He tugged at the waistband and glanced down. He performed his best wolf whistle. "Ooh, sexy. Gray. That's practically like silver. On another planet."

Randa slapped at him, laughing. "Stop it. And if you keep stretching them, I won't have any at all."

He pulled his hand out of her pants with great regret. "We only have a few minutes before daysleep, and as much as I'd love to explore the ins and outs of gray general panties, I want to run something past you."

She propped on her elbow and rested her hand on his thigh, then moved it higher. "Go on."

Shit. That was not helping him be serious. "Ah...I can't think when you do that, sir."

She gave him a squeeze. "Haven't we thought enough for today, soldier?"

"We need to talk about your father."

"Jeez, Will. Talk about a mood killer." She flopped onto her back. "OK, shoot."

It was probably a bad thing to spring on her right before daysleep, but it wasn't like they dreamed—or not often, anyway. Wasn't like she'd lie awake fretting all day. But he wanted her to think about this. Their lives might depend on her answer.

"What would his reaction be if you went to see him? If *we* went to see him." Because no way he'd let her go alone.

He waited for her to argue. Maybe hide behind a wall of snark. But she was quiet—so quiet, in fact, that he raised his head to make sure she hadn't already dropped into daysleep. But her eyes were open, her gaze fixed on the ceiling.

"I *have* been thinking about it, ever since the whole Richard thing came up with Hannah." She shifted around to look at him. "I honestly don't know what his reaction would be. He might be supportive. He might see us all as a huge threat to life as he knows it. He might spare me and kill everyone I've come to care about. I'm having trouble separating my love for him as my dad from my fear of him as someone who could destroy us while thinking he was doing his duty."

Will slipped an arm underneath her shoulders and pulled her to him. She nestled into his chest, and damned if she didn't feel perfect there. "You don't know if he'll react as a father or as a colonel?"

Randa's nod was a sweet scrape of soft curls against his collarbone. "That's it exactly."

☙CHAPTER 27❧

No doubt just as Will had planned it, Randa went into day-sleep thinking about her father and woke at dusk with his image in her mind. Tall, broad-shouldered Rick Thomas, who had his boys on the firing range by the time they were old enough to hold guns but never quite knew what to do with his daughter. She'd learned early that her best tactic was, as much as possible, being one of the boys.

Will had fed from her on waking, before going to check on the water system. But he'd stopped her when she'd tried to feed from him, telling her the story about how Glory and Mirren accidentally became mates by having a blood exchange after sex. "We don't want another accident," he'd said.

Randa clamped down on the urge to point out they'd barely found time to have sex in any normal sense of the word, although what time they'd managed to find for each other had been amazing.

She wasn't sure how she felt about his "accident" remark. On the one hand, she felt rejected, which she knew was stupid.

They'd never gone into this thing—whatever they had—with any long-term plans. After months of sniping, they'd finally learned to enjoy each other's company. She respected him and knew she'd misjudged him, and thought he felt the same. He was sexy and an amazing lover, from what she'd been able to see, although she didn't like to think about how much practice he'd had.

So she had no right to be hurt that he wanted to avoid mating with her. Not only did Will have a lot of issues surrounding his father that he'd mostly avoided dealing with, but he reacted to perceived threat the same way she did—by putting up a wall of words and attitude.

She sighed. Everyone had baggage. They would be a freaking disaster as a real couple, so why did she feel so disappointed?

A knock at the door broke her out of her funk, and she opened it to find Krys—smiling for a change. "I think Aidan is ready to talk without yelling, and he's promised Mirren won't hit anybody." She glanced down the hall. "Although, I probably wouldn't hold him to that part."

Randa nodded. "Think they'll agree to talk inside the silver cell? It's fairly soundproof, and Will and I have an idea we don't want too many ears to hear."

"This have something to do with what Hannah said yesterday? Want me to get her?"

"Definitely find her and Cage." Will appeared in the hallway behind Krys. "Fumes are worse in the water-filtration room this morning. I put a sign on the door telling everyone to stay out because of a malfunction, and cut off the water supply to all the pipes."

He led the way down the corridor to the silver cell and unlocked the door. Randa waited a heartbeat to make sure

Mirren wasn't going to barrel out, fist first, but when nothing happened, she opened the door and went in.

Mirren sat on the floor in the corner, with Glory's head in his lap, stroking her hair away from her face. He narrowed his eyes at Will and Cage, but didn't say anything.

Aidan kissed Krys, and Randa felt a stab of jealousy at the long look they gave each other, full of love and forgiveness. No time to mourn what would never be. She believed people were put on earth for different reasons, including vampires, and she'd accepted a long time ago that her role was not to be a soul mate to some adoring male. She suspected she'd be unsuited to it.

Once Hannah and Cage arrived, Will closed the door and took a seat on the floor next to Randa. They all sat on the painted concrete except Glory, who'd moved to the bed next to Mirren, her hand draped over his shoulder.

"First, don't ever pull a fucking stunt like that again." Mirren's gray-eyed glare shifted from Will to Cage and back. He didn't give Randa a second look.

"It was my plan." By God, she was not going to be over-looked, even if it meant getting chastised or punched. "Call it a mutiny if you want to, but we all agreed you and Aidan weren't thinking as leaders. You were thinking as friends and mates."

The room's silence fell thick and tense. Aidan stared at her with raised eyebrows, and she'd definitely gotten Mirren's attention. Except, instead of scowling, his mouth finally curved up in something approximating a smile. "Well, well. Aidan, you were right. About damned time, little soldier. We've been waiting for you to come to the party."

Randa would have turned the color of a carrot and sunk into the floor had either been possible. Will coughed into his hand in a pathetic attempt to cover up a laugh, and she glared at him, daring him to make a smart-ass comment.

Aidan had been quiet, but he took back authority with a single look. "I can't say I like your methods, but you did what you thought was right. With some time, and Glory's persuasion, we realized going directly after Matthias wouldn't save the rest of you. You'd always be looking over your shoulders. So, thanks. Just don't do it again."

A wave of relief washed through Randa. The practical side of her knew Aidan would take this calmly, but some insecure core feared he'd send her back to the rank-and-file scathe or would at least regret making her one of his inner circle. He might feel that regret, but he wasn't showing it.

Krys cleared her throat. "I think Will and Randa have an idea."

They'd talked about it after waking from daysleep. It was so risky she couldn't imagine Aidan going for it. But she and Will had agreed: they had to make it Aidan's call. Penton had been his idea, his dream, had been made possible by his hard work and, sometimes, sheer force of will.

She nodded at Will, reflecting that, even as recently as two weeks ago, she'd have chafed at letting him take the lead. Now she not only trusted him, but recognized that he was more likely to be listened to by Aidan and Mirren, not because he was better than her or because he was a man, but because Aidan and Mirren had known him for decades. He'd already earned their trust.

She'd wasted a lot of time being childish and stupid, but she could make up for it now.

"Hannah, remember what you said about Randa and me and someone named Richard finding a way out of this mess?" Will asked.

The girl nodded, her eyes somber. "I dreamed it again last daysleep."

Will and Randa exchanged glances. "The only Richard either of us knows is my father." Randa took a deep breath. "He's a retired army colonel, a tough-guy special-operations type."

Mirren stood up and went to lean against the wall, hands in the pockets of his black combat pants. His defensive stance.

"It's obviously risky," Will said. "And I'm not even sure what we're asking him for, if we decide to talk to him and he agrees to help us. Do we ask for help defending against Matthias in some kind of private capacity? Or would we be asking him to help us strategize?"

Aidan looked at Mirren, then at Randa. "Tell us about him."

She blew out a breath and began to talk. She probably told them more than they needed, including her own rocky history with him. She talked about Richard Thomas the colonel, the father, and—as much as she could—the man.

When she finished, that awful silence filled the room again. Will reached over and squeezed her hand.

Aidan rubbed the nape of his neck and tilted his head toward one shoulder, then the other. The crack of taut tendons filled the room. "Hannah, can you see anything else? Can you see an outcome?"

The girl shook her head and leaned against Cage.

"Randa, you understand that if your father reacts badly, we might have no choice but to either wipe his memories or defend ourselves?"

Randa closed her eyes. She'd been thinking about little else. About whether she could live with it if they had to kill her father. Ironic that she'd asked a similar question of Will not so long ago. She was gambling that her father loved her enough, and that he was fair-minded enough, to step away from his black-and-white world of absolute good and evil.

"I understand."

"They go alone." Mirren's rumble cut through the room. "Randa and Will. Go to the colonel and get him used to the idea that vampires exist. Tell him you need help, but not our location. Not our names. If you decide you can trust him, he has to agree to come here, to Omega. Aidan and I have to approve everything."

Randa swallowed hard and nodded. "And if he doesn't agree to that?" Her father was used to leading, not following. Especially not following a type of being he didn't know existed and wasn't likely to trust.

"Then you know your options."

☙ CHAPTER 28 ☙

Clouds obscured any moonlight that might have otherwise reached the rural two-lane highway that stretched across East Alabama toward Columbus, Georgia, where Colonel Richard Thomas made his retirement home. After slipping out of the Omega exit one at a time just after dusk, Will drove the pickup he'd been hauling supplies in, Randa rode shotgun, and the literal shotgun was wedged into the storage area behind the seats. They didn't plan to take it to their meeting with the colonel, but then again, being prepared never hurt.

The digital clock on the truck's dashboard read 7:30 p.m.

They'd spent most of the previous night talking with Aidan and the other lieutenants, especially Cage, about possible scenarios and psychological reactions the colonel might have, not only finding out his daughter who died five years ago was still alive, but that she was a vampire. It would be a lot to take in.

Afterward, Will and Randa had returned to their room and made love with a frantic, frenzied urgency, neither of them saying what Will knew was true for both of them: If this went badly, they might not have another chance to be together, to feel their skin heat with the friction of their movement, to taste, to touch, to love.

If this went badly, even if they survived, their relationship might be tainted.

If this went badly enough, Will might even have to kill Randa's father, and she might not be able to forgive it, even though she understood the necessity of it.

Will had been shocked that Aidan and Mirren agreed so readily to approaching a human for help, even with the colonel's connection to Randa. He had gone into that meeting prepared to argue, and the fact that both senior leaders of the scathe considered it a viable option without hours of debate told him how close they were to giving up.

Damn it, he wasn't ready to give up. Before finding Aidan and helping him get Penton established, Will had spent decades on the move, avoiding his father, never settling down anywhere for very long, determined to never again get sucked into a life of recriminations, self-hatred, and fear.

He'd found a life he wanted to fight for and maybe somebody he wanted to share it with. That realization caused him to swerve out of his lane, and he pulled the steering wheel sharply to straighten their path. Ending up wrapped around a tree in Nowhere, Alabama, wouldn't help matters, but hell, when did *Randa* and *future* become intertwined? Yet thinking about what she faced, confronting her father with some hard truth, made him fear losing her, if not to death, then to a family and a life with which he couldn't compete.

"Would you watch where you're going? Jeez." Randa braced an arm on the passenger door. "Pull over and let me drive. Get your head out of your ass."

Or maybe he was being a sentimental twit. The woman was seriously bossy. "Have you figured out what you're going to say to him?"

Randa groaned, banging the back of her skull against the headrest. "No. Maybe knock on the door and see what he says? You got any better ideas?"

"Well, there is one thing that might help."

She gave him a narrow-eyed look that radiated suspicion, even through the darkness of the truck's cab. "What?"

"Let's stop at an all-night salon or something in Columbus so you can get your hair back to its real color." He liked the short haircut now that he'd gotten used to it. It suited her. But he wanted his redhead back. "It might make it easier for your dad to believe it's really you."

"I hadn't even thought about it." She ran her hands through the tangle of loose waves. "Good idea, but there's no such thing as an all-night salon, not in Columbus, Georgia, anyway. Look for a drugstore or a Walmart."

Once they got near the bridge that crossed the Chatta-hoochee River and took them from Alabama into Georgia, Will spotted a superstore and pulled the truck into the mostly empty lot. "You got cash?"

"Yeah, I took some from your Robin Hood stash. Need anything?"

Sure he did. Clean water. No pandemic vaccine. Matthias to disappear in a cloud of dust. World peace. "I'm good."

While Randa shopped for hair dye, Will tried to visualize his worst-case scenario. The colonel wasn't likely to haul off and shoot them—he was too well trained and, if Randa was any indication, too disciplined. The hardest thing they might face initially was getting him to believe it wasn't some kind of twisted scam.

Dye must have been easy to shop for; Randa was back inside of fifteen minutes. "Bombshell Bronze," she said, holding up the white plastic bag. "Let's hope it doesn't turn into Passion Fruit Pink or Oragutan Orange."

Turns out Bombshell Bronze was sexy as hell. Randa had locked herself in the bathroom as soon as they'd roused a grumbling, sleepy clerk at a small roadside motel and checked into a room at the end of a row of units that had seen better days a few decades ago.

She emerged forty-five minutes later with painted nails, her army T-shirt and khakis, and hair that reminded him how beautiful she was. He wished they had time to hang around the motel so he could show her an appropriate amount of appreciation.

"You ready?" She was practically bouncing off the wall from nerves.

"Let me tell you something first. I...um...you..." He hadn't been tongue-tied around a girl since his human life at about age sixteen, but he struggled to get the words out. "I just want you to know that..." What? That he wanted to find out what they had when they weren't injured or running for their lives?

"You want me to know what?" Randa pulled him into a tight hug and laughed. "That you'll love me no matter how big an asshole my father is?"

He pulled away from her, cradling her face in his hands. "That's exactly it." He pressed his lips gently against hers, a sweet kiss full of hope. "Exactly."

They held each other for a few minutes, needing to leave but not wanting to let the moment pass.

Finally, Will huffed out a breath. "OK, we gotta do this before it gets any later."

"Right." Randa dug her cell phone from her pocket and punched a couple of keys. "Just going to make sure he's home."

Good thinking. "Will he recognize your number and freak out?"

She shook her head. "It's a new number that I got—" Her face froze a few seconds before she ended the call. "It was him. He sounds just the same. Will, I don't know if I can do this."

He took her hand. "You can do it. *We* can do it." True, he didn't have a big role other than providing backup. A lot of this was going to depend on her. All he could do was keep her safe.

The Thomas house where Randa's grandparents had lived was the only stable home she'd known—she'd described her childhood and youth as a series of army bases all over the country, interspersed with a year here or six months there with her paternal grandparents, who'd died before she was deployed. Her dad had moved here when he retired, probably because it was near Fort Benning and he could still be around the army even if he wasn't in it anymore. At least not in any official capacity.

The redbrick ranch house anchored the end of a cul-de-sac in a gently aging middle-class neighborhood full of mature oak trees, broad lawns, and SUVs. Will drove to the end of the circle, rounded it, and retraced their path to park in front of 23 Spruce Street, facing out. In case they needed to leave in a hurry.

Randa got out of the truck and squared her shoulders. Will's heart broke a little as she assumed a facade she'd gradually relinquished over the past couple of weeks: the tightened jaw, the hardened eyes that challenged whatever they saw, the rigid back that wouldn't bend in a strong gale. In a matter of seconds, she'd once again become Randa Thomas, the tough-as-nails soldier, and that step backward made Will hate the man they were preparing to confront for making her feel she couldn't be strong and still be herself.

Maybe Rick Thomas had more in common with Matthias than he'd thought. But Randa believed her father to be a fair and honorable man at heart, which Matthias wasn't. And if Rick Thomas sold his daughter short, Will had two knives and a pistol within easy reach.

They didn't talk as they followed what seemed like an impossibly long set of paving stones to the front door. Randa looked at Will, and he nodded. She rang the doorbell.

Its ring seemed to echo through the house beyond. A dog barked inside the door. A man's voice calmed it. The fall of footsteps grew louder. The outside light clicked on, making Will blink. The door opened, and for a moment, it was as if the world had stopped.

Richard Thomas, US Army colonel (retired), was a tall man in his late fifties, dark hair turning silver at his temples, a strong jaw, broad shoulders, rigid posture. Will tried to see Randa in him. Maybe the slightly upturned nose, the shape of her mouth, the hazel-green eyes.

Eyes that were wide and staring through a storm door at what must surely seem to him a ghost.

"Dad?" Randa's voice shook. "It's me."

He cleared his throat, and Will saw him blink several times—tears? "What kind of fucking joke is this? It's not funny."

Randa looked down, then back up. Her voice was trembling but clear. "I was in Kabul in 2009 on a night patrol when I was caught in a botched ambush. My body wasn't ever found because, obviously, I survived. I was born on March fifteenth, 1984, in the Fort Benning infirmary. I just learned that my twin brother..." She stumbled, paused, continued. "I just found out that Rory died of a similar cancer to the type that killed our mother when we were two years old."

The colonel made no move to open the door. His face was the color of chalk, but his voice held steel. He flicked his gaze at Will only once, but Will would have bet his Robin Hood take that if he made a move, the man would be ready.

"Anybody could've found that information," he said. "What do you want? You have thirty seconds to give me a reason not to call the police."

A voice came from inside. "Everything OK, Dad?"

Will put a hand on Randa's back to steady her as the door opened wider and another man stood next to her father. Younger, taller, more muscular, tanner. A medium-sized dog—a boxer, Will thought—began whimpering and scratching at the door. The dog might do more than anything to convince them this was really Randa. The younger man stepped closer to the storm door. "Holy shit. Ran?"

Randa swallowed so hard Will could feel it in his palm as he rubbed small circles on her back. "Hi, Robbie." She took a deep breath. "Dad, it's really me. I'm sorry to spring this on you, but what can I say to convince you this isn't a scam?"

The colonel seemed incapable of speech, so Robbie answered. "What did I give you for your sixth birthday?"

Randa smiled. "A turtle you'd named Colonel Thomas. I took it to show-and-tell in Miss Michaels's first-grade class."

"My God, Randa." That finally broke through the armor. The colonel fumbled with the lock on the storm door, threw it open, and wrapped his arms around his daughter. He won points with Will by not trying to stop his tears, or hide them.

Will felt like an intruder or a voyeur, but he wasn't going to do the polite thing and sit in the truck while the Thomas family had its reunion. He wasn't letting Randa out of his sight. So he stood and waited.

Finally, Randa turned and motioned him inside. "Dad, Robbie, this is my friend Will—William Hendrix." They'd agreed to play it safe on the last names as long as possible, and since Will had been a Jimi Hendrix fan back in his human days, this had been one of his frequent aliases.

The colonel studied Will an uncomfortably long time before finally reaching out a hand to shake. "Thank you for bringing my daughter home, Mr. Hendrix. I would ask you to stay, but Randa needs to be with her family. You understand we have a lot of catching up to do."

Will gave him the most guileless smile in his repertoire— the just-an-innocent-guy, aw-shucks smile. The colonel didn't smile back. "Sorry, sir, but Randa asked me to come with her and I need to stay."

"Ran, are you in some kind of trouble?" Robbie was giving Will the evil eye now. *Terrific.* The dog was jumping so high he could almost lick Randa on her chin.

"Will needs to be here," she said. "He can help me explain where I've been and what happened to me. And don't call anyone else yet. The conversation we're about to have is need-to-know only, and Robbie, I hate to ask you this, but I need to talk to Dad alone."

Randa the soldier had reappeared, and Will was glad to see her. He'd been squelching a fear—so deeply he hadn't put it into words or coherent thought—that she might forget why they were there if she got overwhelmed by family and the tantalizing prospect of resuming a seminormal life. Once again, he'd underestimated her.

Robbie wasn't happy. "Ran, whatever's wrong, I can help."

She pulled him into a hug, and Will had a flash of insight into the Thomas family dynamic. She'd been the only girl in a family of dominant men who weren't challenging her to compete with them, as she'd grown up thinking. They'd half smothered her trying to protect her. She might resent them for it, but Will certainly couldn't hate them for it.

After some discussion, Robbie finally agreed to go but got Randa's cell number.

Once he was gone, the colonel closed the door and locked it behind him. He pointed them toward the dining room table, where he and Robbie appeared to have been playing cards. Two beer bottles sat opened and half-emptied.

The living room they'd passed through spoke of comfortable middle-class roots. Early American furniture, lots of oak, oval braided rugs on shiny wooden floors. The eat-in kitchen wasn't modern, but it was comfortable.

Will gathered the cards and stacked them on the edge of the table, and they all took chairs. The house was tense, quiet, awkward.

"I'm sorry to do this, but do you have your identification? Both of you?" The colonel didn't make assumptions or accept things at face value, and Will respected that. Those were traits that would come in handy should he decide to help them.

Will pulled out his wallet and his beautifully faked Alabama driver's license for William Hendrix and handed it to the colonel. It showed the address of what was in reality an empty lot in Montgomery.

"I don't have a current license anymore, but I have a few things." Randa had anticipated her father asking for proof of identity, and she pulled out the items she'd had with her when she managed to get herself smuggled out of Afghanistan. Military ID, dog tags, her old Georgia driver's license, and a scarf that had belonged to her mother. Her dad would recognize it, she had said, and she'd been right. He took it from her and fingered the blue wool.

"Rory had one just like it, except it was tan," Randa said softly. "We used to fight over who got to keep the blue one."

The colonel nodded, and when he looked up, his expression said he believed her. His face softened when he looked at her, and Will knew that Rick Thomas loved his daughter. He might not have known how to raise her, but he loved her. That would help.

"Where have you been? I don't know where else to start. Why didn't you tell us you were alive?"

Randa sighed and looked at Will, who nodded his encouragement.

"I wasn't killed in that ambush." Randa's voice rang like a small stone in a deep well as the quiet, empty house seemed to swell around them. "I was abducted. Taken by a man, or what I thought was a man."

"Why weren't there hostage negotiations? Why didn't your CO know about this? I'll have someone's job..." Rick pushed his chair back, obviously ready to wage war against whatever military screwup accidentally reported soldiers dead.

"Dad, sit down. It's not what you think. The person who abducted me wasn't human. He was...He was a vampire."

The colonel's face registered surprise, but quickly morphed to anger. "What kind of joke is this? How dare you come in here, rip our hearts open again when we just buried your twin brother, for God's sake, and pull some kind of sick, freakish..." He turned furious eyes to Will. "You're behind this, aren't you? You have smart-ass written all over your face."

And Will thought he'd left his inner smart-ass at home.

He grinned at the colonel, making no attempts to hide the delicate, curved fangs that extended about an eighth of an inch below the rest of his upper teeth. The Penton vampires could mainstream well enough to pass for human, but it was by choice. Will could vamp it up as well as the next guy.

Rick's face hardened. "So you have fake fangs. You think I don't see all kinds of shit with these kids who think they want to be soldiers? Or who do things like have fake fangs implanted to pretend they're vampires? All that proves to me is that you're a sick freak."

Man, what a sweetheart.

"Dad, it's true. I wouldn't have believed it either. But that's who attacked me in the alley in Kabul. He was a local. He dragged me into a small house, and he turned me into one of them. I didn't know what to do. I couldn't come home because I was afraid I'd hurt you accidentally. I thought it was kinder to let you think I'd died."

Randa stood and walked to her father. "I want you to look at my eyes. They change color when I'm stressed or...or other things. They should look silvery because I was so nervous about coming here tonight."

She sat next to him, and after a hard glare at Will, Rick turned to look in his daughter's eyes. Her face wasn't visible from Will's angle, but the colonel saw something he didn't like. He shoved himself away from the table with enough force that Randa was startled. Her chair toppled, dumping her on the floor, where she sat blinking up at her dad. He stood over her with clenched fists and frightened eyes.

Will was on his feet without thinking, moving to stand next to Randa. He reached down and helped her to her feet, then stepped within biting distance of the colonel. "Sir, it took a lot of courage for your daughter to come here tonight. I can tell you love her, but you need to accept what she's telling you. She needs your help—*we* need your help. But only if you can accept what she is."

"Or what?" Rick met Will's gaze, then looked down.

"Yeah, my eyes get all funny too. It also happens when we're angry." *And hungry or sexually aroused*, but he wouldn't add that. "Now sit down and let us tell you a few things about vampires. Nobody's threatening you, but we're not here to *be* threatened, either."

The colonel sat hard, took a sip of his beer, looked at the bottle, and then drained it. Will went back to his chair and shoved Robbie's unfinished beer across the table to him. Randa set her chair upright and gave Will what he hoped was a thank-you look and not an I'm-going-to-chew-you-a-new-one look. He wasn't sure.

"Randa." The colonel reached out a hand, and Randa placed hers in it. His fingers curled around hers. "Is this the God's honest truth? You swear it?"

She nodded. "I swear on Rory's memory."

"Then explain it to me."

☙CHAPTER 29☙

Well, at least nobody had been shot yet. No blood. No broken bones. Randa hadn't been forced to put on a show of feeding from Will—or worse, feeding from her father. She'd go sunbathing before that happened.

But now, here they sat, and he was waiting for an explanation. "Vampires are real, but they—we—work hard to keep our identities secret."

"Why?"

She'd forgotten her father's annoying habits of treating conversations like interrogations. But this might be easier if he asked questions and she answered them. "Will can tell me if I'm wrong because he's been turned a lot longer than me, but I think the feeling is that humans would feel threatened and try to kill us. That we'd end up in a war. That it would stir up more problems than it would be worth."

The colonel's hard gaze slid to Will, who returned the stare without flinching, his golden-brown eyes calm and steady. Randa had never seen him so fierce as when he stood up to her father, and she realized he was a lot stronger than she'd ever given him credit for.

"How long have you been a vampire, William?" the colonel asked.

Randa gave Will an imploring look that she hoped conveyed *play along*. "I was born in 1947 in New York City," Will said. "I was turned vampire when I was twenty-two, in 1969."

Rick picked up Robbie's beer bottle and drained it. "You're telling me that you're..."

"In my late sixties, in human years." Will smiled at him. "Obviously, we don't age." He pushed his chair back, walked into the kitchen, and pulled another bottle of beer from the fridge. "Here, you might want this."

Rick took it without comment. Great, they were bonding. Or not.

"Here are the basics, Dad. Hollywood has some things right. We don't age. We're extremely strong, we—"

"How strong?" He was frowning, so that meant he was thinking. That was good. At least, she thought it was good.

She shrugged and walked into the living room, making sure her dad could see her. She leaned over and picked up his recliner without strain, then lifted it above her head.

"Jesus H. Christ."

Randa set it back down and returned to the table. "As I said, we're extremely strong." She refused to meet Will's gaze, because he'd laugh, and then she'd laugh. Dad would not laugh. "We can't tolerate sunlight—"

"You don't sparkle? Do you burst into flames?"

Randa bit back the urge to tell him he'd learn more if he'd actually let her finish a sentence. At this rate, it would take them a week just to fill him in on what they could and couldn't do. And he'd been watching too much cable TV.

"No sparkles. No flames." She waited to see if he had another question, but he motioned her to go on. "We are not damned, as far as I know—religious objects don't affect us. We can be photographed. We can see our reflections in mirrors."

"Do you drink blood?"

Ah, yes. There was that little issue. "Yes, we do. But we don't kill those we feed from." Well, a white lie. Some did, although, these days, unvaccinated humans were too valuable to waste. She wouldn't be sharing any of those details for a while.

"So you don't eat or drink, and to stay alive, you could feed from me?" He stuck his arm out. "Show me."

OK, Dad was getting a little out of hand. Randa looked at Will, who'd stared off into space. She saw the dimples starting to form. Glad he was having fun.

Feeding could be positively orgasmic, as she'd recently learned, and she did not intend to share that with her father. Thankfully, she had an excuse. "I can't, Dad, which sort of leads us to why we're here."

He slid his arm back. "I'm listening."

Randa wet her lips and looked at her hands, which rested on the table. "I haven't come before because I didn't want to endanger you or put you in a position where you were forced to change how you looked at the world, the way I was forced to."

Rick picked up the beer bottle, looked at it, and set it back on the table without drinking. Randa was relieved. He was taking her seriously and realized he needed to be sharp. "But something changed, because you're here now."

"Remember the pandemic a few years ago, the one that killed so many people?"

Rick nodded. "Right. There was a good vaccine developed. I got it. That was about the time you died—changed."

Randa looked at Will. "You might be better at explaining this part." She'd just gone through her transition when the vaccine crisis began. She'd never known any other situation.

Will leaned back in his chair. "The pandemic vaccine changed human blood chemistry. Just slightly. Not enough to impact people, but it made the blood of any vaccinated human deadly to vampires. If Randa fed from you—or if I did—it would kill us."

Rick began to peel the label from the beer bottle, which was sweating small rivulets of water onto the wooden table. "That vaccine was widely distributed," he said. "So I'm guessing the vampires have a bit of a food shortage."

OK, he'd handled it surprisingly well so far and had seen the dilemma quickly. "We do," she said. "There's a lot of panic. Desperation. Power struggles." In their meeting the night before, they'd agreed to not mention some of the real problems—the human trafficking for unvaccinated humans that was being considered for sanctioning by the Tribunal, the violence that wasn't tied to Penton. And there was a lot of it, she imagined. They'd been pretty isolated the last few months.

"Are *you* starving?" Rick's eyes roved over his daughter. "Mr. Hendrix looks healthy enough."

Randa shot Will a warning look. He usually followed his raised eyebrow with a smart-ass comment. "No. I was lucky to have met someone, a vampire named Aidan Murphy. Aidan bought up all the land around a little ghost town in Alabama, and we moved there. The vampires who are part of his scathe— it's kind of like a family—and their human familiars live there together. Familiars are humans that willingly feed us. In exchange, we provide them jobs, health care, friendship, protection. So, no, I'm not starving."

Rick pushed the bottle away from him. "Now, what are you *not* telling me?"

They'd agreed that Will would talk about the Tribunal. He'd had longer to understand the power structure. "There is a ruling body over all the vampires—each country has its own representative. It's sort of like a vampire version of the United Nations."

Rick Thomas snorted. "Sorry. It's just hard to imagine a group of vampires sitting around a conference table arguing politics."

Randa smiled. "It's a lot like that, from what I understand."

"This group, the Tribunal, makes vampire law—like not letting humans know about our existence, not turning humans and creating new vampires without approval, that kind of thing," Will said. "They see Aidan's town—our town—as a threat to their authority. Normally, a vampire is a loner. The fact that Aidan has, or had, more than a hundred living together in peace alongside humans is something they couldn't tolerate. So they started a war."

Her dad had been sitting in a relaxed position—well, relaxed for him—leaning back in his chair. At the *W* word, he straightened slowly. "The vampires are having a war in this country, under our noses, and we don't know about it? That's not acceptable."

Here was the crucible upon which their future rested, and Randa was tempted to grab the beer bottle and drink it herself. Unfortunately, she'd have to down about a case to even get a whisper of a buzz.

"No, it is not acceptable—we agree," she said. "And that's why we need your help."

For the next three hours, without divulging names or locations, Randa and Will took turns talking about what Penton had endured at the hands of Matthias, how the humans of Penton had been treated, and why they were there.

Randa hadn't been surprised that her dad had picked up on Aidan and Mirren's success in rehabilitating people with drug and alcohol dependency. He didn't ask, but she knew him well enough to practically see the wheels turning about programs for veterans.

Will caught Randa's eye and tapped his watch. She glanced at hers and saw it was almost 2:00 a.m.

"We are going to have to leave, Dad. We have to be somewhere safe when the sun rises."

The disappointment and disbelief struggled on his face before he got it under control and replaced it with the mask. It made her want to cry.

"There's no way you could be safe here? Even in the basement? Do you really have to crawl back in some underground hole in order to be safe?"

Randa hesitated. The basement of her grandparents' house could easily be made lighttight, but did she trust her dad yet? Would he be tempted to open the basement door, let the sunlight stream in, thinking it better to get this mess away from his home and his remaining family? Would he try to kill Will, thinking he was somehow helping Randa?

"No, sir, I'm sorry, but the members of our scathe know we've come to you, and they will come looking for us if we don't return to our planned safe space before dawn." Will's voice was friendly and respectful, but unyielding. "Randa and I have to go."

Rick let out a long breath, but nodded. "I understand. What's next?"

"Does that mean you'll help us?" God, Randa hated the eagerness in her voice. She wasn't sure if it was the possibility of ending the standoff with the Tribunal somehow or the chance to see her father again, another chance to earn his respect.

"Yes. I don't know what form that help can take. I need to think, and I need to talk to these leaders of your...your town. Can that be arranged?"

It was the question they'd hoped for. Randa slipped a piece of paper from her pocket and slid it across the table to him.

He opened it, frowned, and cocked his head at her. "You're living in a Walmart in West Point, Georgia?"

Randa smiled. "No, but it's as close an address as I can give you right now. I want you to think about this whole situation hard tonight and tomorrow, and I have to beg you, as your daughter, not to tell anyone. If you help us, think about the ramifications it can have. The dangers for everyone." She reached out and took his hand. "I'm sorry I didn't come to you sooner. I thought I was doing the right thing by staying away."

He stood up and pulled her into a long, tight hug. He still smelled of the aftershave that threw her back to childhood, when he was still comfortable holding and touching her, before he grew awkward and distant. "I love you," he whispered. "I thank God for bringing you back to me, however changed. And I'll do what I can to help."

Will cleared his throat. "Ran, we have to go."

They paused at the front door. "As Randa said, think about this very hard, sir," Will said. "About not only how you can help, but how many people you think need to be told of our existence without endangering us or anyone else."

Randa still held on to her father's hand. "Dad, if you change your mind, I won't blame you, and I promise I won't disappear.

Somehow, we'll find a way to be in each other's lives. But if you still want to help, be in the parking lot at that address"—she pointed at the paper he still held in his hand—"at eight tomorrow night."

"If you come, come alone," Will added. "Bring a change of clothes and an open mind."

❧CHAPTER 30❧

Shelton picked at a scab on his cheek and flicked it at the ground. He itched from the whip marks as they slowly healed, his stomach had practically imploded from hunger, and he was standing in the woods in the fucking rain just after dusk, waiting on a dog.

Matthias, the vengeful son of a bitch, had not only refused to let him feed again, but also locked Shelton's favorite plaything in one of those rooms beneath the clinic—tantalizingly close, but out of reach.

He just sat in that clinic office like a big, ugly spider, daring Shelton to screw up.

"Where you want us to hunt?" Matthias's hired dog handler, a thin, sallow-faced human with a name like Bobby Lee or Billy Joe or Tommy Sue, held the leash to a droopy, slobbering bloodhound he called Nosy.

Shelton eyed them both with distaste and set Cage Reynolds's backpack on the ground near Nosy's twitching snout. "He needs to track this scent, fanning out from this spot."

"Where's Mr. Ludlam? He said I was to report only to him. Plus, it's raining. You know that will weaken the scent. I want to make sure he knows that."

Like Shelton cared what he wanted. "You report to me. I'm to stand out here and wait for your findings." Shelton pointed to his scabbed-over wounds. "It's part of my punishment."

Actually, it wasn't. He was under orders to make sure the dog did its job, then have his handler report to Matthias at the clinic. Tough shit. Shelton was changing the rules.

Ever since Matthias had discovered Reynolds was spying for the Penton crew, and that he had the backing of the UK Tribunal delegate, the man had taken paranoia to new heights. He needed to rely on the people who'd always been loyal to him, people like Shelton. Instead, he'd beaten him, starved him, and now had him babysitting a bloodhound-wielding redneck in a fucking monsoon.

Shelton had always prided himself on being able to identify and back a winning horse, and for years, Matthias had led the pack. But the man had let his obsessions—first with William and now with Aidan Murphy and Mirren Kincaid—blind him to the bigger picture. Shelton thought it might be time to find a new horse. The rules of the race had changed, and he didn't think Matthias had been paying attention.

Shelton knew he'd have to be careful. He was blood-bound to Matthias, so if he moved too blatantly against His Highness, the man would know and Shelton's immortal life would cease to be immortal at all. His greatest advantage was that Matthias was too preoccupied with what the Tribunal was doing to keep up with his own people too closely.

The only way he'd ever truly be free would be if Matthias fell from power altogether and the Tribunal forced him to unbond his handful of followers. It might be time. Someone like Edward Simmons or that old cow Meg Lindstrom might be grateful enough to give Shelton a new horse on which to bet.

Shelton wrapped his jacket more tightly around his itchy torso and wedged himself against a tree with dense branches that gave him a bit of shelter from the rain. The longer he sat, the more pissed off he got.

Where did Matthias think this was going to end? Even if he destroyed the Penton scathe and got William back under his roof, what then? It wouldn't make a difference in the endgame.

The vampire world was on the verge of collapse. They'd be able to survive for a few years by bottom-feeding from disenfranchised humans who hadn't been vaccinated—the homeless, the insane, the criminals, the addicts. But to truly bottom-feed, one had to live in a city, so all the vampires now combing the rural outposts looking for viable feeders would eventually flock back to the urban areas.

Shelton had never claimed to be the sharpest vampire in the land of the fanged, but he knew this: wherever too many vampires gathered, problems followed. Territory battles, power struggles, coups and countercoups. Hell, maybe Aidan Murphy had the right idea.

Nosy nosed nearby, snuffling along the ground. The dog stopped and bayed, bringing his handler into view. "Whatcha found, buddy?"

The dog scratched in the pile of leaves and mud, whining until the redneck reached in his pocket and pulled out what looked like a miniature cake wrapped in cellophane. "Good boy. Good old Nosy. Ready for a treat? Got your favorite Little Debbies."

He unwrapped the cake and fed it to the dog in big white-frosted chunks.

The fool rewarded his bloodhound with cheap pastry? Somehow that made Shelton's decision easier.

While Nosy chewed on his Little Debbie, Shelton slipped the small Smith & Wesson carry pistol from his pocket and took aim at the dog's head, bracing his arms on his bent knees. Nosy the bloodhound hadn't even scented Shelton sitting a few feet away, or didn't consider him worth watching.

At the last second, he shifted his sights to the head of Nosy's owner and pulled the trigger twice.

With the silencer, the greatest noise came from the unfortunate Billy Sue, or whatever the hell his name was, crashing atop a leafy bush, the crumpled Little Debbie package in his hand. Shelton sat in place a few seconds, waiting to see what the dog would do. He had no argument with the beast.

Nosy sat and looked mournfully at his owner until Shelton approached. He howled once and ran into the woods.

Smart dog.

Shelton dragged the body into a ditch near the spring Matthias had sent him to poison a couple of days earlier. He rifled through the man's pockets, keeping a folding knife and the cash from his wallet. Credit cards were too easy to track down, so he left them and returned the wallet before covering the corpse with leaves. Maybe something would eat it before it was found.

❧CHAPTER 31❧

Randa and Will were quiet on their walk back to the Omega hatch from the factory parking lot. Her dad wasn't the only one with a lot to think about, and only two hours remained before dawn.

Being in that house had stirred a lot of memories, good and bad. She wanted a chance to talk to Robbie again, if her dad thought it would be OK. Maybe her other brothers. But she couldn't live among them. To her surprise, she didn't want to.

If Dad didn't show up tomorrow night, or if he didn't think her brothers should know, Randa would have to live with that. If he wanted them all to be a part of her life, she had to figure out how to live with that too.

Some part of her had expected to go into that house and reclaim some semblance of her old life. She hadn't expected to go in and realize she no longer wanted it. She always thought she'd latched onto Aidan's scathe because there was nowhere else for her to go.

Maybe that *was* the reason she'd joined them, but she stayed because she'd come to love them and consider them her family, albeit a kind of dysfunctional one. Aidan, with his serious strength and unbending moral code. Krys, with her soft heart and sharp sense of humor. Mirren, who, for all his curmudgeon act, had a heart as big as the man himself. Glory, with her joy for life and hardheaded practicality. Hannah, for the innocence she had somehow managed to hold on to. Cage and Melissa and Mark. All of them.

And Will, who'd faced down her father tonight with a ferocity she'd never seen in him. Who'd gone in there prepared to kill Rick Thomas if he'd needed to so she wouldn't have to either make the decision or do something for which she couldn't forgive herself. Who'd somehow taught her that she could be strong without being hard. And who'd let her tear at least a small chink out of the wall he'd built around himself.

She reached over and looped her arm through his as they walked.

He smiled down at her. "You OK?"

"Better than I expected to be. Part of me was afraid I'd want to stay."

"So was I." He stopped and turned to face her. "But?"

Randa stood on tiptoe and pressed a kiss against his lips. "But I realized that I belong here."

"That's a conversation we need to continue inside." He kissed her again, and they walked hand in hand toward the hatch.

"Go ahead and finish your conversation, kids. I was getting all choked up."

Randa froze at the sight of the man in front of them; they'd both been so preoccupied with each other they'd let their vigilance slide. Even Will's supersenses hadn't alerted him.

The guy was vampire, very thin, medium height, with pale-blond hair, a series of healing cuts across his face and neck, and blue eyes fixed on Will.

Will had gone still. No, not just unmoving. He was paralyzed. Was this a starving vamp out in search of food or one of Matthias's men?

"Good to see you, William. You're looking as pretty as ever." The man had a sarcastic drawl, and if he knew Will, he definitely wasn't a random starving vampire.

"Who are you?" Randa didn't like the look on Will's face. His nostrils flared, and his jaw was clenched so tightly she expected to hear teeth cracking at any second.

"I'm Shelton Porterfield." Shelton finally wrenched his gaze from Will and looked her over. "Looks like you two are close. Can't believe Will hasn't told you about that special summer we spent together. Maybe some memories are just so beautiful you want to keep them all for yourself. Right, William?"

Will's body vibrated with tension, and Randa waited for him to react. This guy was obviously someone who knew Will well enough to push his buttons. *Shelton.* The name sounded familiar...Wasn't Shelton the name of Matthias's second-in-command? If he was standing ten feet from the Omega hatch, shouldn't they be killing him? Shouldn't he be killing them?

Her left hand still rested in Will's. She pulled it free and raised the shotgun she'd been carrying in her right hand.

"You'd do better to let me to go on my way, girl. I can be of more help to you alive. See these stripes on my face? Matthias went too far this time, thanks to your buddy Cage Reynolds. Just ask William how far his daddy can take his punishments."

Will moved so fast Randa couldn't track it. One second he was standing beside her, radiating pent-up emotion. The next he was on the ground with Shelton pinned beneath him. His knife was in the man's chest, angled below the rib cage and up into the heart. Shelton died with a look of utter surprise on his face, blue eyes wide, mouth dangling open.

Will's arm lifted and fell, lifted and fell, stabbing repeatedly with a feral bellow that didn't sound human *or* vampire. His lips were pulled back in a grimace.

The smell of blood filled the clearing and would draw other vampires if any were nearby.

Randa circled Will and approached him cautiously from the front. She'd seen men lose it, big army guys who were tough as old leather until one little thing had finally triggered the release of months of pent-up rage.

If she startled Will from behind, he might easily turn the knife on her.

"Will? We need to leave." She knelt, not sure he could even see her. Should she go into Omega and get Aidan?

He never looked at her, but he stopped stabbing Shelton and climbed to his feet, straddling the prostrate man and staring down at the body, his face still and haunted. The knife fell from his hand, hitting the ground with a soft thud. Randa picked it up and used a handful of wet leaves to wipe it off.

"Leave him, Will. Let's go into Omega." She needed to get him away from that body before he lost it again.

She walked to the hatch, uncovered and unlocked it, and pulled it open. "Cage?" she called down. "You on watch?"

She hoped so. Something way out of her depth was going on here. Will had skated awfully close to the edge of a precipice she couldn't identify, and somehow she knew it wouldn't take much to push him over. Shelton might be dead, but Will was still locked in some kind of battle.

"I had started to worry about you lot." Cage climbed up the ladder and spotted Shelton's body before getting halfway out of the hatch. "Well, hello. That's a sight I didn't expect to see."

Cage went to stand beside the body, looking from Will's face to the knife in Randa's hand, to the bloody mass of hamburger that had been Shelton's chest. He put a hand on Will's shoulder, and he flinched. "Go on down with Randa. I'll take care of this."

Will didn't move. He didn't look up. Randa met Cage's gaze and shook her head.

"Will." Cage stepped in front of him, also straddling Shelton's body. He rested a hand on each of Will's shoulders and stepped close enough that Will was forced to look at him.

Cage's voice dropped to such a soft timbre Randa struggled to hear. "It's over now. You finally ended it. He can't hurt you anymore."

Will's face was a blank, his eyes more pale honey than deep amber.

"Go with Randa." Cage nodded at her, and Randa took Will's hand.

"Let's go and see Aidan," she said, mimicking Cage's soft tone. "We need to tell him about my dad. Make plans for tomorrow night."

That seemed to jolt Will out of whatever trance he'd been in. He gripped her hand almost to the point of pain and stepped away from Shelton. Randa mouthed a thank-you to Cage before following Will down the ladder into Omega.

☙CHAPTER 32☙

Will moved on autopilot, walking when Randa walked and stopping when they spotted Aidan and Mirren sitting in the common room.

"Good. We've been waiting for you." Aidan was halfway to the conference room before Will realized he had to focus. He had to get the ghosts out of his head long enough to talk strategy. Their survival depended on it, and they'd only have a few hours after daysleep before it was time to meet the colonel in West Point. Randa wasn't sure he'd show, but Will thought he would.

Randa kept looking at him as if she feared he'd lose it again and start stabbing everybody within reach, but he couldn't look her in the eye, couldn't reassure her. Not yet. He owed her an explanation, and after that, she wouldn't want him to look at her.

Will glanced at Mirren on his way into the conference room, and the big guy grabbed the back of his sweater on the way in, staying behind him. Will had no choice but to stop inside the door while Mirren turned back to shut it. Everyone was still standing, but Will couldn't sit as long as Mirren had hold of his sweater, pinning him in place.

"What happened?" Aidan finally walked to the far end of the table and sat, leaning back in his chair. Randa sat to his right, glanced at Mirren and Will with confusion on her face, and began talking.

"We got to my dad's house at—"

Aidan gave her an apologetic smile. "Not yet. First, why is Will covered in blood? Vampire blood. I tried to contact you a half hour ago mentally and got a big black void."

Will wet his lips and tried to make the words come out. "Shelton. Dead."

"About goddamned time." Mirren slapped Will on the back and took the chair to the other side of Aidan. "Where'd you find him?"

Will managed to sit in the chair next to Randa, but his mind still spun in a dozen directions at once. "He was outside the hatch."

There. He'd spoken a complete sentence. Good for him.

Randa reached under the table and squeezed his leg. She didn't let go when he tried to jerk away. She shouldn't have been touching him. But then, she didn't know the truth about him yet, did she? She still thought he was strong.

"When we got back to the hatch after visiting my dad, we stumbled on Shelton standing near the hatch to Omega." Randa picked up the story, and Will closed his eyes, reliving it. "He was acting weird, sort of hinting that he'd had a falling-out with Matthias and wasn't going to try to stop us. We couldn't let him go back to Penton, though. So Will took him down."

Will blinked at her attempt to cover for him. What was it she'd said her father always taught her? *Own what you do.* "I didn't take him down. I murdered him. He didn't even pull a weapon on us." He looked at Aidan. "I stabbed him so many times I lost count. I couldn't stop."

Aidan steepled his hands in front of his face, elbows on the table, and didn't speak aloud. His voice came through loud and clear in Will's head. *I know why you did it. I know what he did to you. I'm proud of you. Now, you have to let it go.*

Will couldn't raise his voice above a whisper. "How?"

Did he really know, or was he guessing? Will wanted to sink under the table. Cage must have put it together from that smart-ass comment he'd made a while back and gone blabbing to Aidan.

None of it was your fault. And Cage was right to tell me.

Will couldn't look at him, but nodded.

"Now, Randa, let's talk about your father." Aidan moved on, and Randa gave a thorough replay of the meeting with her dad. When Will finally lifted his gaze, he found Mirren staring at him. The big guy gave him a solemn, slow nod before turning his attention back to Aidan. Did he know? Or did he just think Will had finally grown a pair of balls big enough to kill somebody who needed it?

"What's your take on the colonel, Will?" Aidan's subtext: *Get your ass back in the game.*

Will cleared his throat, forcing the whole Shelton issue to the back of his mind and mentally locking it down. He'd done it for decades, after all. What were a few minutes more?

"I think Colonel Thomas loves his daughter, enough so that he was able to be more open-minded and accepting than I expected." Randa's hand squeezed his knee under the table, and he hazarded a glance at her. Instead of the fear or doubt he deserved, her face showed only warmth. "I do believe he'll show up tomorrow night. And I think he probably stayed up all night after we left—he's probably still up—weighing different options."

Aidan nodded. "We only have an hour until daysleep, but spend that time asking yourself some questions, all of you. We'll have a little time to talk again tomorrow night before you go to pick him up."

The questions were the ones Will had considered himself, plus a few others. Would it be better to reveal the vampire world to the public at large, to a limited group of officials that included military and political figures, or only to the colonel and enough men to help Penton out of its current crisis?

How much, if anything, should their allies on the Tribunal be told?

If the Tribunal suspected the Penton scathe was about to make their whole society public, would they retaliate fast and end up killing Colonel Thomas and his men as well as everyone who'd ever been involved with Penton?

What was the endgame?

><+>-0-<+>-<

Will lagged behind after the meeting. Randa paused in the doorway and smiled at him before disappearing into the hall, headed for the room they still shared. He had to figure out what to tell her. Or maybe he should just come clean and accept that they'd had a great thing together while it lasted.

He owed her an explanation for what she'd seen tonight. And then he owed her the respect of walking away and not trying to force himself on her. Once he let her see who and what he really was, she'd be glad to see him go. All the empty rooms had been taken up by sick people, but maybe he could sleep in the silver cell.

Finally, he hoisted himself out of the chair and walked into the hallway.

"Good, I'd hoped to run into you." Cage was reentering Omega from the exit tunnel.

Will sighed. "You told Aidan." He was too tired of the whole drama to be angry. Hell, he should have told Aidan himself. Instead, he'd only hinted that his hatred for Matthias went deeper than what had happened with his mom and Cathy. "It's OK. He needed to know."

"How are you?" Cage put a hand on his arm, but when Will tensed, he removed it.

How did he expect Will to feel? He'd just turned into a slathering sociopath in front of the one person in the world besides Aidan and Mirren who he wanted to think well of him. "Just terrific. I'm going to try to explain to Randa why I turned into a nutjob, and then I'm going in search of a place to bed down for the day."

He brushed past Cage, but the vampire grabbed his arm. "You didn't ask for it, but I'm going to give you a little advice. Tell her the truth—all of it, even the stuff you've never told another soul. It'll be good for both of you. And let her decide how she responds to it. Don't decide for her."

Fucking shrink. Will jerked his arm away and walked down the hall toward his room. Their room.

He took a deep breath outside the door, knocked softly, and turned the knob. Randa sat on the bed in her army T-shirt, her legs bare. "Thought you'd want to wash some of that blood off."

She pointed to a couple of gallon jugs of water she'd set next to the bathroom door.

Well, he wouldn't pass on an opportunity to procrastinate. He nodded, pulling the blood-soaked sweater over his head, balling it up, looking around to throw it...where?

Randa stood up and held out her hand. "Here, I'll take it to the trash room."

"No, I..." He didn't want her tainted with Shelton's blood. She'd already had to get Cage to clean up the mess he'd made outside. He couldn't let her take this too.

She pulled it out of his hands. "Go ahead and clean up." The door closed behind her with a soft click, and Will was alone.

He shed the rest of his clothes, pulled out some clean jogging pants, and went into the small bathroom. Since the vampires weren't susceptible to the poisoned spring water, they probably could have continued using the water supply and saving the bottled water for the humans to drink and cook with, but there was a fear they'd somehow pass it on to the humans who fed from them, that it might somehow live on their skin or in their clothing.

They'd never had hot water in Omega, though, but instead of chilling him as it usually did, tonight the bottled water helped clear his head of the fog he'd been trapped in since he saw Shelton in that clearing.

The shirt had been what pushed him over the edge. Shelton had been wearing a blue silk shirt under his jacket tonight— not just blue, but a clear cerulean, wet and clinging to his body as if he'd been sweating. The man always liked wearing that shade. He thought it made him look handsome with his blue eyes. Thought it made him look safe to the boys he'd...

Shit. Will stuck his head under a cold stream of water—
more like a trickle since he didn't want to waste any—and let it
wash the thoughts away.

Finally, he dumped the rest of the second bottle over his
head. There couldn't be more than forty-five minutes left before
dawn, and he wanted to talk to Randa before daysleep. That
way, they could start fresh tomorrow night, coworkers again,
partners in work only. If she still trusted him.

He'd killed Shelton Porterfield tonight, but Shelton and
Matthias had killed some part of him a long, long time ago.
He'd been deluded to think he could come out of it whole.

After drying off and shaking as much water as he could
from his hair, Will pulled on the clean pants, gathered his courage, and opened the door to the bedroom. Randa had returned
to her previous spot, her face calm.

He sat on the other bed, facing her. "I owe you an explanation for what happened tonight."

"Only if you want to talk about it. Only if you're ready."

He'd never be ready, but she needed to know. Hell, maybe
he needed to say the words. "Shelton has been in charge of my
dad's Virginia estate for years. He was already bonded to him
when my dad turned my mom and my sister and me."

Randa picked at the light blanket that stretched across
the bed. "What happened that summer, the one Shelton mentioned?"

Will kept his eyes on the floor, trying not to let the ghosts
back in but failing. "Shelton likes—liked—young boys. By *like*,
I mean..." He couldn't say it.

"He likes to sexually abuse young boys." Randa's voice
didn't hold judgment or anger or disgust. Just calm. It helped
Will go on.

"I'd been turned about a month and was twenty-two but looked younger. I was angry at everyone. At my dad for turning us. At my mom for going along with it so that Cathy and I would go along with it too. At Cathy for dying. At myself for helping her die."

Will got up and paced the room. "I acted out. Fought my dad on everything, just to piss him off. I hadn't...hadn't learned how to read that well, so he said he couldn't give me a place in his business in New York. That I was too stupid, even if he'd been able to trust me."

Randa grabbed his wrist on one of his paces past her, and tugged until he sat beside her. "So Matthias sent you to Virginia."

"Matthias sent me to Virginia." Matthias had lured him there with the promise of some light work on the property and the chance to stay in a house removed from authority. "As soon as I got there, Shelton had me in silver cuffs and threw me in that silver-barred cell in the basement."

Again, calm voice. Quiet. "How long did he keep you there?"

"Until I broke." *Like a pretty little girl*, as Shelton had said. He'd still been able to cry then, and he'd cried. Begged. Until he'd been beaten enough, until he'd been violated enough, that he finally admitted it was his fault, that he was as useless as Matthias had always told him, that he deserved whatever Shelton did to him, that he wanted it.

"Did he rape you?"

"It wasn't rape. I wasn't a helpless kid." That's what Shelton kept reminding him. *You're an adult, William. You want this, or you'd find a way to leave. You just pretend to fight it because that makes it more exciting for both of us.*

"Age has nothing to do with rape." Randa shifted on the bed until she faced him, and laid a hand on his arm. He pulled away. He didn't want her touching him.

Randa's voice was soft. "Here's what rape is. It's when one person takes power over another person, against his or her will. The rapist might take that power physically, by restraint or force. Or he might take it emotionally, by telling lies and then convincing his victim he wanted it and it's his or her fault."

Will swallowed hard. He kept his eyes on the floor, but he didn't avoid her this time when she took his hand. He needed her warmth.

He thought about her words. Shelton had taken his power. He'd used the whip, waited until Will healed a few hours later, then used it again. He'd withheld food, which right after transition was painful. He'd cuffed him facedown to the bed and left him for days before he came and took him, pants around his ankles and one of those goddamned blue shirts hanging open.

"Will, did Shelton rape you?"

He took a deep breath, let it out. Closed his eyes.

"Yes."

Randa's voice was vicious. "Then I'm glad you killed the son of a bitch. If he could die twice, I'd go out there and do him myself."

Will finally looked at her, and her fierce expression shocked him. He'd expected disgust or pity, and he'd rather disgust than have her feel sorry for him. But she looked like she wanted to put a serious beat-down on somebody. He couldn't help but smile a little. "You look like a she-bear."

"I'll take that as a compliment and not that you're insinuating that I'm big and hairy."

He kissed her hand, the one she'd kept locked on his, and stood up. "Is it OK with you if I get the rest of my stuff tomorrow night?" He felt dawn approaching. Maybe fifteen minutes, but no more. He needed to find a spot to crash.

"You're not going anywhere." Randa stood up, grasped the hem of her T-shirt, and pulled it over her head. He paused at the sight of those breasts that fit perfectly into his palm, then dropped his gaze to a black lace bikini.

His mouth suddenly felt dry. "Where'd those come from?"

"Funny thing about superstores. You never know what you might find when you go in late at night looking for hair dye."

Will closed his eyes. He'd just killed a man, in a brutal way. Yeah, maybe he deserved it, but there was still blood on his hands, not taken in self-defense. He'd just told her what had been done to him and his part in it. Maybe he had been raped, but it was going to take Will a while to get used to the idea of himself as a total victim. He'd spent too many years hearing Shelton's words and believing them.

Her hands felt warm as they slid around his waist, her breasts pressed against him, her mouth planting open kisses on his collarbone. "Randa, I—"

"Shut up, Will." She smiled up at him. "You thought telling me all that was going to make me hate you?"

He shrugged, realizing he'd probably sold her short. Again. "Or just be disgusted. How do you know all that stuff? I mean, were you ever...?"

"Raped?" She shook her head. "But I was a counselor at my division's rape crisis center. Those victims were not children, either, Will. And they weren't all women. You don't disgust me. In fact, I think you're the bravest, smartest guy I know. Not to mention sexy."

She pulled him to the bed, and he lay beside her. He wished he could show her how much it meant to him that she didn't judge him. Explain to her that it was going to take him a while to put all the baggage of his past behind him—maybe a long while. But he'd work at it, and not only for himself, but for them.

For now, Randa nestled in his arms with her head tucked under his chin, their legs tangled in what had fast become their favorite daysleep position, and it was enough.

❦CHAPTER 33❧

Randa's slow-beating vampire heart thumped at almost human levels as she and Will pulled into the lot of the West Point, Georgia, Walmart just before 8:00. The Penton leaders had talked through different options, but needed to hear what her father had to say.

Assuming he showed up. Part of her feared he wouldn't show, and the other part feared he would.

"Shit." Will stopped at the edge of the lot. "He didn't come alone. Black SUV, far corner."

There were clearly two figures sitting inside it. Both male, about the same size. "I think it's Robbie." Damn it, she should've known her brother wouldn't accept being shut out.

"OK, we improvise. Tell me about Robbie."

Randa took a deep breath, thinking of Robbie as a dossier subject, not a brother. "He goes by 'Rob' and left the army after his second tour was up so he could work with Dad. He's a former Ranger, thirty-three, divorced, no kids. I thought he was engaged, or so his Facebook page said. Can be a loud-mouthed smart-ass." She looked at Will. "You two have a lot in common."

"Ha-ha." Will's eyes stayed on the SUV. "Go on."

She thought of her big brother, of his relationships, what had gotten him in trouble the most. "He's a risk-taker, a brawler, not as cold and calculating as Dad, but more creative. He owned a construction company and made a lot of money before the economy tanked back in 2008. He saw it coming and sold the business before he lost his shirt. I think he was already doing"—she held up finger quotes—"security work for Dad when I got deployed, mostly because he seemed to have plenty of money but wouldn't say exactly how he'd gotten it. My guess is Dad brought him in to lead the missions."

"So you trust him?"

Of all her brothers except for Rory, she trusted Robbie the most, and he'd been the one to first accept that she had really survived Afghanistan, even though he'd missed the vampire reveal. "I do trust him, and if Dad decides to help us, he'd probably bring Robbie into it anyway. I say we go ahead with the plan."

Will nodded. "Good enough for me."

He shifted the truck into drive and approached the dark SUV slowly, stopping next to it. All four of them got out, and Randa approached Robbie with something akin to fear. She assumed Dad had told him but wasn't sure what his reaction would be.

"Come here, fang-face." He grinned, and Randa heard Will behind her, laughing. Great, now she'd have two smart-asses to deal with. But she hugged her brother, relieved he wasn't afraid of her. "Let me see 'em."

She laughed. "You better watch out. You didn't get the pandemic vaccine—I can bite you." Not that she would. Getting her brother all orgasmic was every bit as squicky as her doing it to her dad.

He frowned. "You can tell that? How—by smell?"

She nodded, looking at the ground, avoiding his eye. It really sounded freakish—their whole lives sounded freakish.

"Well, how seriously cool is that?" Robbie stepped around Randa and held out his hand to Will. "Sorry, we weren't properly introduced last night, William. Robert Thomas."

There was a long pause as Will sized up his new potential ally. Finally, he smiled. "Actually, it's William Ludlam—Will. Sorry, but we were being cautious last night."

This whole time, Rick Thomas had stood back, leaning against the rear door of the SUV, watching them all. "It's understandable," he said. "You're trying to decide whether or not to trust us, same as we're trying to decide about you."

Randa hugged him. "I wasn't sure you'd come. I hate that I've brought this to your doorstep."

He kissed her forehead. "If changing the human world as we know it is the price of getting my daughter back, well, what the hell."

Dad made a joke? She looked up at him, and damned if he wasn't smiling.

The smile faded quickly. "The more I thought about this last night, the bigger it got. That's why I wanted Rob here. Whatever we decide to do is going to be complicated—the more minds working on it, the better."

Fifteen minutes later, Will and Randa pulled the pickup into the automotive-plant parking lot, the black SUV following close behind. When they got out of the vehicles, she saw both her dad and brother checking firearms and was sure Will had seen it as well. But she shouldn't have expected them to come unarmed, just as they shouldn't have been surprised to know she and Will carried guns and knives. Trust didn't come easily.

"Stop." They'd been walking silently, but Will halted inside the tree line about a hundred yards from the hatch clearing. He closed his eyes, nostrils flaring. He kept his voice low. "Two vampires—neither of them ours—plus a dog just ahead, between us and the hatch. No humans."

Which was weird. Search dogs usually had human handlers.

Both her dad and brother were looking at Will with renewed interest. "Son, maybe you better tell us how to kill a vampire," Rick said.

Damn. Randa hadn't thought about it, but her dad was right. If they were going to ask him for help and expect him to fight, they also had to equip him to kill. Even if it meant telling him their vulnerabilities.

Will looked at her father long and hard before giving a curt nod. "With a gun, the only way to truly kill a vampire is to shatter the heart with a large-caliber bullet at close range— think raw meat—or do the same thing to the brain. If you can remove the heart, even better. With a blade, you need to be sure to pierce the heart, and the blade has to be silver or silver coated. Otherwise, we heal too fast for it to be lethal. Oh, and beheading works quite well. And sunlight."

Robbie's eyes had grown wider with each new detail. "Holy shit. What happened to the wooden stake?"

Will raised an eyebrow. "It works in theory, but it's pretty slow, and chances are, any vampire worth his fangs would tear your head off before you got it all the way in."

"Good to know." Robbie's voice was subdued.

Randa pulled her pistol from the flat holster that fit inside the waistband of her cargo pants—impractical with something tight like jeans, but otherwise handy. Will, Robbie, and her dad retrieved guns from ankles, inside jackets, and beneath a shirt. Randa fought back a grim smile. The family who hunts vampires together stays together?

They fanned out and approached the clearing in a semi-circle. The two vampires were both males and weren't familiar. The dog, a bloodhound, sniffed around the area where Will had killed Shelton. About two feet from the Omega entrance. They could trip over the hatch if they stepped in the right spot.

Randa looked at Will, pointed her forefinger from herself to the vampire on the left, and then held up three fingers. They'd worked out their signals during the early days when Aidan had forced them to patrol together. To her dad and Robbie, she used her flat palm toward them: *Stay*. They both nodded, although if her father frowned any harder, his eyebrows and mouth would meet.

She suspected not many people had issued a "stay" command to Colonel Rick Thomas.

Will held up one finger, and she raised her gun in a shooting stance. He raised a second finger within his own stance, and she aimed. From her peripheral vision, she saw the third finger go up, and they fired simultaneously.

Will's vampire dropped, missing sizable portions of skull, but the other vampire shifted at the last second and took a hit to the shoulder. He disappeared before Randa could get another shot off. *Damn it.* The guy would run straight to Matthias.

"Go after him or go in Omega?"

Will shook his head. "He's probably halfway to Penton by now. We have to consider ourselves compromised. Let's go down."

Robbie stopped next to the dead vampire. "Shit. His blood's pink. Why is it pink?"

"Our blood is more magenta than crimson. The hungrier we are, the lighter the blood. This guy was starving." Randa knelt and clicked her tongue to call the dog. He came from beneath a bush, slow and wary. When she held her hand out, though, he slinked to her. They couldn't leave him out here to pinpoint the hatch, but she wasn't about to let them kill him.

Mirren and Aidan would have a cow, but she was taking him underground.

While she'd been luring the dog, Will and Robbie had been dragging the dead vampire away from the Omega hatch. No point in making it any easier for them.

"All right, let's get moving." Will knelt in the leaf-covered clearing and felt for the tiny loop to pull up the hatch. Beneath it was the real hatch of locked steel. He unlocked it and pulled it open.

"Cage? You there?"

A deep rumble of a voice answered. "Me, junior."

Oh boy. Mirren was the welcoming committee. Randa hoped her dad and Robbie were truly ready for this.

"We're coming down—there's four of us, plus a big ugly dog, so don't get trigger-happy." Will turned and flashed a brilliant smile at her dad and Robbie—the heart-stopping smile that showed his dimples and would have made her weak in the knees if she hadn't had a mental image of her dad and Mirren, face-to-face.

"Get ready, Dad," she said. "You're about to meet your vampire equivalent."

❧CHAPTER 34❧

Will wasn't sure what he thought about Colonel Rick Thomas. He'd laughed when Randa called Mirren his vampire equivalent, but it wasn't too far off the mark. The colonel wasn't as big as Mirren, but he'd mastered that same ability to mask emotion and reduce people to blithering idiots with a single look.

They'd given each other a cool assessment when they met, and it had warmed up to something Will might liken to, oh, the Arctic Circle. If they'd been bulls, they'd have been butting each other with their horns and seeing which one could paw at the ground and stir up the most dirt.

If there hadn't been so much at stake, it would have been funny.

Aidan and Mirren had done a good job of not only telling the scathe members and fams that new humans would be in their midst, but also getting most of them to stay in their rooms. A few sat in the common room. Some were still in the medical ward with Krys, but once they'd put them all on bottled water, they seemed to be holding their own. A couple were in serious condition, but none had died yet. Thank God Matthias didn't know much about poisons and Krys had been sharp enough to catch it early.

Now they'd all gathered in the conference room, which Will had begun thinking of as the war room. It's what they were planning, after all. Or maybe he should call it the coup room.

First, they had to report on the vampires up top and explain why they'd come in carrying a dog. Mirren had threatened to shoot it, until Glory got between him and the mutt, and then Hannah had taken over.

Watching her with the dog, pulling its ears and scratching its belly, Will wondered why none of them had thought to get Hannah a pet before. It didn't seem very vampire-like, but she wasn't your ordinary vampire.

"I think we have to assume Matthias knows where the hatch is, or will very soon," Aidan said. "The exit room on that side is not as vulnerable to something like a grenade as the one beneath the church because of the steel superstructure, but it's going to make it impossible to go in and out safely. I think you can safely say we're trapped. They can just sit out there and pick us off."

On their tour of the facility, they'd filled in the colonel and Rob on the cave-in, the attack, and how they'd ended up in the stupid position of having only one exit. "How long can you survive down here without leaving?" Rick had asked.

"If the air-filtration system holds up, a week. Months if we had water." Will thought about the other systems; everything else was in good shape, including their food supply. "Water's definitely our biggest problem."

Robbie had a notebook and had been sketching out the Omega floor plan. "Any reason me or Dad couldn't go out during daylight and bring bottled water back in?"

Will might not be sure of his feelings for Randa's father, but he liked Robbie a lot. He reminded Will a little of Glory— practical, straight talking, but with a surprising sense of humor. "I think that's a great idea. You have any objections, Aidan, Mirren?"

Aidan gave Robbie his most serious look. The vampires of the Penton scathe knew to pay close attention when they saw that expression. "You realize we're putting ourselves at your mercy if we do this. If we give you a key to Omega, it leaves us vulnerable."

Robbie nodded. "Anything that puts you at risk also puts my sister at risk. I won't take any chances." Yep, Will really liked Randa's brother.

"No key. We leave the steel doors locked," Mirren said—his first contribution to the discussion. "Rob can take the key to the hatch but not the steel door. He can bring the water to the exit room before dusk, and we'll open it and let him in immediately after."

"That acceptable to you?" Aidan looked from the colonel to his son. "I haven't seen any signs that Matthias has humans working for him, so your risk is minimal. My vampires can't go out in daylight, but neither can his."

The colonel nodded at Mirren, and unless Will was mistaken, there was a grudging respect there. Caution recognized its kin.

"Let's talk strategy, then." Aidan did his "mayor of Penton" routine, welcoming the visitors, thanking them, apologizing for dragging them into this mess, and acknowledging that he realized the only reason they'd come was because of Randa, who spent a lot of time looking at the floor.

Colonel Thomas cleared his throat. "Rob and I came up with three main options, and of course, you might have more."

Aidan smiled. "We have three as well, with a lot of variations. Each has its pros and cons. Why don't you start?"

The colonel rose from his seat and began pacing the length of the walls. Will exchanged an amused look with Randa. If Mirren started his habitual pacing, they'd have either a parade or a collision.

"First option is going public," the colonel said. "I mean, *really* public—media public. Get fucking Brian Williams and NBC News down here with a satellite truck."

Mirren pushed his chair back and fidgeted. The man wanted to pace so badly he was practically twitching. "Won't work," he finally said. "Humans would freak. You'd have panic. And if the humans panic, the vampires panic." A dramatic pause. "You really don't want that to happen."

The colonel gave Mirren a half smile. "Exactly the conclusions we came to. It might be a necessary move at some point, but it would require a lot of negotiations, a lot of time. And we need to move quickly before this Matthias guy and your Tribunal strike again."

"Speaking of which." The colonel turned and pinned a glare on Will, which Will didn't like any better coming from him than from Mirren. "Matthias is your father—your human father—but also a vampire?"

Not a father in any way beyond donated genetic material. "He was turned when I was seventeen. He turned me, my mother, and my sister when I was twenty-two. They didn't survive. I did." *Barely.*

"You can't negotiate your way out of this?"

If he thought that was a possibility, he'd have turned himself in a long time ago. "My father doesn't negotiate. And my allegiance is with Penton."

The colonel nodded. "I figured it had gotten past the negotiation stage. Just had to ask."

Aidan cleared his throat. "Matthias, and a majority faction of the Vampire Tribunal, want Mirren and me dead, so this goes a lot deeper than Will. You should know the charges against us, just so everything's up front. I illegally turned a woman vampire in January—my mate, Krys. She was dying, attacked by someone Matthias had sent in to kill me, and it was the only way to save her."

The colonel studied him, then turned to Mirren. "And you?"

"Long story. I killed someone to save my mate—also involved Matthias." Mirren crossed his arms over his chest and said no more.

"Will?" The colonel paused. "And Randa? Are there charges against you by the Tribunal?"

Will thought about Shelton. He couldn't exactly blame that death on self-defense, unless belated self-defense was legitimate. But no one had witnessed that, and he wasn't sure the Tribunal would care once they'd learned Shelton's history. "We're clean."

"Regardless, what we're saying is that, for Matthias, nothing short of the destruction of this community will be enough," Aidan said. "We have enough dirt to bring him down if we can get the Tribunal to listen to us without sounding like it's our word against his, but there are several Tribunal members on the fence. They're afraid to act until they see who's most likely to win. And, as you just heard, our hands aren't completely clean."

"Sounds like Congress, and most of their hands aren't clean, either." The colonel started pacing again. "OK. The next option we came up with was for me to pull one of my special-operations teams together, come into Penton, and help you clean house."

A growling dissent rose from Mirren's end of the table. "That's the most—"

The colonel held up a hand before Mirren could go further. Will looked up and found Robbie biting back a smile. Will wasn't the only one who thought the colonel and Mirren were cut from the same length of steel pipe.

"Even though we discussed it, I realized this was an unviable solution, Mr. Kincaid. It's a short-term answer that would lead to more problems. You'd lose whatever support you have within your Tribunal and, ultimately, be in even more danger."

"It wouldn't even work if you took control of the Tribunal," Randa said. "I haven't been turned that long, but I know that the vampires would band together against a common enemy. Kind of like in the Middle East. The individual countries hate each other, but they all hate us more."

That made sense. Will couldn't imagine the Tribunal accepting anything that had been rammed down its throat. Even Meg Lindstrom and Edward Simmons, their greatest allies, wouldn't go for that. "So what's left? What's behind door number three?"

The colonel smiled and propped his hands on the table. "A compromise. Think of it as the Hatfields teaming up with the McCoys."

❧CHAPTER 35❧

Cage studied the faces of his scathemates in the silence following the colonel's pronouncement. Most of them looked as confused as he felt.

"The Hatfields and McCoys is an old story about two feuding families," Randa said. "Dad, don't forget these guys are older than they look. Besides me, the youngest here is Will. Aidan and Mirren have lived more than four centuries. They don't know the Hatfields and McCoys."

The colonel stared at Mirren and Aidan with what Cage recognized as fear, even though it was well camouflaged. For the first time, maybe, the colonel realized his daughter's kind were more than regular guys with fangs. Would it make a difference?

Rick Thomas looked at his daughter and nodded. "It's a hard concept to wrap my head around. But it doesn't matter. I have a half-dozen elite teams that plan and execute covert operations, which you suspected. We work mostly for the government, on jobs that never have a paper trail, but we're an autonomous group. I'm in charge, and Rob's my second."

"I joined up five years ago, right before you were killed—changed," Robbie added.

Cage could tell Randa was torn between being daughter and soldier. Part of her wanted to know why she hadn't been told the truth, but the soldier in her knew it was safer for everyone.

The Hatfields and McCoys, working together. Cage had judged a lot of military leaders over his life. If anyone could pull this off, it would be Aidan, Mirren, and the colonel.

"So how would this work?" Aidan leaned back in his chair, his pale-blue eyes fixed on Rick.

"Your Tribunal agrees to work with me to help establish a joint operations team. Let's call it Omega Force—part human, part vampire. It would be jointly run by me and by your Vampire Tribunal or their representative, assuming you can get their support. Robbie and I had already been thinking about putting an elite team together to handle domestic terrorism threats; they're growing daily. A human-vampire team would be perfect to do that kind of operation."

Mirren finally couldn't stand it any longer and rose to prop himself against the wall. He'd be pacing within fifteen minutes; Cage would bet on it. "What would Omega Force do, and how many humans would you have to involve?" Mirren asked.

"Only the team members would have to know about you. The beauty of it is that my government contacts, mostly army and CIA guys, honestly don't want to know how I get the jobs done they send my way. That way they can have squeaky-clean hands if a mission goes south. I'd say ten people maximum, including Rob and me."

Cage listened as the colonel laid out his ideas, and the others contributed suggestions. Gradually, he could see from the animation on everyone's faces that the idea was taking hold.

He liked it too. The vampires on Omega Force could help with intelligence operations and carry out dangerous night-time missions where their speed, strength, night vision, and invulnerability to injury could save the lives of human team members. Domestic threats from terrorist cells, from religious extremists, from average psychopaths—those cases were exploding as more crazy people had Internet access to things like bomb-building instructions, weapons, and chemical agents. This kind of force could be just as effective in England as in the US. He only saw one drawback.

"I see the benefit to your team, Colonel." Cage stared at the notes he'd been making. "But I can tell you from working with the Tribunal in the past, their question will be what's in it for them? And how does it fix our problem here in Penton?"

The colonel nodded. "We were talking about that this afternoon. What would your Tribunal value the most?"

Cage thought they'd like nothing better than world domination and unlimited power, but that probably didn't fall within the colonel's power to provide.

"A possible solution to the pandemic vaccine problem," Aidan finally said. "Our people are starving, and it will be a good nineteen or twenty years before the children born after the vaccine can be tested to see if the blood abnormality is gone. If we could find relief to the feeding issue, and it could be made to look like the Tribunal came up with the solution, they'd go for it."

That was a tall order, but Aidan was right. Even Cage's mentor worried about the criticism the Tribunal was taking as the years dragged on without any answers and vampires growing hungrier.

"Well, we can't provide you with a human food supply, obviously." The colonel spoke slowly, thinking as he paced. "But can you only feed from a living source?"

Aidan and Mirren exchanged frowns. "As opposed to what?" Cage asked.

"What if we set up a new company, a blood bank that handled only unvaccinated blood? Could the vampires feed from a source like that?"

Aidan nodded. "It could work. A lot of vampires wouldn't like it, but then again, if they get hungry enough, and the Tribunal buys into it, they might have no choice. My mate, Krys, didn't get the vaccine because she was allergic to one of the common ingredients. Maybe that's the public rationale for setting up something like that. We'd need a human to oversee it during daylight hours, but if the Tribunal could have a codirector or something that would give them an equal hand in running it, they might accept it."

The potential for abuse was great, and how many unvaccinated people would contribute was an issue that would have to be addressed, but it had possibilities.

Hope bloomed in Cage's gut. By God, this could work. "If I might ask a question?"

The colonel turned to him and nodded. "You're wondering how this would impact vampires outside the United States, I'm guessing, Mr. Reynolds?"

The guy was sharp; Cage had to give him that. "I think this arrangement would greatly interest Edward Simmons, the UK representative on the Tribunal. If I were able to participate in your Omega Force and we are successful, I could see him finding someone from MI6 and setting up a similar arrangement."

Aidan stared into space as he clicked the end of a ballpoint pen in and out, in and out. "I think the Tribunal's US delegate, Meg Lindstrom, would go for it as well, especially if we can figure out a fair distribution system for the blood supply. The other nations might be a harder sell. What's in it for Frank Greisser, for example? He's head of the Tribunal and represents the European Union."

They all pondered that for a while. "Offer them help," Will said. "Describe Omega Force as a pilot project. If it works in the US, then we provide the model and the support to set up teams in their countries. It will make the Tribunal look as if they're doing something proactive to help their starving people instead of talking about things like systemizing human trafficking."

Rick Thomas frowned. "They're seriously discussing that?"

"They're a bunch of asswipes," Mirren said.

Aidan smiled. "They are, it's true. They're also out of ideas. We'd hoped if Penton worked—and it was working before Matthias came after us—the Tribunal might use it as a model for surviving the crisis. But finding unvaccinated feeders is still a problem. This gives the Tribunal something that makes them look like geniuses."

Randa cleared her throat. "This all sounds good, but one thing hasn't been mentioned. What happens to Penton? What happens to Matthias sitting up there in the ruins of our clinic, in the ruins of our town, waiting to kill us all?"

The silence that followed her questions lingered a good thirty or forty seconds. Cage tipped his chair back and thought about it. He wanted Melissa to get her life back, as near as she could, and that meant rebuilding Penton into a safe place.

His heart sped up, and he let his front chair legs hit the floor with a thud. Damn it, that was the answer.

"Melissa," he said. "Melissa and Glory can talk to the Tribunal. And Krys. They've all been victims of Matthias's vendetta. If they go with Aidan to talk to the Tribunal—behind Matthias's back, of course—it will help sway them to our side. Between this potential solution and the testimonies, we might not destroy Matthias, but the Tribunal can keep him away from us."

Mirren flopped back in his chair and grinned at Cage. He was such a sourpuss that when he did grin, it was sort of unsettling. "And make the pardon of all our so-called crimes a condition of the whole deal. This could be fucking brilliant."

The colonel grinned, and his happy face also was kind of unsettling.

"Let's make plans, then," Aidan said. "I'll slip out to Atlanta with Krys, Glory, and Mel and set up a meeting with whatever Tribunal members I can. If Omega's been compromised, getting out could be a challenge, but we don't have any choice. Mirren, you should probably come as well; they need to see you looking all happy and cooperative."

He gave Mirren his stubborn, authoritative look, and the big man shrugged. "Whatever."

"I'll start calling my team," Rick said. "Robbie, make a list of the guys you think are best suited to learning about vampires and taking on a new kind of project. We'll want them in place here in Penton within forty-eight hours. Mr. Reynolds, can you and Randa and Will work with my team on the proper way to kill a vampire?"

Bloody hell. The enormity of what they were doing hit Cage like a semi to the forehead. They'd have to share tactics, however. No way around it. This was going to require a lot of trust on both sides and, especially in the beginning, a lot of blind faith. "I will," he said. He just hoped these new humans, whoever they were, didn't want to practice on him.

Randa nodded. "Me too."

When Will didn't answer, everyone turned to look at him. "I think there's something else I need to be doing while all these negotiations and meetings take place." He lifted his gaze to Aidan's, and some unspoken words seem to pass between them.

Randa reached over and touched Will's arm, her expression asking the question for all of them. Cage had wondered how much their relationship had progressed, and the possessiveness of that touch, and the way they looked at each other, told him everything. They might not even realize it themselves yet, but another Penton lieutenant was about to go off the market of eligible bachelors.

Aidan nodded. "I don't like it, Will. Not at all. But you're right."

"Right about what?" Randa asked, looking around the table, looking fierce and ready to kick some butt. "What is it Will needs to do?"

"We need to keep Matthias busy so Aidan and the others can get out of here safely to meet with the Tribunal. It also might prevent him from taking another strike at Omega while we get everything in place."

Will spoke to everyone, but he looked only at Randa.

"I'm going to give my father something he really, really wants. Me."

☙ CHAPTER 36 ❧

"You really think you need to pack a bag to take with you into martyrdom?" Randa slammed the door into the hallway after following Will into their room. The sharp crack of the door settling into its frame sapped her anger and filled her instead with cold fear.

Will set down the small bag into which he'd thrown a few clothes. "I have to do this, Ran. I'm the only one who can keep Matthias occupied and away from Omega long enough for your dad and Aidan to do what they need to do."

He tried to slide his arms around her waist and pull her to him, but he wasn't going to charm his way out of this one.

"Will, you don't have to prove anything. You took Shelton out. Your dad is going to lose his power over us. We can handle anything he tries to do to us in the next forty-eight hours while my dad and Aidan get everything set up."

"I know that, but—"

"I'm not finished." She shoved both hands against his chest, causing him to take a couple of steps back to keep his balance.

"We can't assume they're going to be successful. What if the negotiations don't work? What if none of Dad's men agree to it and we have to go out and try to erase all their memories—if we get to them before word about vampires starts spreading? What if the Tribunal can't get enough support? What if they see it as a threat and don't agree to it? Then you're stuck with your father and I couldn't..."

He ignored her protests and tugged her against him, his arms warm, his hands rubbing her back like one would comfort a frightened child. "You couldn't what?"

She couldn't stand it, that's what. She couldn't live in Penton without him. She couldn't stand to think of Matthias touching him, belittling him, maybe rebreaking the pieces of his heart he'd finally started mending.

"I couldn't stand breaking in a new partner." The hard words cleared her mind. What was she doing, acting like a helpless little woman begging her soldier not to go to war? Her heart settled back into its normal vampire rhythm, and she knew she'd never let him go into this alone. He'd once knocked her out to keep her from following him on a job. This time she'd play it differently.

"You'd manage. Besides, you're not getting rid of me that easily." He cupped her face in his hands and leaned down to kiss her, his tongue mimicking the rhythm of what they didn't have time for. He was pressed hard against her, and she slipped her hand down to stroke him.

He groaned. "I can't believe you're sending me off to meet my father with a hard-on."

She squeezed him hard enough to hurt and got a satisfying *oof* in response. "That's to remind you what you're leaving behind."

"Just for a while. Promise." He kissed her again, then leaned over and picked up his leather bag. He looked back at her as he opened the door into the hallway. "Stay safe."

"You too." She'd see him again before he imagined it, but first, she had some more good-byes.

After Will disappeared up the ladder of the Omega exit, Randa walked down the hallway to the common room, where a dozen people, vampire and human, sat scattered around the chairs, watching Hannah play with the bloodhound.

She looked up when Randa approached. "Thank you for bringing Barnabas to me." The child vampire had never looked more human—and hadn't looked this happy in a while. In fact, Randa realized, as she glanced around the common room, almost everyone wore a smile, even Cage.

"I can't believe we never thought about getting a dog." She settled into the chair next to him and watched for a while, wondering if he was house-trained. Too late to worry about that now. "Why Barnabas?"

Cage grinned. "She's been watching *Dark Shadows* DVDs on Will's laptop."

The Penton people's endless fascination with pop culture's interpretations of vampires had always amused her. Before Matthias had ruined everything, the *Twilight* movies had been playing back-to-back for over a month at the little walk-in theater downtown. She'd gone a couple of times and laughed as people quoted lines of dialogue with the movie and howled at the glittering vampires. It was like the vampire version of humans doing Saturday midnight viewings of *The Rocky Horror Picture Show*.

The thought of Matthias, however, reminded her of why she was here. "Cage, I have to tell you something, but you can't breathe a word to Aidan or Mirren or my dad. I'll be having this same conversation with Robbie."

He settled moss-green eyes on her, such an unusual color, almost like a dark jade. "When are you going?"

How had he known? "Going where?"

"Don't be coy, and don't look so surprised. I figured once you got used to the idea of Will turning himself in to distract his father, you wouldn't stop him—you'd follow him."

Hmph. Sometimes Cage was too damn smart. "You won't tell?"

"Nope. It's a good idea." He watched Hannah holding up Barnabas's long, floppy ears like they were pigtails. "But be careful and don't underestimate Will. He's proven that he's a survivor."

"I'm not underestimating Will. I just don't want to underestimate Matthias." Randa looked at her watch. "Will can scent me following him if I go too soon. I'll see the others off, then try to find what Matthias has done with him before dawn. I might have to spend daysleep somewhere else, though."

She took a deep breath and asked the question no one had verbalized. "Do you think Matthias will kill him?" She thought he might, if Will provoked him enough. Not fast, though. He'd try to break him first. He'd try to break him *again*.

"I don't think so, unless Will's mouth gets the better of him and he pushes too hard. My guess is that Matthias will lock him in the suite beneath the clinic where he had Melissa." Cage lowered his voice as Mirren and Aidan walked past, deep in conversation.

"I'd try to access it from Aidan's greenhouse. There was a cave-in, but the exit room is clear, and you might be able to tunnel through it. You could even spend your daysleep in the exit room there. Just be careful. Matthias is staying across the street, and they know about that tunnel. But you'd never be able to get at Will from the clinic side. Why don't you take Robbie with you?"

"You're going to need him here." Randa had thought about taking Robbie, but she didn't know if the guys on the future Omega Force, whoever they were, would accept the existence of vampires, much less training with Cage. Robbie needed to be there to smooth the way.

This had to be a solo mission for her.

"Anything else I need to know?"

Cage watched Hannah a few minutes without responding, but finally answered. "I think when I'm not working with your brother and his team, I'll get a crew to start excavating a path through the exit room under the church. I don't think they're watching it anymore. If you guys can't get away through the greenhouse, go there."

He thought a few minutes longer. "One more thing."

Randa saw her father and brother heading toward them and knew it had to be quick. "What?"

"Look for a human kid named Evan who's locked in the clinic if you get a chance—Shelton's latest victim. And if you get a chance to take Matthias out without risking yourself or Will, do it."

≈CHAPTER 37≈

Matthias poured a glass of scotch and set it atop the clinic office desk, rubbed his temples, and focused again on contacting Shelton mentally. The lazy sod was either out of range or ignoring him, and neither of those was going to win him his little boy back.

Maybe he'd gone too far with the beatings, but Shelton had been getting obsessed with his little blood-junkie feeder and unfocused on his business—namely, doing whatever Matthias wanted.

Shelton's last fuckup had been dropping the ball on the dog situation, and Matthias couldn't let it pass unpunished. All he'd been asked to do was make sure Billy Joe Mickler and his bloodhound arrived, direct them to the area where one of his patrollers had scented Cage Reynolds, and then return to Penton. Instead, he'd never come back, and after making some phone calls, Matthias learned Mickler and his dog were both missing. Had Shelton been killed?

Matthias pushed up the sleeves of his sweater and rubbed his eyes. He'd never paid much attention to his blood bonds with his people, but he couldn't sense the bond with Shelton. Had it recently disappeared? Or had it never been strong enough to detect? No answers, but if he found out the weasel was ignoring him, a beating would be the least of his worries.

There was one good piece of news, though. Those two fanged morons he'd put on patrol duty near the poisoned spring had run into some of Murphy's scathe. One of them had been killed, but the other had made it back to Matthias.

William was one of the vampires, plus a woman and two humans. When Will had shown up, the dog had found a bloody patch of ground and what was probably the missing Billy Joe Mickler's bloodhound.

He finished the scotch, pulled his pistol out of the desk drawer, and headed out of the clinic. It looked as if the only way things would get done around this fucking place was if he did everything himself. If he saw Shelton, he'd shoot him.

What a godforsaken shithole this whole town had turned out to be. A fine, cold mist wet his face as he walked to his car, and he pulled his jacket around him more tightly. Buying this little mill town had been a genius move on Murphy's part. No vampire in his right mind would want to live here. Yet they had, hadn't they? And some of them were still loyal enough to Murphy to follow him into some underground pit.

Including William.

Matthias tried to figure out where he'd misjudged his son, at what point he'd miscalculated what it would take to break him without driving him away. Maybe it was the summer he'd sent the boy to live with Shelton. After he'd let William return to New York, he'd been docile, even skittish. He'd followed orders, kept his smart mouth shut, and seemed to be becoming exactly the follower Matthias had needed him to be. A month later, with no warning, he'd disappeared and had proven very adept at eluding his father.

Will had dropped off the map for more than two decades before showing up as one of Murphy's acolytes.

Yes, Matthias was almost sure the summer with Shelton had been the thing that pushed William over the edge, again proving what a shortsighted, weak man his own son had become. Well, he'd find him again, and he'd break him once and for all. And if he couldn't break William, he'd kill him. This game between them had gone on long enough.

He pulled two more projectile grenades and slipped them into his pocket. First, he had to find the hole and figure out a way to extract William. Then he'd blast the whole thing shut and cut off their water supply altogether. Murphy and his friends could live under there until they drained their humans and the humans died of dehydration. Then Murphy and all his pals would starve into dried husks, neither alive nor dead—all together forever in their little hole with their dead fams.

Long live Penton.

Matthias cranked his car and drove out of town, heading east. He watched the odometer until he'd reached eight miles out, then parked and exited the car. This spot was near the Alabama-Georgia state line, and there was an automotive plant not far from here. So he began walking a pattern of circles, back and forth, using the full moon—dim due to the heavy mist—as a guidepost.

He stilled at the sound of footsteps in the leaves a few hundred yards ahead of him. He scented the air. Humans? Two of them, if he was reading the situation right. Why the hell would humans be traipsing around in the woods at midnight in this weather?

He had the sensory advantage on them. To himself—and only himself—he'd admit he wasn't the strongest master vampire. He'd never honed the skills to scent the way some masters could, nor was he strong at mental communication. But he was a master, nonetheless. He could roll human minds and wipe memories easily enough.

Which might or might not be necessary. Matthias slipped behind the trunk of a massive oak and watched the humans approach. Two men—one middle-aged, the other younger. Both had that erect, purposeful walk that hinted at a military background. Maybe some military unit was on maneuvers nearby, or one of those crazy survivalist groups Matthias had heard about. The last thing he wanted to deal with on this cold, wet, miserable night was a horde of walking human testosterone.

He stayed in his spot and was relieved to see the men continue eastward in the direction of the automotive factory. He waited to see if any more arrived. When they didn't, he moved on toward the clearing they'd passed through.

The smell of blood was strong here, but it was vampire blood, not human. Matthias knelt and scanned the carpet of wet leaves.

A sound to his south caught his attention, and he rose to follow it. Deeper into the woods, under a tree canopy so dense the mist didn't reach him, he saw a flash of color through the trees and scented vampire.

And it wasn't one bonded to him. Had his luck finally changed?

Moving with stealth, Matthias edged from pine to oak to pine, keeping a tree trunk between him and his prey.

The sense of movement stopped, and he knew the vampire had scented him as well. He stepped into the open and cocked his pistol.

"Whoever's there, show yourself."

A flash of light clothing moved among the dense brush. Matthias's heart stopped at the sight of his only son stepping into the clearing.

❧CHAPTER 38❧

Aidan tossed his cell phone on the dining room table of the small safe house he maintained in an unassuming subdivision an hour north of Atlanta. He'd finally gotten a call from Rob, with a mixed bag of news.

The good: After a few hours of disbelief and posturing, the human members of their team had finally accepted that not only did vampires exist, but they had a lot of advantages over humans and might help them do their jobs better. "It was Hannah who convinced them," Rob had said. "She sat there playing with that freaking bloodhound, looked up at Max Jeffries—the biggest guy I ever saw until I met Mirren Kincaid—and asked if she could feed from him. He'd never had the vaccine and still didn't believe, so he told her to knock herself out. So she did, and he was convinced."

The bad: No one had heard from Will. Forty-eight hours had passed since he walked into the woods with the plan of turning himself over to Matthias. On the positive side, there had been no other sign of Matthias around the Omega entrance. Whatever was happening with Will, he'd been able to keep Matthias occupied.

The ugly, and Rob was not happy about it: Randa had followed Will, and nobody had heard from her, either.

"What happened?" Krys settled next to Aidan on the sofa and wrapped an arm around his shoulders. As guilty as it made him feel, sitting here in a normal house with his mate felt nice. Omega was as comfortable as they could make it, but it was still a steel-lined hole in the ground. It was a bloody miracle no one had gone stir-crazy yet.

"Everything's going well with the new team, but there's been no word from Will. And Randa went after him."

"Aw, fuck." Mirren walked in from the kitchen with a glass of whiskey. Glory was lying down on a second sofa next to Melissa, still half-sick from the water contamination and tired from having to feed four vampires, even though they'd fed sparingly. They hadn't wanted to risk bringing anyone else out of Omega in case the Tribunal meeting about to take place turned ugly and the new Omega Force had to fight Matthias, after all. That was the whole point of training them before the Tribunal had agreed to it.

After talking to Meg Lindstrom and Edward Simmons, they'd insisted on coming to Atlanta to meet with the Penton foursome in person and were bringing with them the Tribunal members from Canada, Australia, and Mexico, as well as Tribunal director Frank Greisser.

It was risky. Mirren had argued against it, but Aidan was out of options. They had to make a stand now and try to reach an agreement, or they had to fight Matthias, break up the scathe, and scatter—if it wasn't already too late.

"They're here, in a fucking limousine. That's a great way not to draw attention to yourself." Mirren stood at the window, looking out on the street.

Aidan kissed Krys, nodded at Glory and Melissa, and went to the door. "Mirren, I swear to God if you do anything to piss them off, I will use that bloody sword of yours on some body part Glory would really miss."

Mirren grumbled something Aidan couldn't make out, but he figured it could be shortened into two one-syllable words. His point had been made, however. Mirren walked to the far wall and propped against it in his favorite stance, arms crossed over his chest. Glory moved to sit beside Krys and Melissa.

Aidan opened the door and stepped aside as the six vampires—half of the Tribunal and the most powerful members—filed in. They took all the available seats and fidgeted in the awkward silence.

Edward Simmons stood up, a tall, thin man with straw-colored hair cropped short, an accent straight out of London's toniest suburbs, and an air of restless energy. "I insisted on this meeting, so I'll get it underway, shall I?" He didn't wait for an answer.

"We have two issues at play here. First is the future of the Penton scathe that is pledged to Aidan Murphy, the charges against him and Mirren Kincaid, and the allegations they're bringing against Matthias Ludlam."

Frank Greisser shoved a shock of blond curls off his forehead. "Edward, I think—"

"Please, may I finish?"

Frank pressed his lips together and gave a nod. Every vampire in the room felt his flare of disapproving energy, and Aidan wondered, not for the first time, exactly how old he was.

Edward ignored it. "The second issue is a proposal Aidan Murphy has brought forth on behalf of his scathe and an American private security firm that does highly classified military missions for the government. It has the potential to help the Tribunal solidify its position among our vampires and provide a means of weathering the postpandemic crisis."

Meg Lindstrom had been a middle-aged college professor when she was turned vampire by a colleague. Her hair was the color of iron, and her backbone was just as strong. "I believe we need to settle the first matter before moving to the second."

She turned to Frank. "As this is our first chance to hear Aidan Murphy's side of the story, I propose we do that."

The Austrian had long been an ally of Matthias's, and Aidan could see him trying to figure out a way around this while still looking objective.

"We have processes in place to try criminals, and I believe we should use them." His German accent clipped off the words, but his English was perfect. "I see no reason to have this farce of a meeting and now regret that Edward talked me into it."

Aidan looked at Edward—should he go ahead and speak? But the Englishman shook his head slightly.

"Frank, here are some hard truths for you to ponder as you think of ways to defend your old friend Matthias," Edward said. "First, the Tribunal is divided. I did not ask Russia, China, or Japan because their political organizations are different. Their votes, however, are with us. If the Tribunal falls, there is no leadership and our world will slide further into chaos.

"Second, our people are losing faith in us as their leaders. If we don't reach some forward-thinking solution to this postpandemic crisis, the Tribunal will fall.

"Finally, I have heard the charges against Matthias Ludlam, and I have heard the explanations of why our so-called Penton criminals committed their crimes. Let me assure you that you do not want to side with Matthias going forward."

The implied threat took root. Frank blinked twice. Then his shoulders sagged inside their navy sweater. "Aidan, tell us your side."

Showtime. Aidan looked at Krys, walked to the center of the circle, and began to talk.

Matthias had commuted Owen Murphy's death sentence in exchange for killing Aidan, and Aidan was forced to kill his brother in self-defense. During the struggle, Owen had injured his mate, Krys, and he could only save her by turning her vampire.

"It was against vampire law, I now realize, as was keeping her with us in the first place," he said. "But I swear the only thing I thought at the time was that this amazing woman who'd never hurt anyone had gotten caught in our shit. She didn't deserve to die for it."

Krys told her account of being taken by Owen, who'd implied he was brought there to kill Aidan in order to save his own life.

Glory swayed a little when she stood, and Mirren supported her while she told of Matthias kidnapping her from her job at a convenience store in North Atlanta. Of his addicting her to drugs, then giving her to Mirren to feed from. How Mirren saved her, how Will had saved both of them.

She told of how she'd been kidnapped again by Tribunal member Lorenzo Caias, to use her against Matthias. How Mirren had killed Renz in her defense.

Melissa talked about how Matthias had come into Penton with bombs and killed human and vampire alike without discrimination. How he'd ordered her neck broken, then secreted her away and turned her vampire, torturing her for information.

"And he did these things in the name of the Vampire Tribunal," Aidan said into the room that had become still and alien. None of the vampires were playing human. No fidgeting. No rustle of clothing or coughs or head scratching. Just stillness and, now that he'd finished, silence.

All eyes were on Frank Greisser. He locked his dark-blue eyes onto Aidan's pale-blue ones, and Aidan thought he was weighing him, measuring the truth of his words, probing at his mind. Aidan opened his will to the older vampire. He had nothing more to hide. He'd made mistakes; he'd made bad choices. But he'd never betrayed the Tribunal or worked against them except in self-defense.

Finally, Frank broke eye contact. "He tells the truth."

"Then might I suggest that we vote to remove Matthias Ludlam from the Tribunal and bring charges against him for kidnapping, murder for hire, and abuse of office?" Meg rose from her seat. "I'm sure we can add to those charges later. I'd also like to vote that all charges against Aidan Murphy and Mirren Kincaid be dropped. We have the proxy votes of three members who are not here, which gives us the majority, Frank."

The Austrian nodded. Aidan suspected he'd decided that defending Matthias Ludlam might lead to his own downfall. Thank God politicians were, human and vampire alike, mostly concerned with their own preservation. "Are Krys, Glory, and Melissa willing to testify to Matthias's actions?"

If Mirren's eyes had lasers attached, they'd have burned a hole in Frank Greisser's forehead by now, but he didn't voice an objection.

"We will," Krys said.

"But only if Mirren and I are allowed to accompany them and we receive your guarantee of their safety, before these witnesses." Aidan had finally joined Mirren on the don't-trust-the-bureaucrats train.

"Agreed." Frank settled back in his chair. He might as well not get too comfortable. Aidan hadn't even mentioned the humans yet.

"All right then," Edward said. "Let's talk about Omega Force."

Four hours later, the Tribunal partnership with Colonel Thomas had been approved, pending a meeting between the colonel and key Tribunal members. The meeting would be tomorrow after dusk, at Omega. They just needed word from the colonel that his people were in place.

Mirren had already taken Glory down to one of the two rooms walled off in the basement as lighttight daysleep spaces, and Aidan relaxed with Krys.

"The phone's not going to ring just because you keep staring at it." Krys elbowed him in the side and laughed as he trapped her beneath him on the sofa. He could think of a way to get his mind off the damned phone. He kissed her with real hope in his heart that, for the first time in months, they could have a future away from death and fear.

Krys tugged his shirttail out and slid her hands underneath, scraping nails across his bare back. She smiled up at him, dark-brown eyes dancing. "Think Mirren and Glory and Mel can hear us?"

Aidan jerked the shirt over his head and threw it on the floor. "Do I care?"

When the phone finally rang, she'd distracted him enough that it took him two rings to answer. "It's him." He pressed the Talk button. "Murphy."

The colonel's voice was buoyant. "I'm on my way back to Penton to welcome the new recruits to Omega Force. They're all in place and a business plan for the blood bank is in progress— we just have some legalities to handle. Do I have the all clear from my new partners?"

Aidan smiled at Krys. "You do."

"Good. Let's go back to Penton and break the news to Mr. Matthias Ludlam."

❧CHAPTER 39❧

Cage grinned as Rob Thomas chewed Max Jeffries a new asshole. Max had five or six inches on him, and probably fifty pounds of muscle, but he stood with his eyes on the ground and a lot of "yes, sirs" coming out of his mouth.

Cage climbed to his feet—make that his bare feet, to match his bare chest. He wore combat pants, but nothing more, because he'd wanted to make some points to his new teammates. They'd cleared all the furniture from the big common room except for some chairs around the perimeter so they could teach each other new moves.

Among the onlookers was Melissa, minus Mark. Cage had seen them briefly before and after daysleep, but he hadn't had a chance to be alone with her since their first night back. No, make that he had avoided any chance to be alone with her. If she and Mark didn't make it, it would not be because Cage Reynolds had gotten in the way.

He felt the weight of her gaze on him, and they looked at each other briefly as he went to stand next to Max. She almost made him light-headed—she'd lost the haunted, starved look she'd had in the clinic suite. Her cheeks had a little color, and her eyes were bright and clear. God, she was beautiful. And married. And unavailable.

He forced his focus back on the vampire at hand. "Max, look at me." Jeffries hadn't taken the news well that vampires were more resilient than humans, so Cage had made himself the guinea pig.

"Do your worst, as long as you stay away from the heart and the brain," he'd said, standing still as Jeffries punched the hell out of his gut, cracked two ribs with a roundhouse kick from his steel-toed combat boots, and finally fell only after the second stab wound with a nice, shiny steel blade.

He'd told Robbie not to interfere, and he hadn't.

The stab wounds were scabbed and would take another hour to heal. The ribs were sore but mended. The bruises were lightening.

Max glanced at Cage, then did a double take. His face flushed a dark shade of red as his embarrassment brought blood close to the surface. It made Cage hungry, although Max certainly wasn't his type. He'd been feeding Hannah, however, which was just strange.

"Shit, those bruises are fading so fast I can see it happening." Max watched, his face a study in both fascination and horror. "I can see what you bring to the team. Now I'm not sure what you need us for, besides blood."

Cage decided to throw him a bone. Max had had a hard couple of days. "For one thing, we can't move about in daylight, which limits what kind of interaction we can have in terms of setup. If we need to infiltrate a company or a terrorist cell that meets during daylight hours, the vampires would be useless. If I'm pretending to be a recruit in a cult of religious extremists, how do I explain that I have to be in a room without lights, unconscious, from dawn until dusk?"

Max looked relieved. "Well, yeah, I can see that. And you can't conduct business over dinner."

"Well, we can, but often our business partner *is* dinner."

Robbie's laughter filled the room, and Max joined in after a minute. Cage was starting to like these guys.

"The big dogs are back," Robbie muttered, and Cage turned to see Mirren striding down the hall, followed by—*holy shit*—Frank Greisser. Talk about an odd couple. And Mirren looked...well, OK, not exactly pleased. But he wasn't scowling as much as usual.

There was a whole freaking parade of vampires headed for the conference room, and Cage suddenly wished like hell he were wearing clothes.

Edward Simmons broke from the parade and came over to clap him on the shoulder. "Cage, glad to see you looking so"—he looked at his mussed hair, bare feet, and scabbed-over knife cuts—"active."

Cage found himself uncharacteristically at a loss for words, but Robbie stepped in. "Robert Thomas," he said, shaking Edward's hand. "My guys are working with Cage and some of the others to form Omega Force."

"Excellent." Edward gestured toward the conference room. "Perhaps both of you will join us? We're going to discuss your first mission. Oh, but Cage..."

Right. "I'll get dressed and be right in."

He shot a dark look at a snickering Max on his way past; a smile from Melissa cheered him. But, oh, it shouldn't.

By the time Cage returned to the crowded conference room, the colonel had arrived, wearing fatigues. It took him less than thirty seconds to see who *wasn't* there.

"Where's my daughter?" He zeroed in on Rob. "Where's Randa?"

Damn. Well, Cage owed Robbie a save. "Sir, she slipped out two nights ago, following Will Ludlam. He turned himself over to Matthias to keep him occupied so we could get in and out of Omega as needed."

The colonel's glare was as intimidating as Mirren's, but he shifted it back to his son. "And you let her go?"

Robbie shrugged. "Dad, have you ever been able to talk Randa out of anything once she set her mind to it? The woman is as stubborn as...Well, she's as stubborn as you are. Plus, she and Will are partners, and partners back each other up."

The colonel had obviously drilled that lesson into his kids and didn't appear to enjoy having it thrown back at him. He nodded and turned to the crowd of vampires watching him closely. If it made him nervous, he didn't show it. Hell, it made Cage nervous, and he knew most of them.

"Gentlemen, and Ms. Lindstrom, I assume, I'm here on behalf of Thomas Securities to officially offer you a partnership. I propose forming a highly skilled military unit to neutralize threats of domestic terrorism in the United States and its territories. You will supply operatives for our missions on a combined vampire-human team to be known as Omega Force. In return, we will pay your operatives a salary comparable to our human team members. Our clients respect our privacy, and your existence would never be compromised."

A murmur of approval washed around the room, and Cage couldn't help feeling proud that Edward had taken the lead on this. They'd make Omega Force work, and they'd be able to take it to the UK within six months. He felt certain of it.

"What about the provision of blood?" Meg asked.

The colonel nodded. "As we speak, the wheels are in motion to set up a blood bank of unvaccinated blood to which your people will have access. We will purchase from existing blood banks and begin a recruitment process for donors. As it turns out, a number of humans were allergic to the vaccine and might benefit from unvaccinated blood themselves. It gives us a logical cover."

Cage spoke up, asking a question he, Robbie, Max, and the rest of the new team had been wondering about. "What type of missions do you foresee?"

The colonel talked about domestic terrorism and how it was on the rise. "Even disturbed high school kids have access to bomb-making instructions," he said. "We need people to infiltrate online groups, monitor and even infiltrate extremist groups both foreign and domestic, and be ready to act when we receive word from our government clients that a threat has become real."

Rick Thomas looked at Aidan, who spoke for the first time, a smile playing at the edges of his mouth. "But your first mission will be to take Matthias Ludlam, former head of the Tribunal's Justice Council, into custody."

Cage grinned. "That will be a pleasure."

☙CHAPTER 40☙

For the second night—or was it the third?—Will awoke on the cold concrete floor of a storage room off the partially collapsed corridor of the clinic suites.

Good old Dad. Matthias was nothing if not consistent. Starvation, intimidation, and incarceration. His favorite methods of persuasion.

Will struggled to sit up, his hands and ankles wrapped in silver chains. He studied the dozens of tiny bite marks on his bare chest, his legs, even...He stared at his groin in horror. Matthias had released fucking rats into the room just before the second daysleep. Two of the goddamned things had been chewing on his stomach when he awoke and scared them off. He'd heal during his long, solitary night when he could scare them away, and when dawn came again, they'd feast.

Just in case he didn't have enough Matthias-induced nightmares to relive during his downtime.

Almost as bad as the rats—not quite, but almost—was the isolation. He wondered how Randa and Cage were doing with the new team. Whether the puffed-up peacocks on the Tribunal would see this opportunity for what it was. Whether they'd be willing to band together and move against Matthias.

A key rattled in the lock, and a stream of light blinded Will as it poured through the opening door. The dim fluorescent lantern that had been placed in the otherwise-empty room was no match for the flashlight shining right at his eyeballs.

Two figures were silhouetted in the doorway, one tall, one short. Will inhaled. Both vampire. Both bonded to Matthias. Awesome.

"Put on some clothes. Your father wants to see you upstairs."

Man, Matthias had picked some winners. "My hands are tied behind my back, and my ankles are chained together. You got special pants for that?"

"Shit." Mutt handed the flashlight to Jeff and felt in his pockets, finally fishing out a key. He flinched at the sight of a rat running along the far wall, and Will knew how he felt. "Better do a good job, or you too can spend your daysleep naked and being chewed on by rodents. Can't recommend it highly enough."

"You're a major smart-ass, you know that?" The chain on his ankles loosened, and Will shook his legs free, wincing at the stiffness in his left leg from being in the same position for however long he'd been here. That leg would probably never be the same despite Dr. Slayer's best efforts. On the bright side, he might not live long enough to be bothered by it.

"So I've been told. I'm just misunderstood." Will grunted as Mutt jerked him to his feet and removed the cuffs. Will rubbed his raw wrists and bent over to pick up the pants. Looked like he'd be going commando, but it was an improvement over rat bites down under.

"Where are we going, gentlemen? Dinner? A movie?"

The sound of a cocked pistol sounded incredibly loud in this empty cavern of a room. "Shut the hell up and walk," Mutt said. "We're going upstairs."

Better and better. Will stumbled a couple of times as he tried to remind his feet how to walk. What would these two clowns do if he fought them? He had no doubt he could take them. Could maybe even roll their minds, although that was questionable since they were bonded to Matthias. He hadn't been a master vampire long enough to explore his new skill set.

Instead, he walked along like a good boy. No point in making a move until he got topside. The only thing he'd accomplish by acting too soon would be to get himself thrown back in solitary confinement as a rat entree.

Actually, he should thank Matthias for the rats. Instead of being frightened or intimidated or wondering if he deserved nothing better than to be his father's eternal acolyte, he was simply and righteously pissed.

They crossed the basement level, and Will followed Jeff up the ladder into the clinic office, with Mutt and his pistol following. Matthias sat at Aidan's big desk, which pissed off Will even more.

But if he'd learned anything in the years he'd spent with Aidan, it was how to bide his time and plan his moves.

"Have a seat, William. You two wait outside." Will took the chair and faced his father across the desk. Neither of them spoke until the two guards had walked into the hallway and closed the door behind them.

Interesting. Matthias wasn't afraid to be alone with Will. If he thought his son was the same boy who'd run away in shame all those years ago, he had a surprise coming. A long-overdue surprise.

Before he could take on his father, however, Will needed to know how much time had lapsed since he'd been here. Amazing how fast the hours got muddled when one's routine was out of whack. If this was the beginning of his second full day, he needed to stall and give Aidan and the colonel time to put things in place. If this was day three, he might as well try to make a move. If negotiations for Omega Force had failed, he was as good as dead anyway.

He would really, really miss his fiery redhead.

"I hope you're in a frame of mind to cooperate now." Matthias lit a cigar and leaned back in the chair. It had developed a new squeak. "I'm not buying your insistence that you missed me. However much I'd enjoy your filial devotion, it's never been the nature of our relationship."

As much as Will wanted to be a smart-ass—and he wanted it so badly he practically had to stick a fang in his tongue to shut himself up—he had to play it smart.

"You're right." He assumed what he hoped was a contrite expression. "Here's the deal. I had hoped if I came back into your organization willingly, you'd agree to leave the rest of them alone. Let Aidan and the others get on with their lives, and I'll do whatever you want."

He looked down at his hands so his father wouldn't see the lie in his eyes.

"I don't understand how that stupid Irish farmer inspires such devotion." Matthias poured himself a glass of scotch from the decanter on the desk and took a sip.

A knock on the door made Will jump. OK, so maybe he wasn't as calm as he pretended.

"What is it? Damned fools." Matthias stood as another vampire came into the room; Will had never seen this one. How many did he have? This was the third one here at the clinic, and he was sure there were still patrols being done.

"Sir, I thought you'd want to know we found the remains of a human and a vampire near that spring in the woods. It's hard to tell because, well, some animals got to them. But I think the vampire was Shelton."

Matthias looked genuinely surprised. Once the messenger had gone, he resumed his seat. "Shelton had been with my organization for a long time, but I recently realized that I made an error in judgment when I sent you to him the summer after you were turned."

Will had been picking at the hem on the cuff of the baggy cargo pants they'd given him, but those words froze his movements. "An error in judgment?"

Matthias took a sip of his drink. "Shelton had a cruel streak, and I wanted him to bring you to heel."

Like a fucking dog. He'd been brought to heel, all right. Did Matthias regret his actions? Would it matter to Will if he did?

"Obviously, you weren't able to handle his authority. You never did handle authority well. I'm surprised you've lasted even with someone like Murphy for this long. Maybe I should ask him his secret for keeping you under control."

Nope, he didn't regret a thing, except that it hadn't completely broken him. Will raised his eyes to meet his father's, and Matthias saw the truth. "You hate me that much? Should I just kill you, then, instead of trying to make you see reason? You could have everything if you came back into my organization, but I won't promise to let criminals like Murphy and Kincaid run free. Frankly, you're not worth it."

So much for a father-son bonding moment. "Don't you want to know what happened to good old Shelton?" He was past caring what day it was or whether the Omega Force or the whole fucking US Army was on its way. "I killed him. I shoved a knife into Shelton's heart so many times I practically bathed in his blood. Funny thing is, he died trying to sell you out. Looks like you *don't* inspire such devotion."

A flash of rage crossed Matthias's face before he got it under control and replaced it with his usual maddening stone face. His cigar had gone out, and he relit it with steady hands. He didn't give a crap about Shelton, or about anyone but himself. Will knew that, but it was a nice reminder lest he think Matthias wouldn't kill him.

An interesting truth hit Will with a sudden, harsh surety. "Shelton had been bonded to you for a long time." He reasoned it out as he went. "You should have known if he was in trouble. If he was dead, you should have felt that bond disappear."

Matthias stared at him. "Aidan Murphy and Mirren Kincaid have been telling you tall tales about master-vampire skills?"

Will smiled and struck at his father with his mind. They weren't blood-bonded, but his father was his maker and therefore had genetic ties. It might work, and it might not. *You are afraid of me, you little weasel. You're afraid of me, and you'll do whatever I tell you.*

Matthias's face grew slack, his eyes glazed. He gripped the scotch glass so tightly that it crushed beneath his fingers, the clear shards cutting into his skin and drawing bright welts of blood. The pain of it was enough to snap him out of his trance, and his eyes grew wide.

"How did you...You can't be a master vampire. You can't even read a fucking menu."

"I can do better than that." Will smiled, feeling weightless enough to float as the burden of decades of feeling inferior lifted. "I can read you, Dad."

Another knock on the door broke the strained quiet that followed. "What?" Matthias's voice revealed his rage. He was not a happy man. How would finding out his son was a stronger vampire than him change his plans?

Will suspected he'd just gone from potential acolyte to enemy number one.

"We just found this one poking around that greenhouse up on the circle." The same messenger from before shoved a woman into the room, and Will didn't need to see her face to recognize her. The red hair was enough.

The stakes had just been raised.

❧CHAPTER 41❧

A t least Randa had taken two of them out before the third one wrapped a silver chain around her neck and cut off her ability to breathe.

She'd taken Cage's advice, using the exit room beneath Aidan's greenhouse for her daysleeps and spending the rest of the time trying to tunnel through the rubble into the subbasement hallway.

Nice idea, but Cage had greatly underestimated how thick that wall of debris was. If Randa dug for a month, she wasn't sure she'd be able to get through it. So she'd finally given up and decided to scout around town. When she climbed the stairs and stuck her head out into the greenhouse, three vampires on patrol were waiting.

Now here she was on the floor, and she'd bet the shiny pair of lace-ups visible underneath the desk belonged to Matthias himself.

Randa struggled to her feet, and her world dropped away at the sight of Will in a pair of loose black cargo pants, small healing marks all over his body, horror in his expression. Not exactly the dramatic rescue she'd envisioned.

"How interesting." Matthias stood and walked around the desk.

He wasn't that much taller than Randa, maybe five nine, several inches shorter than Will, and she looked to find some trace of Will in him, much as he said he'd done upon meeting her father. Matthias was very polished, even sophisticated. They had the same color eyes, only while Will's were expressive—soft when he made love to her, sweet when he teased, filled with dancing fire when he was excited—his father's were cold, hard, and calculating.

"I remember you from the day of the takeover." Matthias circled her, and she flinched as he slid his fingers around her throat and pulled her toward him. He buried his face in her hair and inhaled. "And you have my son's scent all over you."

From her periphery, Randa saw that Will was already half-way out of his chair. She shook her head slightly. The last thing she wanted was for him to get himself killed trying to save her. *Damn it.* She couldn't believe she'd let herself be taken. They'd stripped her of her gun and two of her knives. The one strapped to her ankle? That one, she still had.

"What's your name, girl?"

One thing the army taught its people was the protocols if taken captive. The first rule was to survive. "Randa Thomas."

"You're a Pentonite." Jeez, the guy said it like it was a four-letter word. "I remember you standing alongside Aidan Murphy that day. One of his lieutenants, perhaps? Another vampire blood-bonded to him, I imagine. I can tell you're bonded to someone."

Would that information help, hurt, or make no difference? She decided it was irrelevant. "Actually, I'm bonded to Mirren

Kincaid." Of course, since Mirren was bonded to Aidan, it was virtually the same thing.

Will had remained on the edge of his chair, but she saw his posture relax as Matthias returned to his seat behind the desk and motioned her into a chair. She wanted to study Will, make sure he was OK, reassure herself that he was whole and that Matthias hadn't screwed with his head too much, but she didn't dare. The less Matthias suspected about their relationship, the better. Their feelings for each other would be an exploitable weakness.

"Well, this brings up an interesting situation." Matthias smiled at her, the shape of his mouth so similar to Will's and yet his smile so utterly different. "William tells me he's willing to come back to my household if I leave his Penton friends alone. But I assume that doesn't include the ones who are out snooping around places that don't concern them anymore."

He turned to Will. "So if I agree to let the rest of them go, will you kill this one? I'd consider it a show of good faith on your part."

Will's face was expressionless. "If that's your price, yes. I'll kill her. What's one life taken against many saved?"

Randa shifted in her chair. She wished she and Will had become mates so they could share thoughts, because she'd really like to know what he was thinking. He wouldn't kill her. Of that, she was sure. But what did he plan to do?

A chill passed through her, and it took Randa a second to realize it was coming from Will, who exuded some kind of raw power as he stared at his father. Matthias froze as if caught in the glare of an oncoming train, powerless to move away as it barreled toward him. Only Will didn't barrel—not physically, anyway.

He was trying to enthrall his father, and doing a pretty damned good job of it.

Apparently, the hired muscle still standing in the doorway must have thought so as well. "Mr. Ludlam, are you all right?"

Matthias blinked, awareness seeping back into his eyes.

Damn it, he was coming out of it. Randa moved slowly so neither the guard nor Matthias would notice, reaching down to scratch her calf. Sliding her fingers lower, she slipped them under the hem of her jeans, unsnapping the safety on the scabbard and sliding the knife out.

"Take out Matthias if you can," Cage had told her, and this might be her only shot.

Randa reached him in three fast steps, hoping to slice the silver knife across his throat to slow him down before lowering it to his chest. It would have given her an extra second or two to fix the awkward angle of her knife to the heart, but she realized before the knife scored more than two inches across his throat that she'd underestimated his awareness and his reflexes.

Matthias grabbed her arm and snapped it like a twig, sending Randa into an ocean of pain. The knife bounced off the hardwood floor and slid under the desk.

The room blurred around her. Will screaming as he flew at Matthias. A gunshot. A guard on the ground in front of her, his brains spilling out onto an area rug three inches in front of her eyes. More gunshots.

Will falling.

Silence.

❧CHAPTER 42☙

William blinked at the ceiling. As many meetings as the Penton lieutenants had held in this office, how had he never noticed the elaborate crown molding before? Dentil, that was the pattern. He sure had spent a lot of the last couple of weeks lying on his back, staring at ceilings.

The rest of the room came into focus, and he shook away the cobwebs. He had to see about Randa. She was hurt.

Climbing to his feet, he was distracted by the bullet wound in his chest. His father had freaking shot him. Since Will was standing here, Matthias must've missed the heart, but it hurt like a son of a bitch. He'd bet his next Robin Hood stash the bullet was silver.

Trying to press the wound closed with his fingers, Will finally raised his head to a sight so bizarre he had to be hallucinating. Maybe the bullet had hit his brain.

Matthias stood behind the big wooden desk, Randa sat against a potted plant cradling her arm and smiling, and in the doorway stood at least five guys in fatigues, holding rifles and looking as serious as death itself. Four of them were human; the fifth was Cage Reynolds.

In front of them was the strangest sight of all: Frank fucking Greisser, who Will knew only because he'd seen a photo of the guy shaking hands with his father. Now he was in the office of the Penton clinic, standing shoulder to shoulder with Colonel Rick Thomas.

They'd done it. They'd fucking done it. If he hadn't feared something would fall out of his chest, Will would have done a celebration dance.

If Matthias thought the sight strange, his face didn't show it. "Frank, not that I'm not pleased to see you, of course, but what's going on? What are you doing with human soldiers as your bodyguards? And Mr. Reynolds, of course."

Greisser stepped around the desk and stood next to Matthias, his voice low, hard, and probably unintelligible to the humans. Will could hear him just fine. "You arrogant bastard. You didn't even try to cover your tracks. There's nothing more I can do for you."

Matthias still hadn't gotten it, but understanding began to dawn when Aidan and Mirren eased through the line of soldiers, both wearing shoulder holsters with those big-ass Smith & Wessons they liked so much.

"Frank, I demand to know what's happening. These men should be disarmed and put under arrest." Matthias blustered and puffed out his chest in indignation, but his eyes darted from Aidan to Mirren and back to Frank.

Greisser unfolded a paper and began reading. It was a formal piece of bureaucratic tripe, but it was the nicest bit of tripe Will had ever heard.

"*Matthias, I have been charged by majority vote of the Vampire Tribunal to strip you of your seat on the Tribunal as chief counsel and head of the Justice Council. I'm also to inform you that you're to be taken into immediate custody and will be duly judged in Tribunal court within thirty days. This is witnessed by both myself, representing the Tribunal, and Colonel Richard Thomas, representing a new human-Tribunal partnership known as Omega Force.*"

"You fools. You've brought humans into our business?" Matthias reached for the spot at the edge of the desk where his pistol had fallen, but Mirren was too fast. He crossed the room in two strides, grabbed Matthias's wrist, and twisted it behind his back. The click of silver cuffs was like a choir of angels.

"What am I being charged with? This is preposterous! William, you're behind this, you ingrate, you stupid...Do you know my brilliant son can't even read a comic book? A dullard and his farmer friend and a professional murderer—these are the people you're listening to, Frank?"

"May I?" Will held out his hand to Frank Greisser, who raised an eyebrow and handed him the paper.

He could read this just fine. "*You are hereby charged with kidnapping, murder by contract, and abuse of office, with additional charges pending.*" Will tossed the sheet of paper on the desk and crossed the room to where Randa had gotten to her feet. He had nothing else to say.

Together, they walked toward the door, Randa holding her broken arm and Will with blood running down his chest and pooling at the waist of his pants.

Colonel Thomas gave him a solemn nod as they passed.

>—◦—◦—◦—◦—<

With an hour to spare before dawn, Will and Randa lay squeezed against each other in their twin bed in Omega. Krys had treated Will at the clinic, removing the silver bullet and packing the wound to hold it until daysleep. She'd offered him a bison-sized dose of morphine, but this time he'd passed. Randa's arm was a clean break, so Krys had set it and put it in a cast.

"Think my dad's enjoying his locked suite in the clinic sub-basement?" Will nudged her with his shoulder.

She grinned. "With Mirren sitting outside his door, daring him to try and escape? Oh yeah, I bet he's enjoying it plenty."

Will didn't know how long it would take them to rebuild Penton, but he'd already envisioned the training facility he'd design at the site of the old community center. A state-of-the-art place for Omega Force to work. He'd build a restaurant for Glory and replace the damaged clinic with a new one for Krys to work in.

Randa nudged his shoulder this time. "Will, let me ask you something."

"Yes, I'll buy you some new granny panties."

"Stop it. I'm serious."

He sighed. He was so damned tired of serious. He just wanted a daysleep where rats wouldn't gnaw on him. "OK, spill it."

"I was thinking tonight how it would have been nice if we could communicate mentally. You know, so we could talk to each other in tight spots. It would be really helpful to us when we're working with Omega Force."

Krys had ordered him to stay on his back, but he rolled over and groaned as he propped on one elbow and tried to keep from slipping off the narrow bed. "To do that, we'd need to be mated."

She flicked a glance his way, then returned her gaze to the ceiling. "I know."

He tried to keep the smile off his face, but his mouth just kept going there. "We'd have to have a blood exchange."

She waved her arm in its cast. "Yeah, we'd have to do that."

"And we'd have to have sex at the same time."

Randa sighed, but her smile kept trying to break out too. "I think I could make the sacrifice. Just to make us more effective in Omega Force, of course."

Will leaned over and took a nip at her earlobe. "Of course. Kind of like a business deal."

"Exactly."

"When would you like to do this business deal?" He figured they had thirty minutes left, max.

"Tomorrow, I think. Since you're injured, you know. I wouldn't want to worry about your stamina."

He leaned over and kissed her, long and hard, ignoring the throbbing pain in his chest and the fact she'd accidentally beaned him in the head with her cast.

He rolled onto his back and nudged her shoulder again. "Yeah, tomorrow. And I'll show you stamina."

❧ ACKNOWLEDGMENTS ❧

A s always, thanks to editor Eleni Caminis and the Montlake team for letting the Penton crew find life on the printed page. To Marlene Stringer, simply the Best Agent Ever. To editor Melody Guy, for smoothing out the wrinkles. To Dianne, for being my alpha reader even though she really doesn't read this genre—really. To Debbie, for being alpha-deux, even though she has horribly miscast Mirren. And to the rest of my Sisterhood of the Traveling Snark (Stella, Lauri, Amanda, and Lora) and the Auburn Writers Circle (Larry, Pete, Julia, Mike, Shawn, and Robin) for your unending support and encouragement.

⚜ABOUT THE AUTHOR⚜

 Susannah Sandlin is a sixth-generation Ala-
bamian with roots buried deep in Scotland,
Northern Ireland, and the piney woods of
Marion County, Alabama. She speaks French
badly, adores Middle Eastern food, and still
considers her longtime residence of New
Orleans the hometown of her heart. A recently
uncloseted fan of reality television, she's in search of her perfect
mate: all gator-hunting ice-road truckers need apply. Find her
online at www.susannahsandlin.com. *Omega* is the third install-
ment of her sensual and thrilling Penton Legacy series.